For those who came through.

Also by Neil Stanners -
'Somewhere Night Falls'
'Visions'
'Assigned Climes'

The
Magic
Room

(Der Magisch Raum)

NEIL STANNERS

Published by Garamonde (new edition) *2019*

GARAMONDE

Production by Media Services

Neil Stanners was born in Sydney.

He lived and worked in Europe.

He now resides once again in Sydney.

CHAPTERS

1	The Search
2	Go Round
3	The Cellar
4	Prepared
5	Moving On
6	Survival
7	Battle
8	The Climb
9	Exploring
10	The Room
11	The First Night
12	The Neighbourhood
13	The Morning and the Afternoon
14	Then Two
15	The Complications of Victory
16	Another Morning
17	Refuge
18	Good LIfe
19	Hunting Party
20	Reunion
21	Settling In
22	Orders
23	Decisions
24	Checkpoints
25	The Move
26	To Pass
27	The Road
28	Moving South
29	Eisenach
30	The Run
31	Rolf
32	Moving On
33	Bad Hersfeld
34	The Corporal
35	Transport
36	Willingen
37	Correspondence

DEVELOPMENTS

In 1937 the Japanese Navy finalised their specifications for the A6M fighter aircraft. It would become known as the Zero.
That same year the age of the airship came to an end with the loss of the German airship 'Hindenburg'.

The next year the US Army adopted the new M1 automatic rifle. At the same time the British Army brought the highly innovative Czech designed Bren Light Machine Gun into service. Frank Whittle was given a contract by the British Government to build a jet engine and German physicist Otto Hahn split uranium atoms to produce nuclear fission.
With some major subsidies from the German Army 1939 saw the establishment of an experimental rocket station at Peenemunde and German Ernest Heinkel saw his He178 become the world's first jet aircraft.
US Engineer Karl Pabst created the GP (general purpose) military vehicle. The GP quickly became known as the Jeep.

In 1940 the British Gloster E28 jet aircraft was tested. It was not considered for production.
This year also saw new Russian fighter plane, the MIG-1 brought into service. The US produced the first P-51 Mustang fighter aircraft.
British Magnetron coastal radar was installed giving quite accurate readings. The British shared the knowledge with their allies. The Oboe radar system was introduced to provide accurate positioning for planes to drop bombs.

1941 saw the trial of the W1 jet engine in another British Gloster experimental jet aircraft. It was decided that the engine was too small.
The Russian Stormovik dive bomber was produced with the first air-to-ground rockets.

The Australian Army was equipped with the revolutionary
lightweight Owen 9mm Parabellum sub-machine-gun.
Allied bombers began using H2S radio waves to give vision of
targets in all conditions. The British began manufacture of the
Sten Gun.

In 1942 the US Army tested the new Bazooka anti-tank weapon.
Harvard chemist Louis Fiesher created Napalm for use in flame
throwers and bombs.
The Avro Lancaster heavy bomber was added to the RAF Bomber
Command.
US shipyards began production of Liberty Ships, building 10,000
ton cargo ships in 10days. The world's biggest artillery piece, the
'Gustav', was used by the German Army to hurl 5 ton shells at
Sevastopol.
The Russian Army introduced PPSh-41 sub-machine gun. Known
as Papasha (Daddy) it dramatically improved the effectiveness of
close combat.
The German Army deployed the 'Tiger' tank. Large and heavy
with limited maneuverability it still gave a major advantage in
firepower.
Russian shock tactics now widely deployed Katyusha rocket
launchers which allowed their advances to be preceded by
massive opening barrages.

By the following year the US Air Force was flying the B29
'Superfortress' bomber. The British tested the Goblin jet engine
in a Vampire aircraft. German engineers were working on the
super-heavy Maus tank. Allied bombers dropped foils strips to
successfully confuse German radar.
The first of the highly effective Panzerfaust hand-held anti-tank
weapons was used by the German Army in 1943.
Simple items such as the US 'pineapple' fragmentation grenade
and even the KaBar utility knife gave US forces an edge in
equipment.

By 1944 German V-1 flying bombs were falling on London and British ports. After much development the first German V-2 rockets were launched against Britain in September.
The German rocket program was advancing quite rapidly.
The RAF began using the Gloster Meteor, the first, fully operational, jet aircraft. At the same time the German Luftwaffe began flying the Messerschmitt 262, after a failed attempt at a rocket powered fighter with the ME163 Komet.
German forces where equipped with the StG44 (Sturmgewehr 44). The first genuine rapid fire assault rifle.

In 1945 the DECCA navigation system underwent successful trials during the D-Day landings in France.

On July 16 that year the first atomic bomb was detonated in the new Mexico desert in the USA.

Chapter 1

'The Search'

The world has lost its colour. Stolen by evil men.
It is another hard day, black on the edges and grey.
Grimy and dusty, covered in the pounded debris of
conflict. Every touch blackens hands and clothes.
Pools of water in holes are covered in a film of what is
in the air. And the air is a mist this morning blended
with smoke, coated in the drift of explosions and carried
about in swirls, blanketing all the surroundings of the
city.

The streets are broken, their pavements shattered,
buildings gone, nothing but pale images of once solid
thoroughfares.
Now rubble, mixed with all the parts and pieces of
human existence.
On one mountain of bricks a small bird sits with its beak
open as if the air is not sufficient. It has lost its normal
avian alertness. The burden of survival has rendered it
hunched without purpose.
So many bricks from so many buildings. All jumbled in

a vast sea of destructed life. Hopeless waves. Too hard to climb, too numerous to allow movement. Paths have to be navigated through new ways and means to reach a goal. A goal that is often not there or unrecognisable.

The sun may appear briefly later in this day but at this first light, none is evident. In past years such a time would bring a hint of the coming warmth of summer but events have turned the seasons off. It is only a lost, bleak heartless landscape of wreckage, ruin and isolation.
Sitting in a doorway that once had a substantial house behind, there are two women. One seems quite old. Head down, almost all in black except for her blue slippers, she speaks with a husky dried rasp as if her body has no moisture left.

"What can they do with me except shoot me for sport?" She places her hand on the knee of the young woman next to her.
"You, my darling, are another matter."
She hauls in a breath waiting for the effort of breathing to kill her. "God, God, God, what a mess. Such promise, such victories, such glory. They went too far. If they had stopped. Some arrangement could have been made. There's always a way for such things. Half of Europe is not bad. And then the Russian front. Didn't they read their history books ....?"

The young woman is in a simple print frock. Once it had been white with a pattern of small yellow flowers. It is wet and stained. She has some flat, scarred shoes on her

feet. All she owns in the world except for a small brown cloth bag which contains very little. Some photos, a pencil, a little book of poetry, a piece of very dry bread, some raisins and a piece of pale blue cloth holding a wedge of cheese. She is pretty, with dark hair to her shoulders and pure creamy skin. She has soulful eyes. Her elbows rest on her knees and her chin on her hands. She looks pale.
Perhaps she is twenty. It is hard to tell in these circumstances.

In the silence a series of thuds break through the lost world of these two people.
"Where did they come from?" asks the old lady, lifting her head, trying to navigate
"I don't know, they seem all around."
"If they start the shelling again I hope they hit me straight away. I can't take any more of the terrible noise and the uncertainty. When the cursed bombers hit my house it burst into flames and my life just vanished as I stood in the street. I watched everything I owned, all my memories, all my past, all my dignity, together with my husband, roar up into the night sky. I walked. The neighbours were all gone as well, so I walked. I think I was planning to go back to my house once the flames had died but when it came time to turn round I had no idea which way to go. So now I am here. Wherever 'here' is."

In a loose train of thought the woman spreads her arms.
"What do we do with all the dead?"
She waves her arms.
"They just lie about. Nobody cares. It is unfair. They

should have some place to rest for eternity. Other than disappearing into the ground or being simply swept away when the time comes.

I always wanted to be beside my Walther. We could be together, almost holding hands, in a quiet part of some leafy cemetery. Where children would play, unafraid and the dead would lie at peace under their feet."

She gives several little grunts of annoyance or perhaps she is tearful. There is nothing to be said but the girl tries.

"Perhaps it is just the living who concern themselves with these things."

There is no reply to such logic.

While they sit the grey surrounding atmosphere is briefly broken by the appearance of a bright ginger cat.

It slips into their line of vision from nowhere, stops at the sight of them and stays still, frozen by their presence. Finally it decides that chance is on its side and advances, miaowing as it brushes their legs. They can offer it nothing except a reassuring stroke. Quickly realising these creatures are of no value it returns to its cat instincts and moves on. It disappears as rapidly as it appeared. Leaving the two women with their hands still poised for another stroke.

"Cats know a thing or two," says the old woman.

"I suppose they do." The girl gives a half smile to herself.

A silence follows. It becomes so quiet they can hear the mist lift and crawl about.

"I used to know Berlin," says the old one at last. "Such a

glamorous place. I would say I knew my way about the city quite well. Now, as I say, I have no idea where we are. Or which direction they're coming from. It would help, if I could only recognise something or see the sun for some guidance perhaps. Anyway you ....." She waves her hand at the girl as if to add emphasis. "You would stand a better chance with the Americans. That much I say. But first you have to move away from the Russians. Oh God, child, what a dilemma."
She takes the young woman's hand. She squeezes it to try to stop her shaking.
Then she turns to the girl, pushing her face forward. "You must flee, child. Or find a place to hide." She spits on the pavement in front of them.
"I was a lady. I would never have done that a year ago. Listen. Right near us now there are those in cellars, with the doors barred. I don't know where but the Russians will know. They will break down the doors, shoot the men and children and drag the women and girls out. Good German girls and wives, who have done them no harm. They will tear off their clothes, beat them and rape them over and over and over. And when they are done they will kill them. Revenge, pure hatred and revenge. They are sub-human. Unspeakable things will happen. Our fine German culture will mean nothing." She pauses then adds with a sneer.
"Oh, and don't offer a white flag. The SS will denounce you as a coward and hang you."

Now the young woman is shaking severely. Her breathing comes in gulps. The old lady takes her shoulders. "I run away with my mouth. Better I make you under-

stand. You must not be caught. You have made it this far.
You're in a city that you do not know. You're lost. That
is a good thing. No preconceived ideas about where or
what is best."

The women have spent the night together. The younger
one slid into the partly ruined entry hall, past a wall
covered in rose wallpaper. It led to a partly damaged
kitchen. There she found the old lady asleep on some
blankets and bedding. They had only met in the first
hint of morning.
The old lady had simply smiled and said, "Hullo, my
dear. Where did you come from?"

From some point in the gloom that surrounds them in
the street mist there is a slight shape. It flutters near
them. A figure standing so close. Both women stare.
Finally the older one stands and walks forward. She half
vanishes in the grey air then she returns and sits again.
"A lamp post with a National Socialist flag hanging on
it. No doubt it will form part of some Russian invader's
souvenir collection."
She looks at her young companion.
"There's some light coming into the day. Time for you
to go. If you can't see anybody they probably can't see
you. Look for an answer."
"What should I look for exactly?"
"You either work out how to get through our soldiers
and all the fighting and surrender to the Americans or
perhaps the British. In which case you must work out
how to not walk into the Russians. Or ...... you go to
ground."

The girl stands brushing down her dress, as if it mat-
tered.
The older woman stands again. It is an effort.
"Let me hold you and give you two kisses. One for luck
and one for love."
She embraces the young woman and kisses her tenderly
on each cheek in turn.
"I'm sorry, that's all I've got to give. There's a little food
in the kitchen but I can't spare it." After standing for a
moment she adds.
"Perhaps one more thing. This may seem harsh. If it
comes to death. Don't be concerned. It's only another
interesting experience. I don't know what lies beyond
such things. Perhaps it is quite a reasonable outcome."
The young woman let's go of the other's hand.
"Thank you, I want to live a while yet. Maybe we'll see
each other again." She pauses. "You know. When things
are better."
Walking off, she stops and walks back.
"What is your name?"
The old lady looks away then back to the enquirer. She
half smiles.
"Oh - I'm Frau Bohm. My name is Freda Bohm. What's
yours dear?"
"Adriane," she replies.
"Good day to you Adriane. Are you German?"
Adriane looks surprised. "I'm not anything really. But
yes, I'm German."
"It is of no consequence. I just wondered. I had some
very good friends once. They were Jewish. We were near
neighbours. Went to social events together. Their daugh-
ter was sweet like you. You remind me of her. So pretty.

Such rubbish this Aryan race idea. Beauty is not exclusively a Teutonic invention. The Fuhrer was a great man but not all his ideas were sound. I can dare to say things like that now. What harm can it do? So .... then things changed. For us and our neighbours. I don't understand why. So ...... unnecessary."
"My surname is Gerst."
"Well there. A fine name," says Frau Bohm.

As the young woman, Adriane, moves away she realises she is smiling. Then the world she inhabits moves back onto her face and she is desperate once more. She looks over her shoulder. The mist moves away briefly. Frau Bohm is sliding back past the collapsed wall into her half room.
She looks smaller as if she is shrinking.

Chapter 2

'Go Round'

There are only fifty-two of them, stretched over three intersecting street corners. Five have seen battle, twenty are old men of the volkssturm who have finally been called to arms, too fanatical to recognise their situation. The rest are mostly young and very young recruits with little idea.
The remains of the Hitler Youth. They are commanded by one of the old men. He has gained his position of power through party connections. He will not see any of the enemy pass this point. He has told them so.

About them is an endless testimony to the allied forces aerial bombardment. The fifty-two are positioned around one of the rare buildings that is still intact. It is a three storey brick warehouse, positioned on a bend in the road. On every side there are piles of bricks, twisted steel, splintered, shattered wood, the carcases of once solid streets and avenues. Some of the stronger structures are half down or hanging at odd and dangerous angles. Stories abound of death by falling masonry. It is not a scene to encourage optimism in the hearts of most Germans.

There has been word that the Fuhrer has massive reinforcements on standby just waiting to drive the cursed Americans, British and the treacherous Russians all the way back to oblivion.
The old man, the main one, this self-appointed commander, has a shine in his eyes as he tells the small band of defenders of this plan.
"Nothing can pass the superior soldiers of the Reich.
It is in our blood. We are warriors. Europe bows before our might. We will hold our assigned positions with this power."
He pauses for effect.
"I'm no fool," he continues, waving his arm above the collection of blank faces that stare fixedly at the black swirling air about them.
"We small band are not sufficient to drive the invaders back. But we are one of many such groups," he hisses.
"Our fire-power is best used to hold our places and simply wait until the new divisions sweep into this sector and overrun the enemy."

The five soldiers who have fought in other campaigns are given the task of using the scout car to fetch and then distribute ammunition to each of the combatants. They work quickly handing round boxes of ammunition for the old Karabiner 98k rifles and shells for the three mortars.
A quick assessment shows they have very little to go round.

It is decided to give the new recruits a good deal less of
ammunition. They will be the first to die. Better to let
the fanatics have more. They will fight till they are taken
out. There are sixty hand grenades. One each and a few
spares. A lot of the newer recruits have holsters for
Walther pistols but no gun. They have been given new
knives instead.

The five soldiers quietly agree that they will desert the
absurd situation by slipping away from the back of the
building they are defending once the enemy troops first
engage.
Aware the fanatics, who include four members of the
Geheime Staatspolizei, may try to block such a move,
they will have the sniper in their midst 'clean up' the
rear of the building beforehand.
It saddens them that they must take such action against
fellow Germans but after five years of this war, reality
and logic have disengaged any residual thoughts of the
glory they have been sold as their destiny. It is and was
all so wrong. That these ideologues still cling to the
crazy notions that have caused the ruin of their country,
makes them now expendable.

The old man has insisted that they operate two machine
guns on the third level of the building at the end of the
main street. One at a window on each side. The guns are
big heavy brutes on tripod mounts. Maschinengewehr
08's. Remnants of a previous war. Meant for the countryside.
It is hard and difficult to carry the guns up the stairs and
into position.

"A withering crossfire," the old man explains. "Our
flanks will drive them into your ambush."
It is not a point to argue. With only five cases of ammunition on some very old webbing, the guns will not operate for long. It is decided to fire fast and use up all they
have. When they are down to the last case, it will be fed
into the gun furthest from the stairs. A piece of wood
has been shaped and will be jammed in the trigger.
They will get out while it runs down. There will not be
much time.

With everything set up they have spent an uneasy night
listening to the relatively distant thump of heavy artillery or tanks. In the morning they can faintly hear the
rattle of automatic weapons.
"And we have none," says one of the soldiers quietly.
There is a thick mist at dawn, mixed with smoke and the
endless smell of explosive materials.
"If they come now," says the sniper, "We may not notice
them."

Just after dawn there is much excitement. A spluttering
rumble has everybody on edge. Eventually an old field-
car rolls out of the gloom. One of the fanatics has managed to secure it, complete with a shiny Raketenpan-
zerbusche 54 anti-tank gun mounted on the back. They
have twelve rounds.
"That will be twelve less Russian tanks," the old man
opines.

The soldiers are dismayed when he decides to put the
gun in front of their building. Below them now they have

a row of new recruits behind sandbags and rubble and
an anti-tank gun. It is far too much attention for their
area. Does he think the enemy will conveniently march
up the street toward them in formation?
The men always smoke their cigarettes in the front
doorways. They are more visible and not drawing attention to the rear door.

Very few people are about. Occasionally, in the distance,
a figure may appear briefly. With the ominous thuds
of warfare getting closer it is time to be not seen nor
heard. Now with arrival of this black, oily mist there's
little to be seen anywhere. It makes the group more nervous. For what it hides and what may come.

As the morning progresses a silence falls over the area.
It is more unnerving than the sounds of battle.
Perhaps there is no resistance ahead of their redoubt.
The enemy could be advancing quietly, meeting nothing but empty streets. They strain to hear. A weak glow
above their heads signals an attempt by the April sun to
clear the view but it flickers awhile then fades.

The old man eventually pulls two of the new recruits
from behind the sandbags. Possibly because he considers their extreme youth renders them expendable.
He addresses them in the manner of a field marshall and
orders them to go forward of their position and scout
the area.
"Go far," he says, "and come back with some useful
information for me." They pick up their rifles.
"No, no. You don't need rifles. Stealth and cunning.

If they see you it will be death whether you have a rifle or not.

I don't want you starting a cacophony of conflict and alerting others to our presence. I'm willing to sacrifice you to achieve our objectives. Be thankful for the honour I am bestowing upon your young shoulders. The Fatherland expects no more. Now go. Heil Hitler."

The two chosen ones half return the man's rigid salute as if caught off guard by the formality.

They move away timidly into the gloom, hugging the sides of the buildings. At an edge of one more erect building they cautiously peek round the corner then with a fatalistic step they move forward and quickly disappear.

The old man looks at the rest of the young defenders. "They are scouting about, not engaging the enemy." Their faces reveal an understanding that belies their years. They must die for the Fatherland. Those two who have gone are bait. Canaries in a coal mine. The sound of their execution will give advice to the old man.

Over half an hour goes by. There is no sound of death or of life. Alertness gives way to idleness.

The older men smoke, look at the sky, occasionally mutter. The young recruits look anxious and tend to fidget, rubbing their hands and squirming in their positions. One or two will periodically lift their head to look down the street where their comrades recently disappeared. Time ticks.

Then a shot rips through the air. The bullet rattles quite dramatically into a brick wall.

"Halt, halt, schießen Sie nicht."
It is the scouts returning. They call again. "Halt halt."
The old man viciously kicks the recruit seated behind
the sandbags.
"Give away our position, you fool. Shoot only when I
say."
One of the soldiers smiles to the others.
"How ironic, if we'd killed them."

The recruits are breathless. They have run the last
street.
The news is neither good nor bad. They have found
nothing of consequence. They swear that they advanced
many kilometres, past the square and up the hill on the
main road. There is no sign of any living person. One
man lay dead in the street. They checked him carefully
and rolled him over. There were no bullet holes the two
eagerly explain. They suspect he had a heart attack.
The old man gives the impression he does not believe
them but they stick to their story.

The soldiers know they are truthful and know what
stopped them. Beyond the square at the main road is
the railway line.
The Russians are there. They know it. The silence is
simply a lull while the enemy secure the line and look at
its potential.

The recruits would have heard that terrifying enemy
moving about and have quickly beat a retreat. No point
mentioning that they heard something but did not investigate. Exuberance overtaken by self-preservation.

It is now, as they all stand about considering their position that they are stealthily approached.
One of the recruits is first to see the figure but after the wrath of the old man he does not shoot but merely points and makes a nondescript sound.

As the girl emerges from a side street and moves in front of them she looks dismayed to have so many guns pointing at her.
There is a brief moment of obvious concern until she recognises the uniforms of the Wehrmacht.

At some point in the interrogation of the girl, Adriane Gerst, the old man realises that the whole group are circled about listening to the words being spoken.
Not one of his men is taking note of the surroundings.
He flies into a fit of rage, pushing and slapping the recruits, though avoiding the soldiers.

"Do you believe the enemy will conveniently wait while we have a little chat amongst ourselves and listen to gossip? I have an army of fools. You deserve to die. And dammit you all will. The Fatherland will have your blood in its defence."

Having kicked and harassed all but his immediate cronies into position once more he returns to the girl seated on a wall behind their line.

"A country girl. What in hell made you think Berlin would be a viable alternative for your safety and well-being? Every stinking Russian, American, Frenchman,

Englander and all their lackeys are trying to destroy our city and all of us with it. It will take a huge effort to drive them back."

Adriane remained calm. Her eyes are an odd green and quite intense. She has been through too much to have this man disturb her soul. She speaks quietly.
"I watched from our field, hidden in the crops. First they brought out my father and my brothers. They stood them against the wall of our house. My father pleaded with them to spare Ernst and Eric. He's only ten, my father said. And little Eric is eight. They shot them all while he spoke. Then they went inside and I listened to my mother and my little sister, screaming for some time before it went quiet.
Later they carried their bodies out. They threw all of my family over the wall into the pig pen.
A while later they came back out of the house. They must have found my father's wine and spirits
They then killed our pigs and roasted them in some fashion, over a fire. They settled in for a night of feasting and drunken singing. I stayed in the field. I couldn't move.
They were burning all farmhouses as they went. I ran from that day till today. Into a city there are places to hide."

The group still listening remained silent for some time. They looked at their boots, their eyes glistened. Finally the old man said in a hushed voice, "What have we done to deserve such things as this?"

The soldiers at their posts above heard the story with indifference. Four years of war had left nothing but scars and a numbness towards other humans. Looking down they then heard the old man, the ideologue, the believer, the fool, tell the girl what to do.

"You are safe behind our lines. You have stayed ahead of the Russians. You have been good, resourceful and clever. All the features of the Aryan race. Better you are here than facing the Americans. They have firepower and good soldiers. The Russians are a rabble. They will easily be defeated and driven back. I suggest, for your own safety you keep going into the city and find some citizens who will take care of you. There will be bread and soup, vegetables and sausage. You can clean up and sleep in fresh linen."

The old man smiled. It made his face rather comical.

As if he were in pain.

The girl rose and thanked the men for their kindness. She asked if she might have a drink as she was very thirsty. The men bumped each other in an effort to oblige the girl. She drank long from the canteen offered. It's owner looking anxious the more she swallowed.

One of the group looked at the girl and asked, "What is your accent? I can't place it."

"Oh," said Adriane, "my parents were from different parts of the country and I picked up a little of both. I have a mongrel accent. I hope it doesn't offend you."

"Of course," said the enquirer, "I didn't mean to embarrass you."

Handing back the container she thanked them again for their kindness. At that moment a golden light flickered onto their area.

"Ah, see," said the old man, "already the sun is shining on your adventure."

With more handshaking and good wishes the girl moved off.

"What a pretty young German girl," one man said, almost sadly.

"Yes, it's a shame," replied another, watching her back.

She half turned once as if seeking reassurance

Before she had gone fifty metres a swirl of mist slipped Adriane Gerst from their view and the street behind was grey and featureless once more. The gold was gone.

Chapter 3

'The Cellar'

Adriane Gerst is lost in a big city. Within minutes of leaving the defenders and their encouragement she found herself in a pile of bricks and rubble. The street had melted away. She could see no more than five metres and the view gave no clue as to which way to proceed. No street or gutter to follow. A mountain of broken masonry. In the end she found a chair sitting proudly upright, atop some fallen stonework, as if awaiting her arrival. It was a fine beast, made of oak, heavily upholstered in rich blue fabric. The edges of the arm rests and seat were finished in frilled piping and the head-rest had an embroidered white antimacassar.
Seated, she waited for some more of that light that had appeared minutes earlier. She knew that fog and mist dull sound but still she was surprised that here in the inner reaches of Berlin there seemed so little noise.

A series of thuds to her right. More parts of some building falling to the ground. Artillery occasionally but very distant. A bird. How odd. You would think they would

stay silent. Nothing for some minutes and then, much
closer a vehicle accelerating then fading away. Some
shouting off somewhere to the right.

Perhaps, once again closer, the sound of pots and pans.
That is all she could think of with this latest noise. What
war machinery makes a sound like pots and pans?
A secret weapon? Adriane smiled in spite of her predica-
ment. "If I can smile I am still living," she thought.

And then it came. So quickly. A small gust of wind
moved the air. As if a curtain had been drawn and the
stage was lit. A whole street appeared in front of her.
She gasped at how high and precarious her position was
on her seat. She had somehow walked to the edge of a
large hole. The street appeared intact on the left.
Big, flat dull, dark brick, apartment buildings. At least
three in a row. With little ugly piggy windows and small
indented entrances. The right side of the street had
been hit by one very large explosion that gutted the
buildings while leaving their facades dangerously intact.

As she watched, Adriane saw bricks slip and grumble
their way down the piles of debris in their innards.
It was on one of these piles that she was seated.
With light and direction she made her way carefully
down the slope and almost ran to the dubious safety of
the left of the street.
Briefly she leaned against the solid wall of the nearest
building. It was the first she had seen for days that offered some degree of completeness and potential refuge.
Far away down the street at the edge of the visible area

she saw some figures. They were pushing two carts.
Another ran out of a building carrying something. They
examined the item and then it was placed on one of the
carts. They looked briefly at the girl but headed away
and soon disappeared.

Moving along the footpath, running her fingers on the
wall in case the vision vanished once more, Adriane felt
the brickwork change. Her hand rested on the paper of
a poster. A German soldier stared down at her. 'So wie
wir kampfen - Arbeite Du fur den Seig.' it read. Work as
hard for victory as we fight! An emotional plea that now
seemed rather lost. Adriane reached the first entrance.
It was just an opening in the facade, a larger doorway.
Three steps led up to a pair of timber and glass doors,
each with a silver push bar. Inside was a tiled foyer.
There were mailboxes to the right and on the left a set
of stairs led up and away.

The girl stepped forward. At the doors she hesitated.
All seemed quiet. No danger. She pushed the door open
and stepped inside. Nothing happened until she took a
breath. A massive overwhelming stench hit her nostrils.
The sickening sweet smell of rotting human flesh.
She knew it well.
As she stumbled backward Adriane saw bundles of
clothing to the right and the left. Another body sat
propped in the corner. One more lay on the stairs as if
they had fallen. It seemed theatrical.
Outside, bending over, breathing hard, trying to rid her
nose of the awful odour, the girl's body tried to vomit
but nothing came as her stomach twitched and con-

vulsed. It was the first time she realised she had not
eaten for days.

Minutes passed as she leant against a lamp post. Breathing, just breathing. When she looked up, the street was
still clear, perhaps even brighter. Something blocked the
way. A large dark, bearded man stood, his hands on his
hips, staring at Adriane.
Their eyes locked. It was the man who moved first. He
walked forward.
"Oh, you should not have gone in there," he said. He
reached the girl and patted her back. "Awful business.
Here, move away, take deep breaths and hold them in."
She does as she is told, coughing a little. He pats her
back again.
"Are you from around here? I don't recognise you."
"No, I'm from the country."
"Ah," says the man, "keeping ahead of those Russian
pigs. The armies of the Reich will soon have their mea-
sure. You can relax now."
The girl stands up straight once more, still breathing
deeply and deliberately. The mist has obliterated the
end of the street once more.
"I'm not so sure anymore."
Adriane looks at the man. He is large, in stature and
girth. "He could be a baker or sell beer," she thought.
His clothes are grubby. He has a heavy coat despite the
mild weather. His hat is an odd alpine thing but with a
broad brim. He has knee length leather boots with his
trousers tucked.

"Come," he says, holding out his hand in the gesture of

a doorman ushering a guest. "If you are lost and alone, I have a nice safe cellar. It is the place to be. The walls are two layers of brick. When other things have been destroyed my cellar has not moved. There are mothers and children, some old men who would enjoy a chat with a country girl. We have soup, some bread and a good stock of army provisions."
The girl still looks at the large man.
He smiles. He has surprisingly good teeth. Some are gold.

"Oh, you can't be too careful. You didn't get this far by taking chances, eh. What can I say. We're fellow Germans in an hour of need. Somewhere to be amongst friends. That's all I offer. Somewhere to lay your head on a pillow, under warm blankets."
Adriane looks the man in the eye. He smiles again. "My name is Brunek." His hand is outstretched.

He leads the way along the street. At one point where a hole has replaced a building, he tells her that a maternity hospital had existed there.
"One minute a place of hope and birth. Then gone."
They reach a space between two intact buildings. It appears to be a dock area where trucks might have delivered and picked up goods. The man turns in. This small area is cobbled under foot.
"Old and built to last," the man says, slapping a wall with his palm.

Past a raised wooden loading bay with a swing gibbet and ropes and a big pulley wheel, there is a heavy steel door.

Brunek turns and smiles again. "Our secret hideout."
There is a large handle and mechanism that he wrenches up to open the door. He motions Adriane forward.
Once inside he pulls the door closed and they are
plunged into darkness. There is a sound of two bolts
being driven home.
A moment later a torch light comes on.
"We don't have power, of course," explains Brunek,
"straight ahead my dear."
Down five steps and into a corridor of brick. It is surprisingly dry.

"This was a food warehouse. I used to work here. When I
lost my home, I thought' why not come here?"

They pass a glassed off room that must have been some
sort of office or workplace. There are desks and papers
and swivel office chairs. A short distance further on
there is another door that ends the corridor.

"Here we are. You can meet everybody. We're all friends
here."
The man leans past Adriane and opens the door.
She can see only darkness. There is a massive thump in
her back and she pitches forward into the room.

Chapter 4

'Prepared'

At the redoubt, the morning calm is becoming difficult
to overcome. The mist is moving away in patches.
Sunlight breaks out and lights the street then fades
back. It is comfortably quiet. Even the old fanatics can
be occasionally seen closing their eyes for a minute.

The mist is practically gone. Sunlight brightens the
whole area.
One of the soldiers speaks up. "Let the kids have some
rations. Two at a time, it can't hurt."
The 'commander' does not like ideas that are not his.
He looks the soldier up and down but does not meet his
gaze.
"No, they will stay at their posts." He finds a compromise that has authority. "You soldier." He smacks the
nearest boy across the side of the face with his swagger
stick. It catches the boy's eye. The young soldier turns
screwing up his face, squinting.

"God, are you crying? The Russians will rape the likes of

you before they cut your throat. Pathetic." He spits on the ground. "Go to the rations. Open enough tins for two of you each to share. Bring them back and hand them out. ...... Schnelle!"
The boy runs into the building, stumbling against the door, holding his eye.
The soldier stands quietly, then turns and walks away. "Now all the defenders will be eating instead of watching and you've just blinded one of them with your damned stick."

Inside the building the boy is pulling small tins of herring from boxes stacked against the brick wall. There are teaspoons that can be used to dig out the fish. They are not army rations, just acquired tins.
He counts out the correct number and lines them up on top of a box ready to be opened.
He is shaking his head against the pain in his eye, trying to focus. His jacket is too big and he must keep pulling the sleeves up above his hands. Trying to pierce the first can with the opener, the can slips from his grasp and rolls away.
"Scheiße!" he exclaims. He gives an exasperated sigh. Once again he rubs his eye. It is watering and he cannot open it. He turns his head to use his good eye and locate the missing can. The soldier, one of the regulars, a big man, is standing in the doorway holding the errant can.

The man walks over. He puts a hand on the young soldier's shoulder. "Perhaps I should give you some assistance? With your war injury and everything."
There is a brief silence. "You hand me the cans and I'll

open them. Gut?"
The boy nods holding out a can.
"I already have the first one." The soldier smiles. The
boy smiles back, in relief as much as anything.

As the soldier works the opener up and down with ease
he takes note of the boy. He is slim, his blonde wavy hair
that has not been cut for some time. He is pale. He has
not seen the sun in a while. He has quite golden eyes
that are oddly piercing. At least the one that is open
has that quality. It must be assumed that the other eye
matches. His uniform is fairly new and oversize. It hangs
from his frame. When he reaches for another can his
hand disappears into the sleeve. He has a belt with an
empty pistol holster and a Fartenmesser Hitler-Jungen
knife in its sheath. The latter has the brightness of a new
possession. He has a cloth peaked cap rather than a helmet. His trousers are tucked into boots that are also a
size too big. "Allowances for midgets and children were
not part of the plans," the soldier muses.

The boy winces once more as he looks up. The soldier
stops.
"Here, let me look at that."
He takes the boy's face in his hands and uses his
thumbs to pull the protesting eyelids apart. The eye is
red, bloodshot. The welt from the stick has gone right
across the cheek and caught the eye.

He turns the boy's face to his, "You're not going to die
from this or go blind. I can't see any damage. It will
settle down. Here ......" The soldier pulls a net field scarf

from around his neck. He ties it around the boy's head and across the damaged eye. He replaces his cap then pats his shoulder once more.

"Go and hand out the open cans then come back for more."

The boy is concerned. "What about the commandant?" He points to the scarf on his face.

"He won't say anything. It's not wise to injure your own fighting men. Go on." He adds, "Things could be worse you know. The defences either side of us are Waffen SS. Imagine being commanded by those Totenkopf chaps. At least we only have an old man from the Volkssturm."

The boy nods and moves off with his armful of cans. "Superbly trained men, born to kill who seek pleasure in death verses a man with no idea and an ego that will see us all killed." The soldier is talking to the empty room. "The difference isn't all that great after all."

When the boy returns he smiles at the soldier.

"All okay?" asks the soldier.

"Ja, ist gut."

The remaining cans are nearly all open. The soldier holds out his hand. "I'm Dieter Falke. What's your name?"

The boy earnestly shakes the man's hand. It had been a while since he'd held the hand of an adult. It felt comforting. Something that would go unsaid.

"I'm Hauke Kluge. I'm glad to meet you Herr Falke."

Dieter Falke is a tall, broad shouldered man, with dark swept back hair and dark brown eyes. His face is square with a strong jaw. His uniform moulds itself to his frame.

It has the insignia of a Oberleutnant. He has an air of quiet confidence. There is a standard issue knife next to the pistol on his belt. Another larger non-regulation knife is attached to a leather cross strap on his chest. The man seems capable of anything. Somebody to be trusted. Although there is another layer to his appearance. A slightly resigned, worn down presence. From somebody who has seen it all before and knows the inevitability of things. One who has lived in the shadows of fortune for too long.

Soldier Dieter Falke looks at the boy, who is probably going to die soon. "We're both soldiers, call me Dieter." He frowns, "How old are you Hauke?"
"I'm twelve sir, but I'll soon be thirteen. Well next year anyway."
"No you won't," Dieter Falke thinks. "Where are you from Hauke?"
"I'm from here. Berlin is my city. I'm defending it. Are you a Berliner?"
"No," says Dieter Falke, "All my family were in Dresden."
"Oh," says Hauke. All Germans are aware of the Dresden destruction, even these boys.
He searches for some other topic. "Have you fought long?"
"It seems, my friend, as if I have done nothing else. But that's just the way it seems."
Dieter Falke looks at his young companion. His brightness, his unblemished countenance. The child's fingers poking out of his sleeves.
"When the attack comes Hauke, fight bravely and hard. Give all you have for your Berlin." He pauses. "But don't

use up every bullet." He pauses, scratches his cheek unnecessarily. Gives a weak smile.

"You see …… it is best you don't allow yourself to be captured. Think about your situation. Consider all your options. There is always a selection from which to choose. Lots of 'possibilities'."

He is looking into the boy's face, searching for some understanding in their silence.

Hauke Kluge's countenance is hard to read. He is staring at the soldier with his one bright functioning eye. For a moment his focus wanders as he takes in the gravity of the message. He frowns a little. His head bows then he looks back at Dieter Falke and nods slowly.

Dieter Falke meets his gaze. "Good. I'm glad we talked." In that moment the commandant appears in the doorway. "Get back to your posts now please."

It is almost a request.

Chapter 5

'Moving On'

Brunek is a mystery. Lying on the floor Adriane was
confused more than scared. She had landed on softness.
Blankets as it turned out. It was very dark. Lying on her
stomach still stunned from the blow to her back she
became aware of a light, growing in intensity. Lifting her
head she could see that she was in a warehouse-sized
room. Half the floor was covered in blankets. Hundreds
of them. In the distance, next to a table, the dark figure
of Brunek was adjusting a paraffin lamp, pumping up the
pressure. There were cupboards and racking along one
wall, stacked with boxes.

There were no children, no mothers, not one old man
wishing to hear stories of her life on the farm. Just herself and the large, dark man.
For a minute or more Brunek stands in the half light of
the lamp and watches her as she slowly turns and sits
up. He says nothing. Just watches.
For some time he does nothing but stare. Adriane is not
going to ask what, how or why.

The situation is odd and dangerous. She should not be here. Is he mad?

Still he watches from his lighted patch of the room. She tries not to meet his gaze in case it antagonises the man. It is completely silent.

Should she stand? Demand an explanation? Tell him she is angry at this situation. What stupid game is he playing? Her eyes briefly meet the staring man.

Then, as if by some switch thrown in his skull, Brunek strides across to the girl and grabs her wrist. Close up his face has no expression she can recognise. At best she might describe his demeanour as that of a farm animal when presented with a trough of food. Purposeful and focused.

Holding her wrist he plunges his free hand into the front of her frock and rips the light material in one powerful sweep, leaving it in shreds. He grunts as he works. Clutching and tearing off her undergarments. He shakes and throws them aside as if they annoy him.

He runs his hands over her small girl breasts, growling, muttering to himself in a mix of satisfaction and lust. He clutches at her thighs with equal ardor. Adriane makes one attempt to fight, to stand and resist. The man Brunek slaps her so hard across the face she is rendered almost senseless.

Over the next hour he rapes her twice. Going away then like some possessed bull, his breathing increases and he comes back unbuckling the heavy leather belt of his trousers again.

He is big and heavy and brutal. Muttering indecipher-
able sentences as he goes about the job.

When finally he rolls away and straightens up his
clothes Adriane can feel wetness between her legs. She
thinks she is bleeding.
Since they entered the room neither party has spoken.
Now the man goes off to the far side of the room and
oddly stands behind some racking while he finishes
dressing.

Adriane has nothing. She pulls a couple of the blankets
around her body and sits with her chin resting on her
knees. For the first time she allows tears to run down
her cheeks.
She can still taste the tobacco of his breath. The wetness and sweat of his body. She cannot speak, just
breath, her mouth hanging open. Like some wounded
forest animal she is afraid to move for fear of further
attack. She is scared and disgusted all at the same time.
She shakes, unable to bear the feel of her body.

Adriane wants to ask why? It seems a reasonable question. What could make a man trap and attack his fellow
citizens when they are in their time of greatest peril and
greatest need? She quickly realises that this is a naive
thought. There will always be monsters like Brunek who
take advantage of any situation, no matter how cruel
and unfair. They are both Germans. It means nothing.

Was this a sudden impulse for which he is ashamed
or a planned entrapment? No, no, no. Of course it was

planned. All the stories of others, of food and comfort. The girl cannot concern herself with questions. She instead turns her attention to the immediate problem of her safety and wish to depart.

The man is busy at the table where she first saw him light his lamp. She waits. She would try to get to the door if she had clothes or shoes but they are ruined or missing. Dignity and no obvious answers hold her to the floor, wrapped in blankets.
After some minutes watching the dim figure, trying to discern his actions, he turns and moves toward her. He is carrying something. The light is behind him so she cannot make out what he is holding.

He leans down. "Soup," he says, "vegetable soup." He places the bowl on her knees and hands her a spoon. Pride and logic would command that the girl stand and hurl the hot bowl at his departing back.
"You defile me and then offer me soup!?" Her thoughts are mixed. Anger and fear. The smell is too tempting. Adriane has not eaten for days.
Instead as she spoons the delicious warm liquid into her mouth she watches the man as he sits at his table in the faint light and watches her.

When she has finished eating Adriane places the bowl si-lently on the blankets beside her. She continues to hold the spoon in some ritual of comfort. Resting her head on her knees once more she feels so naked, so dirty and vulnerable.

Brunek is sitting at the table. He lifts something to his mouth. He is drinking, the girl realises. She sees the bottle rise and pour, the glass to the lips and the head thrown back. Shots of strong liquor. Schnapps or perhaps brandy.

The effort of watching in the dim light , staying tense and alert makes her back ache. It would be so easy to lay down and sleep but that could be the trigger for more advances from Brunek. Still after many more silent minutes pass Adriane sleeps with her chin still on her knees.

She starts awake. His face is next to hers. She lets out a short scream. He had been touching her cheek. Jumping back Brunek steps on the soup bowl. They both hear the crunch as it shatters under his boot. For a moment he stops, looking down. Then he roars. It is a demented bellow. He smashes his hand across Adriane's face. He pulls at her hair, grunting, shaking her from side to side as she clutches at his hands trying to stop her hair coming away from her skull.

"See what you've done. You damned whore," he cries. "You temptress. Slut! Why did you come? You're like all the others. All the same. I'm a good man. God needs me to be rid of you. And I will be rid of you!"

He finally lets go of the girl's hair and throws her aside. She can smell the stench of alcohol on his breath. He kicks her hard in the stomach blasting the air from her lungs then strides back to his table. Crashing into his chair Adriane can see, as she clutches her midriff, that he has opened another bottle and this time has dis-

pensed with the glass and swigs, in between an ongoing
series of curses and threats. They go on in an endless
stream. His voice is guttural and slurred.
"It is God's will. Damned vile whore. Why? I cannot help
my weakness. Dear Lord I will fight their ways. Crush
them all. ...." He takes great drafts from the bottle
spluttering and giving self-satisfied grunts.
"I am right, of course I am right. Righteous! A soul of ....."
He seems to lose his train of thought and trails off.

Adriane is terrified. The man is deranged. As she watches, waiting for his rage to turn to her demise, she takes
slight comfort from his increasingly slow and slurred
speech and behaviour until she realises he has slumped
in the chair and his head has flopped back in a stupor.
Several times he half lifts his head, tries to shake away
his drowsiness, then finally his head slips back and
stays. His mouth hangs open.

With just the hiss of his pressure lamp in the room she
has time to collect her thoughts. She could try to find
the door in the blackness. It is big and heavy and has
two large bolts that squeak. Possibly it is locked. Out
in the street, barefoot, alone with only a blanket? Could
she find the soldiers again?
It is a chance but not a good one. She cannot stay here.
Her stomach hurts badly from the kick. Could she even
stand?
Without warning, a series of memories fall into line.
Adriane's eyes widen. Here breath comes in small pants
of panic. The building with the bodies? Was that all his
work? Did they all come to his cellar on a string of prom-

ises only to be murdered and then placed in that foyer like a trophy room?

It may not be so but the thought that it was even a possibility gives the girl the motivation she needs. Groping about she locates the steel soup spoon still laying on the blankets. It has a large curved handle. She runs her finger along the edge then moving some of the blankets aside, she locates the concrete floor and begins rapidly grinding the metal on the hard surface.
There is a purpose to her actions and an urgency.

The light is sputtering. It loses some of it's glow for a few seconds then spits back to life. Brunek, the man in the chair is snoring. His head still hangs back. At times his snores are so guttural that they choke his breathing and he stirs only to flop back. But it adds to the tension and the need to complete the job. After nearly an hour Adriane holds the spoon up to catch the light. She feels along one side of the handle and is satisfied.
A childhood in the country is now the motivation and acceptance of her actions. She stands, letting the blankets fall silently to the floor. She draws in a slow, deep breath letting the pain in her ribs subside. A need for both her body and her mind.

Across at the table Brunek still hangs over the back of his chair snoring loudly. As she advances toward him Adriane can see the bottles and a pipe on the table and as she gets closer a knife and a leather holster with a gun shining black inside. The knife is a large, bone-handled hunting device with a viciously curved tip. Briefly she considers abandoning the spoon in favour of claiming the knife but it would involve leaning right past the huge man with the possibility of knocking something over.

The knife is tangled in other pieces of paraphernalia on the table. It may not be sharp.

Reaching the sleeping man Adriane is cowered by the simple closeness to his powerful body. For some seconds she stands behind looking down into his red, bloated face as if willing him to perform one last foul act of treachery to justify her need.

The moment has come. Adriane reaches around the huge head, positioning the spoon handle over his bulging neck. She is thankful that he has no beard or hair on his neck. From experience she knows that slicing through hair is a more laborious process. He has also conveniently placed himself in the ideal sacrificial position.

'Now,' she says to gird her hand into action. Her face screws up. Her teeth are clenched.

Outside in the streets of Berlin a sudden howling sound cuts through the air, followed by a massive thump as the first of thousands of Russian artillery shells crashes into the streets of the capital.

Brunek's eyes open wide. He stares upward into the face of an angel. Before he can comprehend what situation presents itself, he is aware of a terrible, stinging pain across his neck. He tries to lift his head, to move. His hand rises from the armrest of the chair. He tries to call out but only a gurgling nonsense occurs. Something has robbed him of any power, confusing his thoughts. He does not understand where he is in the room. Then there is a coldness in his shoulders and a warm rush from his chest. Then it is nothing. Just black.

Adriane has stepped back. She was as shocked as her victim by the start of the bombardment. Resolute, panicking and too fearful of the alternative, she proceeded rapidly with her plan. Pressing as hard as she could, she drew the sharpened spoon handle from left to right across the man's neck and throat. The gap was satisfactorily large. It opened his carotid arteries and his throat. Blood under pressure rushed from the cut. His heart fought to maintain a flow. The blood spurted then subsided.
Once the body lost it's power to live the man slid then toppled sideways onto the floor with his chair.

For some time Adriane stood motionless. In case some movement might somehow awaken the man once more. She considered the enormity of her deed. Then she dropped the spoon onto the desk and began to look about, breathing rapidly like some scared dog. Naked, ashamed, sore, trembling. So many emotions.

Outside, across Berlin, the Russian offensive hurled explosion after explosion down onto the battered city. Some shells burst close to the building then the guns trained away, only to return in their ugly sweep of destruction.

Adriane carried the light about in the cellar, stopping
once to pump up the pressure. She paused at times
to look back at the body lying beside the table with
the pool of dark red around. Slowly she assessed the
contents of the cellar storeroom. The racks along the
wall contained boxes and in those boxes were blankets.
Adriane opened the cardboard tops of boxes with armed
forces markings and the swastika, right along the range
of shelves. All contained blankets.

Frustrated with nothing to wear, Adriane stood draped
in a blanket once more, holding the lamp. It continued
to sputter, presenting a greater fear, that she may be
suddenly pitched into total darkness with that man. She
still did not trust the finality of her deed.

Adriane walked back to the table and the body of her
attacker. Behind the table the shelving stopped. It
formed a deep alcove. Holding the light high the girl
could see piles of more boxes. Some made of timber,
some cardboard. They were a different size and shape to
those with the blankets.
On the side of one she can see the word 'Hosen.'

As another Russian shell pounded down and showered
debris about, the outer door of the warehouse opened.
In the opening stood a girl in German army pants and
boots. She wore a nondescript cotton vest and a lightweight jacket. Around her waist under the jacket is a
belt with a pistol, though it has only five bullets. She has

a hessian sack. It contains two cans of chicken soup, a
bottle of expensive brandy and a bone-handled hunting
knife with a curved blade.

Chapter 6

'Survival'

From the steel doorway that opens onto the courtyard
Adriane peers out. She opens the door far enough to
lean forward and look about. It is empty and still. For
some moments she cannot understand what is different.
It is silent. The shelling has stopped.
Behind her is darkness and that man. As she left the
room she stood and watched his figure for over a minute, searching for a hint of life. A momentary flicker, a
slight rise and fall of the chest. Her eyes began to sting.
To trick her mind. In the end she ran.
Now there is the thought of Brunek behind or a Russian
soldier in front.

She moves forward, under the wooden loading bay then
along the wall to the street. At the corner she waits and
listens. It is so quiet she realises she can hear her own
breath. The mist that covered the street when last she
walked along has been replaced by smoke and dust
and little glimpses of sunlight. Fires are burning nearby.
Some of the smoke is black as if rubber or fuel is alight.

Waiting at the corner Adriane cannot think of what
to do. To run is an option. But she has no idea where
her legs might carry her. Quite possibly into the arms
of a Russian or his bullet. She looks like a soldier. Her
clothes are heavy and a bit oversized. Her belt gathers
up the trousers in folds. She doubts a Russian would
take note of such inaccuracies in her apparel. There is
no alternative. She must find a sanctuary. Briefly she
considers Brunek's lair but it is too obvious. Nor could
she return to the place. The girl is also desperately
thirsty.

As with other times in her comparatively short life she
takes on a fatalistic mindset. "Dear Mutter," she whispers, "Your words are with me. Nicht reinen." She pulls
the brandy bottle from the coat pocket and takes several gulps. This is followed by some choking and smoth-
ered coughs. It takes a few moments to gain a calm
demeanour once more. But the warmth of the brandy is
spreading through her body.

Then Adriane smiles and walks straight out and across
the street, back the way she had come, back toward the
Russians with the German defenders between.
"Don't do the obvious," she thinks. "Run through the
wall."

After some minutes, past craters belching white acrid
smoke, there is a narrow street that rises slightly as
it curves away on the left. From her position Adriane
can see that most of the buildings facing the street are
just fronts, their rears smashed to the ubiquitous piles

of rubble. Other buildings are broken as if their spines
have been damaged and they await death. The street
is an empty, gutted shell. Why would anybody wish to
enter? There is nothing.

Adriane turns and makes her way in. Bricks and shattered masonry make even following the roadway difficult. For once the heavy boots on the girl's feet with
their two pairs of socks make the treading of such a
path slightly less arduous.
At it's halfway point the road makes one odd turn to the
right, rises briefly then drops away as it moves on to
connect to the next street in a straight line of smokey
light.

On the rise there are a number of intact buildings. One
has a small printery. Inside she can see metal presses,
type formes and stacks of paper. Next Adriane looks at a
building of some height. It shows promise. Perhaps eight
storeys. It seems to have escaped any damage.
A strong set of concrete steps lead up to some impres-
sive doors with ornate iron handles and lead glass.
There are curved sides to the front steps. The bricks are
dark. The foundations with a chute for coal delivery are
of grey granite. Not a grand building but one of substance and quality.
Adriane steps up to the doors, running her hand reas-
suredly along the curved step wall. At the doors there
is a welcoming light. There should not be a welcoming
light.
Pushing the heavy handle Adriane makes a door move
effortlessly back. Daylight. To each side of the entrance

there are parts to the building. A foyer but in the centre where stairs and possibly a lift would be, there is a view of the building's rear wall. To the right, at the side, the wall is missing. It is like looking from the inside of a large cave to the world outside. Walking in. Adriane can see that the structure has taken a massive blow to it's legs and torso. She judges it to be gutted and useless.

Now moving on into the straight line of the last section of the street Adriane can see that this street is empty for a reason. Most of the buildings in the latter half of the thoroughfare are, or have been, fine old German homes from a time when timber beams supported walls and floors. Fire has reduced many to street level. Those that still have shape are shells or fire damaged. Held aloft by their charred but sturdy beams.
Ahead at the end of the street there is activity. Several trucks of German troops rumble past along the adjoining street, heading to that line of defence.
Adriane is beginning to run down. She is weary, starved, thirsty and more than a little drunk. The answers that the street presented are not there. And from here, there is only flight. How long has she got? To outrun the hounds. It never ends well.

A bright moment presents itself. Sitting down on a step the girl hears the clunk of her soup cans.
Placing one on the ground she sits Brunek's knife point on the top and uses a brick to hit the handle, to punch and gouge a hole. The contents will not come out until she drives another hole into the other side.
Oh the joy of feeling the glutinous cold liquid move into

her stomach. This small meal gives hope to a hopeless situation.

Will she ever be free of the Russians? They have chased her unknowingly across the country, through towns and fields, over bridges and rivers. At first with others fleeing, then less as they dispersed. Then just a few, as others gave up or assumed they where safe.

Adriane did not believe she would ever be safe in their hands. She knew.

Now where to go from here?

Sitting waiting for some inspiration, a guiding thought to renew her quest, Adriane is struck once again by the silence around her. A piece of window suddenly gives way from the house opposite. It floats down and shatters on the street. No place for bare-footed refugees. The silence returns.

There is no alternative, she must flee. Perhaps they have not surrounded the city. There may be some place left to go. Find a crowd somewhere. Would they kill everybody? There are no crowds. Those that can, have gone. Those that can't, are hiding.

Time moves, the girl sits. It is daylight. She has no idea what part of the day she is experiencing.

Whock, whock, whock whock whock, whock, whock!

There are sounds, it is no longer quiet. Distant sounds but unmistakable sounds. Rapid now. Men's voices, yelling. It erupts. A crescendo of bangs, pops, blasts. Rapid stuttering of bullets being fired. It keeps building. Blasts and manic firing of guns. The sound washes past.

From a distance gunfire can sound harmless. It appears

to be moving already.

Now the girl is standing. In the middle of the street. A
lone, lost figure. Stooped as if protecting herself. Her
need to flee or hide is now vital. Her head swings to the
right and left. Searching for something. At the end of
the street the intersecting road can take her back but it
is the road where all the death will occur. It is the road
along which they will come.
It is the only choice.

To run you must be light. Adriane is considering taking
off her jacket. She will throw away everything she car-
ries. It slows her down.
A solid whack of some explosive sends a flare of sparks
and phosphorescent fizz shooting overhead. The girl
looks up.
Silhouetted briefly in the display of firepower is the
building with the large steps. The building with the big
doors that led to an emptiness. Adriane has not looked
at the building from this position. She has not seen what
she sees now. For some moments she studies the structure. This view changes her plans.

Here in this bombed-down street in the city of Berlin,
under attack and unsafe, there is a small opportunity.
It is the law of probability. After so many bad things is it
possibly time for the odds to swing in her favour?
In desperate events these are the chances that must be
taken. They may not come again.

Chapter 7

'Battle'

Despite his experience and his alertness, despite the obvious peril of their situation, it is still a surprise when they come. Dieter Falke is looking at his watch. His last view of the street below is of an empty black stretch of asphalted road with sturdy grey or brown buildings on either side.

There is a footpath on both sides. Ornamental trees not much taller than a man are planted along the footpath inside protective iron frames. Both the trees and the street lamps have remained largely untouched by the calamities that have rocked the city. The street has a curve about sixty metres from their position. It is a very slight curve and affords little cover.

The buildings have some pockmarks from bullets in one place but overall the street is intact. There is even glass in the windows of the building.

Through his binoculars the soldier has been able to make out a grand piano in a second floor apartment. It has a bust of Bach sitting atop a pile of what appears to

be sheet music. He knows such a scene. A comfortable
life with academic parents who, despite their respect
for knowledge and a need to make a place in the world,
were able to respect equally the arts and fine music.
They instilled in their children a sense of balance. It was
a gentle life. One that he craved. One that had gone.
This view and the whole street has not changed for days
and for the hours of this day.
After the shelling they waited for the inevitable attack.
It did not come.
Looking back to the street there is something different.
For a moment in time Dieter Falke is staring, compre-
hending the change. Two figures are crouched at the
corner of the building, right at the curve. They are holding something tubular. There is a flash as the soldier
launches himself to the floor.

Their building is rocked by the blast. Masonry and plaster spray across the room. One of the machine guns is
blown sideways.
The machine gun to the left starts up as Falke shakes
his head and jumps to his feet. Another blast hits the
building below them. A third further down must have hit
the sandbags.
Those Russian bastards have an anti-tank weapon.
Probably American or one of their own captured and
put into use. Now everything around Dieter Falke comes
in a rush.
The machine gun on the right is damaged beyond hope.
The snout where bullets would exit the machine is bent
up and twisted. Falke pulls the web of ammunition from
the chamber and drags it across to his comrades at the

left.

"We got the bazooka," the machine gunner cries. The returning Russian fire is withering. Looking down Falke can see Russian soldiers pouring round the roadway. Some have been hit but it does not stop them. They extend their covering fire as others move forward. Above the clatter there is the unmistakable rumble of tank engines. A quick glance below shows the Raketen-panzerbusche 54 anti-tank gun and it's operators have been cut to pieces in the opening exchange.

The vehicle sits exposed and useless. The boys below have managed to get two mortar shells away and both have landed in the middle of the Russian troops. It has briefly halted their progress.

Falke fires his rifle into the confusion, carefully picking targets. Their machine gun is firing very short bursts, to conserve what little ammunition they have. The sound of the tank is drawing close. It will destroy them and their building.

From below, one of the fanatics is standing, firing an MG-42. Where the hell did he get a light machine gun? Initially it has a solid effect on the disorganised troops but like any man who puts ideology before practicalities he is taken out by a Russian bullet. And because he stands on the sandbags to fire, as he falls, he pitches forward and the weapon drops down on the other side out of reach.

Falke and others are firing hard at the Russians while they are temporarily halted.

There is yelling below. The old man is screaming at the boys with the mortar. He yells and points. The boys stand to move the mortar. Both are knocked down in an instant. The old man seems overcome with rage that they should carelessly die in front of him. It is then that his head explodes as a bullet smacks him sideways in a fall like a discarded rag doll.

There are not too many left alive behind the sandbags. They keep firing but it is pointless. The Russians have reorganised and are creeping forward.
Falke picks up a rock and throws it across the room. It clangs on the machine gunner's helmet.
When the men look up Falke waves his arm, calling them to the stairs.
Through a series of hand signals they go about their plan. The machine gun keeps firing small bursts. Falke and another of the Wermacht soldiers run to the back windows to look down.
Despite the ridiculous situation, two of the old fanatics are crouched beyond the back door, waiting to take out any deserters. Near the doorway lay the bodies of two of the boys, shot as they emerged.
The two soldiers rest their rifles on the window sill. One of the men looks up and sees them. They fire. One man is laid flat. Falke's shot has hit his target's leg. The man is squirming in pain and firing rapidly at their window, emptying his Walther in a rage. Bullets clatter around and through the opening.
There is another bang and the man flops back.
Falke acknowledges his companion. He has always been an excellent shot.

As the soldiers move for the stairs Dieter Falke takes

one last look at the scene below them. The tank is rounding the corner. It runs over the bodies of fallen Russian soldiers.

He considers the situation, then scrabbles around to find two of their stick grenades. He hurls them as far as he can past the sandbags.

As they explode it pauses the action. Then the overwhelming rush continues.

The first Russians have reached the sandbags. A few of the Hitler Youth boys try to take them on and are bayoneted quickly and efficiently. A couple more have their hands up. And surprisingly a number of the old guys have surrendered.

Falke momentarily thinks of Hauke and hopes he kept his last bullet.

As they reach the doorway at the back of the building a blast sends a great wall of dust out behind them. The tank is about its business. It seems Russians don't even care if they hit their own men.

The Wehrmacht men shake hands and wish each other luck. "Watch out for the Totenkopf brigades," one of them warns.

"Deserters don't live." It is an obvious comment but understood and appreciated.

They run, each on his own path to hopeful salvation.

Dieter Falke heads straight over a mound of bricks and ruins. He has noted some days before that it affords protection from three sides and leads, like a small canyon, away from their building to an open area some way off. From there a sprint will take him into the remaining frames of several other buildings. He is thankful and surprised that none of his companions have chosen his method of escape. He prefers to take his chances alone. Briefly he wonders if he has missed some dangerous aspect of his chosen route but it seems to be safe.

As he runs, the soldier considers how soon their battle was over. All that silly preparation for such a quick death. There is heroism and then there's stupidity. Judging from the increasing roar of battle each side of their position, the SS soldiers are putting up a much sterner resistance.
Soon the Russians will pour through the hole that their own pathetic effort left in the defences and encircle the SS men.
Falke was glad as he left the doorway to note that neither of the two boys was the body of Hauke Kluge.
He hopes his death was quick wherever it happened.

Crouching he has reached the end of his little canyon of safety. There is a clear, flat open grassy area ahead.
It is of little use looking around. At this point he can't be seen and cannot see. He checks his gun and knives. Who knows?

He is away. Running, upright and purposeful. The grass is short and spongy. A small park? Hard to tell in its current condition. With all the gear of a soldier still hanging from his belt and uniform he is weighed down.
The buildings seem some way off. He is aware that a call, the crack of a rifle may be the last thing he hears.
The battles going on behind seem to have intensified.

His boots thud on the ground. His breath is rasping, his legs weary. The wooden frame of a doorway appears ahead. Half of the surrounding brickwork is missing but it is a goal and will give some protection.
He is through.

Swinging around he presses his back against the wall. He sinks down, spending some time taking deep breaths with his head between his knees. Finally he lifts his head. He fiddles and releases his water bottle, taking careful sips rather than being greedy.
According to his watch their battle lasted a little under half an hour. He gives a snort. Longer than he thought.

Dieter Falke lifts his head and gazes about the buildings and bits of buildings hc can scc.
Now to disappear.

Chapter 8

'The Climb'

Adriane has made her way back along the street. Will it look different when she is close?

"Oh God," she says, "this is impossible."

The building has been hit in a most peculiar way. An expert in these matters might deduce that a large British or American bomb had failed to explode on impact and then gone off some seconds later at the base of the building's side wall. It has had a devastating effect. The side of the building has been blown in, up to nearly the third floor. It has gutted the inside foyer and removed the stairwell and lift.

In doing so the bomb has produced an unusual situation. From the front and three sides the building appears intact. From the one side it appears smashed and dangerous. Yet, for those who are inclined to look for these things, a closer inspection reveals that the building has an inner core. A frame of giant steel beams and concrete. A very solid structure. The brick facade has been built around this core but it has no bearing on the inner strength of the structure. Also, there has been no fire.

Does Adriane notice these fine points of architecture and construction technique? No, she does not. She can however see that the building is reasonably sound. She can also see that it is not in the least way an obvious place to seek refuge. To the brief observer it is a dangerous wreck, best avoided for fear of collapse. With no stairs or means of ascent it is largely useless.
Thus, she concludes, it presents a refuge.

What the girl has seen is a step. Just one. Hidden in the jagged tooth opening from the blast. At the top, almost out of sight, the concrete stairwell continues up into the high floors above. It clings to the steel frame and concrete.

Now she stands at the side of the building her enthusiasm is wilting. From a distance the opening seemed manageable. But beside the great structure it is towering and unreachable. She counts the levels. It is an eight storey building. Thus five storeys are to some extent, intact.
Another blast and the sound of rapid fire drive Adriane into the opening.
She crouches inside while the noise continues. Waiting she can make out the innards and wreckage of the collapsed floors. The foyer had chairs and a lounge, together with a small table. Perhaps for visitors to meet or occupants to await some transport.
Now the whole setting has been hurled to the far side of the space.

There are some pigeons who seem to be crouching in

fear also.

As she watches them watching her, another quite noisy crack takes place outside. The terrified birds can stand their torment no more and do what birds mostly do when in fear. They take flight.

Up, swirling around seeking salvation, they eventually flutter out of the building and away.

"No, you stupid birds," thinks Adriane.

Her eyes rest on the unreachable stairs. So high. The girl has not a great strength when it comes to heights. Below the steps she sees a steel floor joist poking out, cut and bent away by the bomb blast. Below that she sees several holes where bricks have been partially blown out of the wall, below those holes there is a beam with several bent and busted steel protrusions. It lays on an angle from the second to the first floor.

And in front of Adriane is a great lump of timber, possibly part of the foyer. It is long and no doubt heavy but laid far enough out and resting against the remains of the first floor, it may give access to the concrete platform of that floor and the sloping steel beam which could take her to the second floor. This would in turn allow access to the holes in the bricks and if she could climb those holes without falling to her death and get onto the beam that sticks out of the wall, she would reach the stairs.

It takes Adriane over half an hour. The timber that is to begin her ascent is very heavy. At times she considers giving up. The wood seems incredibly dense. The grain is tight. It is hard, like marble. Whatever tree yielded it up must have been a sturdy forest giant. Finally by

building two columns of loose bricks and lifting the
piece from one to the higher one and then to the first
floor ledge, the girl is able to achieve a reasonably an-
gled, possible to climb, point of access.
Before she starts her climb Adriane realises that she
cannot climb in a jacket. She must leave behind the
remaining soup and the brandy. She also dispenses with
the pistol, concluding that knives are more useful and
don't run out of ammunition. All are hidden at the base
of the leaning timber, under some bricks.

Then she begins to climb. She slips and falls several
times before concluding that boots are not for climbing.
They too are hidden behind the bricks. Her bare feet
grip the wood and she struggles up, slides back, tears at
the wood and groans with determination. With strength
she barely possesses she reaches the first floor, laying
for a while her face on the cold concrete.
It is here breathing deep, considering the next part of
her journey that she hears voices. They are distant
and muffled, perhaps carried by the wind but they are
enough to scare this refugee.
She pushes the great piece of timber that took her so
long to position. It falls back to the floor below with a
clattering roar and pleasingly bounces off one her brick
piles, scattering more evidence of her presence.

The act also creates a major barrier to any thoughts of
retreat.
For a moment she pauses, waiting for the noise to bring
soldiers but the greater noise goes on outside as a back-
drop to her quest.

"What have you done?" she says. "You're trapped now. The only way is up. And now I'm talking to myself."
She looks once more over the drop to the ground floor. She might survive a jump back down. For now she must go on.

The steel beam is comparatively easy. There are footholds. Though the round steel rods hurt her feet she quickly reaches the second floor.
Now the folly of the whole idea is apparent as Adriane climbs the vertical wall with nothing to grip except a hand or a foot in some painful hole in the brickwork. Her vertigo suddenly rushes forward and grips her in fear as she looks down at the drop straight to the basement. She hangs, pressed against the masonry for minutes, talking to her inner self that explains that there is no other choice. She must go on. She watches the wall. Counts the bricks as they go past with each move up. Once her hands are on the steel beam solidly stuck in the wall there are a number of easy footholds as if her effort was being rewarded.
From the beam there is one large, don't look down step up and onto the first part of the remaining stairwell.

Now is the moment of concern. Adriane looks up.
It is a beautiful site. Stretching away in neat formed steps and disappearing onwards and upwards, the stairwell awaits her tread. After three steps it is kind to her feet as she moves onto a soft, thick, plum red stair carpet runner. She can see the next landing.

The fighting outside has subsided. No more voices or

noises. A brief piece of silence in a war zone. The building is quiet. It awaits her visit.

Chapter 9

'Exploring'

Could it be that there are people here? Doubt, fear,
suspicion all work their way through Adriane's mind
as she moves up the first steps. There are none of the
tell-tale creaks of a wooden staircase. This beast is solid.
The concrete has tiles at the edge and the central run of
carpet feels soft. Not threadbare or even worn.
Absurdly, Adriane takes out her knife and holds it in
front as she reaches the first landing.

Stretching away to the front of the building is one long
corridor. At the end a large window floods in light along
to the stair landing. The stairwell that started in the
centre of the foyer has wound round to the back of the
building. It is secondary to the lift. From the lift a corridor branches off to allow access to the apartments.
When the building functioned, the stairs would have
been rarely used.
Along the corridor there are four doors. All appear to be
open to some degree. Halfway along on the left are the
cage doors to the lift.

Making her way along Adriane reaches the first door on the left. It is wide open. Inside is a wasteland. The windows have been mostly broken. There is a lounge and cabinet. Papers, dust dirt and sodden rubbish lay everywhere. The curtains have half fallen across the windows. The ceilings are slightly vaulted with a timber beam across. Perhaps an effort to give the main rooms a country manor touch. There is mould on everything. The smell of rot in the air. Broken glass on the floor has almost reached the door. Adriane can see pieces close to her feet.

This, the fourth floor, consists of four apartments all equally damaged, all wet and mildewed. They have been this way for a while. The moisture is causing some of the furniture to expand and fall apart.
One tiny bright note is the appearance of a bottle of some sort of liquid sitting on a sideboard, out of reach across a glass covered floor.
Adriane makes note of a need to find some form of foot covering. Shoes, slippers, socks, even rags. She will come back.

Treading very carefully, noting tiny glints of glass in the carpet, the girl reaches the fifth floor. It is a replica of the floor below. This time there are some pieces of bedding in the corridor as if residents may have temporarily sheltered here from the bombing until they were evacuated. At least there are no bodies. Nothing sinister. The apartment at the end of the corridor closest to the front window has a closed door. It is locked. The corridor window is intact. Could there be people inside this one?

Hesitating, Adriane, a polite person, knocks on the door.
She waits. Knocks again.
Finally she puts her shoulder to the door. The locks are
not strong. It yields. Another mess. Better furniture.
Sturdy, heavy German make. Dark carved wood. Some
mould damage but only one broken window. An optimist
who hoped to return.

For a minute Adriane retreats and lays on one of the
beds in the corridor. It is musty but dry.
She realises how long it has been since she lay on a bed.
Her hand, hanging to the floor, touches something under
the bed. It is a bottle of beer.
Sitting on the side of the bed she uses the hunting knife
to prise the cap loose. The contents foam up. Adriane
does not like beer. Old beer that is stale is even less
appealing but she is thirsty and this is at least a liquid.
It is good, she decides. On the farm such slops would be
fed to the pigs.

After the awful noise of conflict the day has become un-
usually quiet. Perhaps it is the building. It already feels a
little safer.
Occasionally Adriane hears voices. Some yelling. Making
plans, giving orders. Soldiers? Civilians? Distant sounds
drifting in through the broken windows.
It is time to move on. Though without food or water
there seems little point. The building could be a safe
refuge for a while but how does she survive?

On the sixth floor there is the usual corridor with four
doors and the lift gates. Three doors are closed. There

is a single bed near the front corridor window. It looks
cleaner than the bed on the floor below. The apartment
with an open door is completely empty. All the windows
are intact. Just carpet on the floor. These people evacuated early. Adriane can reach the windows without
fear of broken glass. There is little to see. The day has
cleared. There is smoke rising from several positions
nearby. The view is quite extensive. The building sits
on a high point of the street. At the end, near the corner
that Adriane turned to enter the street. She thinks she
can make out people, soldiers, bodies? They are down
and do not move. That is all she can tell.

The door of the room opposite opens to reveal another empty apartment. The two front rooms have locked
doors. In her routine Adriane still knocks on the first
door. It then takes several runs to break the lock. Standing in the entry she quickly assesses the rooms. Near
empty. Moving out when the bombs fell. Just a stack of
chairs. Rolled rugs. A giant cabinet. The windows are
intact. The other rooms are empty.

For the other door Adriane dispenses with her polite behaviour. Once the lock is snapped the experience is the
same. An almost empty apartment. This time the move
out is all but finished. Just a large dining table. And upon
the table a plate of hardened cheese and what was once
a loaf of bread.
The windows are yet again all in one piece. Light floods
in across the empty space.
The cheese is hard, parts are mouldy. Cutting with her
knife Adriane is able to locate a central part that is clean

and still edible. It is good. Aged by default. A rich tangy mouthful.

It is beginning to look bad. Stale beer and a mouthful of cheese will not sustain the girl for long. To go back to the streets is a terrifying option.
There are two floors left. Little hope judging from the increasing absence of higher floor tenants.

On the landing of the seventh floor Adriane stares for some seconds. Something is different.
There are only two doors. There are the lift gates on the right but only two doors, both on the main street side of the corridor.
Moving along, the door on the left comes first. It is slightly ajar. Pushing it back there is debris cluttering the door. The inside of the apartment is fully furnished. Everything is black and charred. The windows and part of the wall is shattered. Something has come through the window. It has caused a massive flash. From what Adriane can see from the door, the apartment is unoccupied. With bare feet she dares not enter.

The door of the second apartment is locked. The apartments on this floor are much bigger than those below. Each appears to cover half of the levels floorspace. Adriane takes several runs at the door but it does not budge. It seems heavier and of greater quality than the doors of the previous floors.
After several minutes chipping at the door jamb round the lock with her knife, she tries again. Still the door does not move. It needs to be unlocked.

The door has four panels. The indents on the panels present a comparatively thinner area on which to work. For twenty minutes the girl hacks at the panel edges. Then the tip of the knife penetrates and slips through. With the help of a blackened table leg from the other apartment the girl smashes the panel. It pops clear leaving a sizeable opening.

In savouring her triumph Adriane is hit by a foul, sickly sweet stench from the door. It is a smell she knows. Encountered time and again on her journey. Death. Standing at the door of the other blackened apartment she takes deep breaths, trying to rid her nose of clinging, pervasive odour.
The initial wave seems to dissipate. After a suitable wait and with her lung filled with clean air, Adriane returns to the door. Holding her vest up and over her mouth and nose she peers in the hole made by the missing panel. The room is a lounge. Unlike the previous apartments it is full of furniture. There are bookcases, lined with large important looking editions. A giant sideboard with expensive vases at either end. In the centre is a bronze eagle in a pose as if poised to take flight. Richly woven rugs on the floor. As the girl's eye moves from the sides of the room she can see a lounge settee with deep cushions in a rich dark green brocade fabric. There are two matching, high-backed chairs. Her eye stops. In one of the chairs, facing her, is a man. He is dressed in a somewhat old-fashioned, Bavarian-style tweed jacket and jodhpurs. His hands are at his sides. His legs splayed. Strangely his head is upright and his mouth open and his eye sockets staring. His body is rotted and decayed.

Still, in death he presents a physical and mental obstacle to any thought of entry.

Stepping back Adriane considers her options. The apartment was occupied. Possibly the old man was too stubborn to leave. He may have died of a heart attack. Alone, he sat down in his favourite chair and just passed away. There could be food. It may all be tainted? There could be no food. He may have starved to death or died of thirst or both. The door lock had a key protruding from it's mechanism on the inside. She could enter. She chooses not to proceed. There is another floor.

At the landing for the eighth floor there is a steel ladder bolted to the wall. It runs up to a trapdoor in the ceiling. A maintenance device?
So, Adriane stands and stares down the corridor of this final floor. Unlike the seventh floor there is a shorter corridor. It leads to the lift gates and nearby there is a single door. The normal light from the corridor window is not there. Instead there is a small window on the side wall, the back of the building. It shows the neat, clean short passageway. It looks somehow elegant. Near the window stand two brass planter pots on dark-stained wooden plinths. The plants, whatever they were, hang over the sides, long dead.
So here is a last chance. Whatever is up on this top level, it is alone. It occupies the whole floor.
As the girl surveys this last floor in her grand plan for refuge there is a sudden crescendo of activity outside. Below in the streets, a massive clatter of small arms fire breaks out. There are shouts, screams, a blast, then

another. This is close fighting. A machine gun is rattling.

Adriane sinks to the floor, covers her ears and waits.
The fighting goes on and on. Whatever is happening it
is not good. People are being hurt, blood is being spilt,
lives are ending. At one stage she uncovers her ears
and jolts. Voices rise up the stairwell. There are soldiers
below, possibly inside her building. There are shouts,
enraged, urgent utterances of men in critical moments.
Listening intently, cowering on the floor, Adriane cannot
make out the words. She screws her face in concentration. Then the realisation of why she cannot understand.
The voices are crying out in Russian.

Chapter 10

'The Room'

Fear can be overwhelming. Despite her anxiety, her need to stay alert, to protect any chance of discovery, Adriane has fallen asleep. Her face lays comfortably on the soft, plum red carpet of the eighth floor corridor. She dreams of a black tunnel which seems endless. Though she can see a tiny light, she cannot reach her goal. Occasionally there are odd windows in her tunnel that show green fields with flowers but the windows switch off as if a light is extinguished and she is once again in the blackness. It is a sudden feeling that she is being pursued and that a black figure is near her and there is no longer any light, that finally snaps the girl awake.

After some disorientation she looks about then climbs to her feet. She leans against the wall listening for any sign of a presence in the building. Still not assured she goes back down the stairs as far as the fifth level, creeping down, stopping listening, checking the various corridors as she goes. It is all quiet, Still as a crypt.
There are noises. Vehicles and voices. They are distant.

After standing for some time on the fifth level landing she decides that her building has not been compromised.

Back at the eighth level, Adriane stands where she had stood two hours before, about to explore this last area. Shadows are starting to lengthen across the hallway as the day progresses.

One door, one choice. It is closed. The door is locked. It is not a door that will yield. It has quality. There is a difference. No other below has a doormat. It is black with some green leaves on a branch built into the tufted surface. It is more a small decorative carpet than a doormat. It clashes with the hallway carpet runner. Standing looking at this odd piece outside a door Adriane is taken by an impulse. Why would you have such a thing at your door?

She reaches down and lifts the mat her eyes searching for the possibility. It is not there. Then could the mat at the door be a decoy? She looks up then reaches to the top of the door's architrave. It is high. This is a big door, made for a bigger, better apartment. The top floor apartment. Her hands are scrabbling along the surface. They touch nothing. Of course. Why would the owner of a top floor apartment leave a key where it could be easily found. They would carry such a key with them.
But what if it were lost? What then? How to get in once more? Adriane looks about this last corridor. She walks and looks at the black emptiness beyond the lift gates then to the corridor itself. The first planter pot is not

heavy. The soil is dry, the plant dead. Beneath the pot the plinth has a circular wood ring to enclose the pot and keep it secure. At the bottom of this circular piece there is a crossed wooden section which supports the pot. Sitting in the centre of this section there is a brass key.

With a satisfying click the door indicates it is ready. Adriane turns the handle and the door opens. She stands, waiting.
No smell, no broken glass, no rot, mould or mildew, no empty room, no blackened, charred damage, no bodies, scenes of chaos or departure. A little dusty perhaps but nothing more.
Somebody left this apartment with a plan to return again quite soon. Did they die in the attempt? Did an American or British bomb end their plans? Perhaps right outside as they returned home.

Adriane stands on the threshold looking about, searching for a reason to be disappointed. The lounge is fat and soft with peach coloured covers in large bright patterns. There is a little table next to one seat with magazines and an ashtray. There is a large bookcase with glass fronts. Heavy dark green curtains at the windows. On a long side-table on the lefthand wall a vase with wilted flowers. Near the chairs against the wall on the right is a handsome radio with a fine timber cabinet. In the far corner on the right, a glass panelled door leads onto the balcony. The carpet is a beige almost brown colour. At the left in the centre of the wall is a mock fireplace with an electric heater. Set beyond the fireplace is

a handsome, heavy desk. It is positioned in the corner
to take advantage of the light from the large front window. A brass lamp with a green glass shade sits on the
desk. A big leather upholstered chair with padded arms
and rollers is back from the desk as if the owner had
only this minute stood to walk to another room.

Stepping in, the girl does something involuntary. She is
momentarily shocked at such a simple action after she
is in the room. She has pushed the door shut behind her
and hears a satisfying click.
Once inside, the room is bigger than first indicated.
Beyond the room itself is a balcony.
This will be the first apartment that Adriane can explore
completely.

A wide corridor runs off this loungeroom all the way to
the side of the building. It is lit by a window at the end.
This is the premier apartment in the building. The first
doorway on the right leads into a dining room. There is
an oak table with eight chairs and matching sideboard.
In the corner is a serving trolley with two shelves. There
is a silver tray on top. The wall has a painting of a forest
with light beams coming through the trees.
From the dining room their is a archway into an extensive kitchen. It has an open door to the corridor as
well. There is a big gas stove with a hood. In the centre
there is a wooden table and four chairs. A wide marble
sink. Cupboards above and below the benchtops. Even
a small refrigerator. Adriane has never seen a refrigerator. She pulls the handle, wincing at the expected
odour. It's contents are shrivelled. Some pieces of fruit

are mouldy. There is an unopened bottle of Moselle. No smell except a musty note in the air.

It is the first cupboard that changes the girl's point of view. Reaching above the benches she pulls open the door. The cupboard is packed with tins. Her eyes widen as she reads the labels.
"This can't be true," she mutters.
The next cupboard is the same and the next all the way to the end wall. At that point in the corner of the kitchen is a giant walk-in pantry that has two wide doors and stretches from floor to ceiling. It is piled with jars of cabbage, pickles, fruit, even preserved potatoes. There are packets of flour and rice, milk powder and custard. There are army packs of egg powder.
Other packets have sultanas, dried apricots, dried apple pieces. To the side, wrapped in muslin-cloth is a leg of smoked ham. Next to the ham a long rope with at least twenty types of sausage. The liverwurst is no good. The others appear dry but still quite edible.
Standing in front of this magnificent find, considering all the possibilities, Adriane slowly turns her head. She stares back into the kitchen at the object that will bring all she is seeing to life. Gleaming above the sink is a tap.

The city is destroyed and fighting for its life.
Occupants are living hand to mouth. Those that remain are about to be subjugated under the unsympathetic rule of the deeply scarred Russian invaders. Not even basic services could still exist.

The tap is stiff. It has not been turned for a while.

There is nothing. She sighs. For a while she could get by with the beer and wine in the pantry but without water to cook, to survive ....
There is a slight noise, a pause, a gurgle and water gushes out.
Shocked the girl jumps back watching the amazing scene. With the realisation that this precious commodity is escaping down the drain she lunges forward and shuts it off. She is breathing hard. Trembling. She is looking about with a new appreciation. The possibilities.

Now Adriane stands back again and makes sense of this event. Her breathing won't slow. Her hand to her mouth. With the turn of the tap handle all the cupboard contents have a new meaning. Food and water. Food and water!

Whoever lived here had planned for a long stay. Possibly a siege. Some doubt as to a great German victory? Maybe they had connections? Party members? Military? Was there a wife or perhaps a cook? Were there small dinner parties in the dining room?
With her hand still to her mouth, still contemplating the enormity of her discovery Adriane glances sideways. The stove sits silent, like some large metal beast, waiting to be disturbed. Could it be?

Turning a tap on the stove top produces nothing. Perhaps a little too much optimism. Still there is food and water. Cold food and water. It is more than could be hoped for in this city in this situation.
Standing in front of the open cupboards the girl can

only marvel, pointing with her finger as she reads the labels on the cans of soup, pork, jam, honey, lard, butter .... She mouths the words over and over.
How long can she last? Will there be an end? A point at which it will be safe. She has nothing, no one and belongs nowhere.
Except here. For now it is a place to be alive, alone and safe.

"What!?"
Her first instinct is danger. The stove?
There is a hissing noise and a smell. She looks about.
Her first thoughts are of danger. A bomb? A trap? Then the answer. It is right there in front of her, coming from the stove. Gas!!! My God, gas!!
Yes, it is flowing out of the open jet.
After shutting it off there is little more to do than contemplate the new possibilities.
Adriane Gerst, an experienced country girl has found a sanctuary in the city. She stands with both her hands over mouth now and laughs quietly. Schoolgirl silly, she shakes until it hurts.
In a moment of supreme optimism she goes to the wall and flicks the light switch. Nothing happens. "Stupid girl," she thinks, "I couldn't have lights on anyway."

Eventually she sits with a glass of water at the kitchen table. It is enough pleasure for the moment to do nothing but sit on a chair at a table, in a clean room and drink clean water from a clean glass.
Still she periodically breaks her reverie to look about and smile.

Chapter 11

'The First Night'

Through a door on the left of the corridor there is a
bathroom and a toilet alcove with a curtain.
The bathroom has a pale green bath with a matching
hand-basin. It is tiled. White walls and a brown green
mosaic on the floor. A dried, cracked cake of soap sits
on the basin.
In a small cabinet there is a razor, a shaving mug, a
strop, some powder in a tin and a some lavender water.
Another packet contains small tablets. Some medication
or possibly just aspirin.
The toilet is a flush operation. In the bottom of the bowl
there is a small grey pool of water.
Contemplating the simple act of flushing the toilet
requires consideration. "It will use water. How much is
there? The noise could possibly be heard."

Finally Adriane shakes her head and grabs the porcelain
ended chain from the cistern. She pulls it down once
and lets go. Water rushes down and through the bowl.
When the stop cock shuts it off the water is back again

to the correct height. The bowl should be cleaned but the water in it is clear. Meanwhile the cistern refills, not with the roar of a pressurised pipe but at least with a satisfyingly strong stream.

It is the next act that Adriane finds most necessary. She lights the stove and boils two large saucepans of water. From a hallway cupboard full of linen she finds a small towel and a large one.
In the bathroom she fills the basin with hot water, saving one saucepan for some refills. She then removes all her clothes. Slowly and thoroughly she washes every part of her body, rinsing and scrubbing. Over and over till her skin is red. Going into herself till it hurts in a necessary effort to rid herself of the smell, feel, taste and memory of the man Brunek, the trickster, the betrayer, the monster. Who had offered her hope and given her misery. German on German.
Her head hurts from his blows and her stomach is bruised. These will heal. But can she forget?

At the end of the ritual she splashes some lavender water on her body to further mask any memories. Wrapping herself in a large, soft, white towel she finally looks at herself in the bathroom mirror. For a moment she is unsure of the person she sees, then her face crumples and she cries. It is a hurt, lonely wail. She sinks back to the bath and sitting on the edge she sobs, screwing up her body, clenching her fists and rocking.
After some minutes the her misery subsides. Now she sits sniffing and trying to get a breath. It comes in shudders.

"Why have I not cried before?" she asks herself. It has
been a cathartic release. She feels as if it were some
burden that she has now expunged.
She glances up at the doorway as if somebody might
have taken a position there while she was offguard.

Finally, dry and clean at last she puts all her clothes into
the bath and runs some water to let them soak.

At the end of the corridor the naked girl looks for the
first time into the bedrooms. Little flashes of uncertainty still flicker into her brain. She had not examined the
whole place. There could be somebody here.
The excitement of seeing all the food had dulled her
sense of caution.

Of course there is nobody there.
The large bedroom at the front has a double bed. Plush
with a fat dark plum feather quilt. A similar colour to the
stairwell carpets. There is a big chest of drawers.
A large, heavy carved chair. Some suit trousers are
draped over the arm. There is a big matching wardrobe.
The decor is coordinated in a way that suggests money
and some privilege.
A cursory inspection of the wardrobe reveals only men's
clothing. Suits, jackets, shirts, heavy winter coats, expensive leather shoes. Not the clothes of a young man
but somebody with taste. A tall man perhaps, not of
heavy build.
Adriane finds a soft woolen dressing gown. It is lined
and feels good against her skin. There is a clean hand-
kerchief in the pocket. It reminds her briefly and for

some odd reason, of her father.
There is a photo in a silver frame. It is small, perched on
top of the chest of drawers. It shows a woman standing
by a gate. She has her hands on two small children, a
boy and a girl, as if she is controlling their exuberance.
She is smiling. She looks well dressed as do the children.

The bedroom on the other side is similarly furnished
but as a guest room with two single beds

Now, with the light of the day failing, with a hot meal
of ham, cabbage and potatoes inside her, sipping hot
milky coffee with a little pinch of cinnamon, Adriane sits
on the lounge of her newly acquired home and contem-
plates the events of the day. From despair to hope. It is
quiet outside. She is tired.
There is a beautiful welcoming bed a few steps away
but the cunning, the caution that has guided her to this
point will not desert her.
So she lays on the lounge, wrapped in the man's dressing gown, wearing a pair of his thick grey woollen socks,
resting her head on one of the man's pillows, warmed by
two bed blankets but holding her knife and watching the
door.
The door that is locked is still a way in for somebody
who may do her harm. Thus she pulls the blankets close
to her face and enjoys the warmth and comfort of the
moment.
Her eyes drift over the bright flowers on the upholstery.
They are quite beautiful she thinks. So nice. Elegant in
fact.

Adriane's sleep would have lasted the whole night had
it not been for the crazed rush of the counter offensive
by the regrouped remains of the local Schutzstaffel the
Waffen SS brigades who at 2am launched into the whole
Russian army.

The battle commenced with a remorseless roar of light
arms fire and a great deal of yelling. Flares were fired to
give some light to their advance as they poured back
down the streets below and around Adriane's building.
The girl woke with a jolt while the room lit up and faded
as each flare into the night sky. Their initial attack was
well planned and successful. Several of the Russian T34
tanks parked in a row just two blocks away were destroyed by SS soldiers using their Panzerfaust anti-tank
weapons and grenades to disable the tracks. Many Russian soldiers were drunk on locally discovered hoards
of liquor. They staggered about and were cut down by
the disciplined German crossfire. Some Russian soldiers
shot other Russians because they had stolen and were
wearing the much more comfortable and better quality German uniforms. Chaos cannot last. The Russians
reacted.

Adriane lay shaking, the blankets over her head. Would
they enter her building this time for some strategic or
survival reason? She waited. Listening to every sound.
Nobody came.

The battle seemed to reach a climax and move on.
It dropped away as if a marathon running team had
merely passed by.
In more rational times the highly trained and fearless
soldiers of the SS units would have used the thorough-

ly drilled tactics of warfare. Their advance would have been consolidated and coordinated. Scouting, taking, holding, positioning, reinforcing.
Perhaps they knew, after all they had each taken the oath. There were no options. It may have simply been a gesture and a way of putting an end to things.

These Russians had not crossed the vast lands of their birth and entered the lands of these people who had done them such terrible harm, without gaining a lot of knowledge, toughness and cunning.

So they let the German soldiers run, let them stretch and thin out. They faded before them and around them. Became a non-target. Ran down their ammunition, their will and their hope. When the SS men were at that point of denial, the Russians reappeared and in one terrible and monstrous blow cut these indoctrinated, lost sons of the Reich, down in their hundreds. They cut off their retreat and simply annihilated them. And they fell as they had lived, in a belief in a system that had turned them into the tools of a hopeless empire.

Even the girl on the eighth floor could guess the stages of the battle and the inevitability of its outcome.

Chapter 12

'The Neighbourhood'

In the morning the fog was back. Briefly it hung about
the buildings and rubble. Little of its content was natural. More a source of gunsmoke and fire smoke.
No prisoners were taken from the night. In a mix of try
or die from the SS and the Russian disinterest in
having Germans to look after, the options all amounted
to death. So now it was the Russians who carried and
stacked the dead Germans and set alight the piles of
corpses.
The local population who may have cared for the
bodies of their dead soldiers were nowhere to be found
and to search them out, bring them out and have them
fuss about trying to make the bodies disappear was too
daunting for the victors.
Better it be done and the stench be over quickly. Bones
in the street were commonplace in this city.

The area of the battle was to be held while other
Russian units moved deeper into the city. In all its obsti-
nacy Berlin had days to live. So, for now, in a neat two

storey, former restaurant, that had escaped all but a few pock marks to its facade, the Russians set up a command post that would serve the area.

Downstairs they used the kitchens, turned the seating into a work area and communication facility and installed the officers upstairs.

War and death can be a very convenient ladder for the ambitious or simply fated few to climb. The latter was the case for Boris Chaban. Four months ago in the Russian motherland he was a minor Lieutenant.

A direct hit on a staff car two months back, an unfortunate explosion in some munitions near their previous headquarters and Boris Chaban was now climbing the stairs of the establishment known as 'Gerostetes Brot', whose sign still hung from its chains outside the window, as a full captain.

Boris Chaban was not a ruthless soldier, a leader of men or brilliant tactician. His mild desire for promotion was based solely on a wish to live for now and come out of the war alive and with a degree of security. He knew the soldiers of the glorious Red Army were a commodity. The higher he rose in the ranks, though not without the alternate risk of being noticed, at least moved him out of the expendable area of current thought into desirable in the new Russia. A homeland already plotting its destiny in the postwar world.

Now as he mounted each step, behind his personal assistant, he hoped that the night's battle with the last, desperate patches of the enemy combatants, would bring an end to his troubles and the danger.

They had been caught out, lost a lot of men and taken some time to regroup and produce some counter measures. It could have looked very bad for his first major test as a Kapitan. But the equation that makes sense of war's chaos had once again fallen in his favour.
General Federoff, the man who would have demanded answers from his new Captain was killed by a suicidal German BDM girl who had been assigned to help in their field hospital. With two grenades under her coat she held out her hand to the General while pulling the pins with the other.
After that, the eighteen other BDM girls working for the Russians were taken outside and shot.
It was a lesson being learnt many times over by all the allied forces. Most of the children, Hitler Jungend and BDM girls, encountered in battle and post battle, were beyond help. They believed in the Reich and the Fuhrer and wished to die for the cause. Their blind fanaticism and lack of wisdom meant that they saw no reason.
It was akin to dealing with the insane. Hard still for soldiers to face killing children. Though as the last desperate child soldiers became fourteen, then thirteen and twelve, eleven and younger, their bravado faded to fear and panic.

The staff were proud of their effort. On short notice they had set up a desk and chair, a separate much larger table with some restaurant chairs for briefings, also a bed and washing facilities.
Smart enough not to look too at ease, Captain Chaban resisted the urge to sit at his desk and moved to the large table.

"Do we have maps yet?" he asked, holding his hands out and addressing all the staff.

"Yes, we do, Sir."

The man assigned to assist this new captain was a regular soldier. Chaban had picked him because the man actually met his gaze when he spoke to some troops. His instinct about the fellow proved correct. The man was both resourceful and respectful and as far as he could tell was loyal.

With an ability to get things done, he also had an ability to find things. A resource of great importance in any theatre of war.

It seemed a cliche. An almost theatrical ability. This able assistant who could 'get things' and 'do things' but thus it was and thus it would stay.

"Good," said Chaban, "let's see what you have."

What they had was a tense situation. The SS brigades still operating in the area had no plans to give up and no plans to be captured. They would all eventually die by inflicting as much misery as possible on the Russian invaders. Unlike the general enlistment Wermacht who knew defeat when they saw it, the blind loyalty of the SS to the ideals of the Fuhrer seemed to match the childlike madness of the Hitler Jugend that would take them all to their graves in glorious defence of the fatherland.

Captain Chaban's problem was a lack of reliable intelligence concerning exact numbers, positions, ability to attack, ammunition and backup of the foe and whether to move forward and engage or wait for them to come to him and meet their fate.

To advance would be desirable. The Russian Army had a very long score to settle and getting closer to that goal was considered the complete focus for all commanders. However, to advance into an unknown situation could be a complete rout and detrimental to a commander's career.

To wait for the SS to try something also had many risks. Another possible crazed battle as well as being seen to be inactive could indicate indecisiveness and not moving forward. A further issue nagging the Captain, was the far too relaxed nature of many of the men under is command. They assumed it was all but over. Despite orders to the contrary they were drunk and taken to looting and vengeful acts.

So, with these burdens at hand Captain Chaban's tactics of the night had, in the end, proved very successful. The German soldiers, spurred on by their initial success, had let enthusiasm overcome caution. Caught in the withering fire of two well-placed ambushes the body count of SS soldiers numbered in the hundreds. How many did that leave? The intelligence was sketchy and unreliable.

Chaban looked at the maps. They were basic street maps with little detail. His section covered a narrow channel of residential areas in what was an affluent part of the city. A main road and several parallel roads connected some kilometres back with a rail siding and station.

It was obvious why the Germans had decided to push through this area. It presented a well covered direct route to the railway. One that could be functioning again very soon.

Now in this room, there were only junior officers and none of any consequence with which to confer.
The Captain leaned over the maps, his arms spread on the table, hoping some enlightenment would occur.
Finally he stood back, then walked to his desk. He dismissed the officers and suggested they continue setting up the post downstairs.
He took off his heavy coat. His adjutant jumped in from his respectful distance to assist. Chaban handed him his hat as well.
He looked at the soldier. "Comrade, what is your name? I've forgotten."
The young man straightened up.
"I am Sergey Kozuch, Sir."
Chaban looked again.
"Well, Sergey Kozuch. It looks like it's up to you and me."
"Sir?"
The captain smiled.
"These are unconventional times, Comrade Kozuch.
Do you see any others in this room?"
The soldier looked about as if expecting there to be others gathered that he had not noticed.
"Ah, no sir."
"Then," the Captain paused, "it's up to us."
The adjutant looked puzzled, slightly concerned.
Chaban put a hand on the man's shoulder.
"Leave my coat and hat on the desk. You and I comrade, we're both Russians, do you agree?"
"Yes Sir, I do agree."

"Then it is only fair that you, as a Russian, one who has
fought all the way from our homeland to this city of Berlin, should have some say in how we go about finishing
this job."
Sergey Kozuch was apprehensive. No commander had
noticed his existence until now, nor wanted to know his
name. Now here was one who had done both also wanted his opinion. He feared a trap.
And Captain Chaban knew the look.
"Comrade Kozuch. My mother often said, 'Two heads
are better than one but three is an argument.' I'm no
genius. There's two of us. The perfect number. If we get
it wrong nobody will ask you why you did what you did
because this situation could not possibly happen. But
right now I would welcome a second opinion from somebody who has some 'experience.'"
Chaban held out his hand. The soldier looked at it in
disbelief. Then the two men shook hands.
"I like you," said Chaban, " because you look people in
the eye. Now let's look at these maps."

Chaban was a dark tall man. He had broad shoulders
and a fleshy, ruddy face. In a better life he may have
been chubby but the exertions of war and slim rations
had removed such tendencies. Kozuch was a man born
of muscle. It showed in his face and his movement.
A restless energy. Like a nervous bird. He had an odd
gentle smile and dark blue eyes. Possibly the reason the
captain had noticed his gaze in the first place.

As the two men leaned over the table, Chaban added,
"Of course, if I get this right, I will take all the credit."

He paused, "But I promise you I will find you a bottle of the best German Brandy and some decent cigarettes, maybe even American."

"Thank you, Sir. I am sure you will. Incidentally, our biggest strategic problem is not the enemy." Kozuch paused. "The men, Sir, they are perpetually drunk and looking for women to rape. That is why we were caught by surprise."

Having said this much the soldier plunged deeper.

"The death of General Federoff may have been avoided if the BDM girls were not raped repeatedly every night. They were even raped again before they were shot. Some of them were not of age. I hate the Germans for what they have done to Mother Russia but surely it is common sense not to give them any advantages they can use against us."

In the silence that followed Sergey Kozuch felt he may have gone past his role as an adjunct to the Captain's planning.

Chaban spoke.

"I know of these things Comrade Kozuch. Sometimes, what we cannot command in life we try to control instead. The answer to nearly all things lies in the middle of the extremes. If we're to continue our advance into Berlin we need discipline while allowing the natural flow of human emotion to run its course.

So the soldiers get drunk sometimes and rape and kill. This is war. Command is getting the balance right to achieve the objective. You are wise and you are right and by God it's good to hear an honest opinion instead of a safe one but I for the moment outrank you. Sadly we must accept the situation."

Captain Chaban then laughed, quite loudly.
"What a situation we have. War does this. I am laughing at something so basic and vile. C'mon now let's think of something. It's the least we can do."
Adjutant Comrade Sergey Kozuch smiled and concentrated on the streets in front of his face.

Behind him Captain Chaban spoke once more, his voice softer.
"Soldiers fight and die but it's the civilians who suffer and die the most. Don't think I'm heartless Comrade. I feel for those girls, obsessed products of an ideology they may have been. All those who have been unfairly caught up in this mayhem. I personally don't think war has winners. We're all losers. Now we have to see it through. The quicker it's over the more chance others will have to survive. And for that matter for us as well."
"Thank you, Sir," Kozuch whispered.

Chapter 13

'The Morning and the Afternoon'

Silence can be loud. The girl on the lounge, lost in blankets and cushions, is woken by a lack of noise. A peace that allows the creak of a hinge or the call of a bird to make its way through the morning without interruption. She lays still for some time, her head wrapped in one of the blankets, just her eyes moving about, searching the room, watching and remembering. If someone were watching they would not know she is alert. Nothing has changed. Everything is as it was when the night's darkness descended.

Sleeping past the dawn is not a concept she is used to or one that affords safety at this time.
Adriane decides she is safe. At least in terms relative to the surrounding area.
She sits up. For a while this is all she does. To be able to sit on a comfortable lounge is reward in itself.
There were dreams. Upon reflection they were sad dreams. She had been at the farm. The farmhouse was much bigger, the rooms huge. Her family were all there.

Looking at her they had smiled and run off down corridors and into other rooms. She called to them and followed but could not catch them. They would stop and smile at her and then run away. Always away.

In the kitchen there is the odd problem of what, from the myriad of choices, she should prepare for breakfast. After standing for some time scanning the pantry contents with a schoolgirl smile, Adriane settles on dried apricots heated with some oats, powdered milk and water. She adds some sugar and then makes more milky coffee. Marvelling all the time at the continued supply of gas on the stove and the water that issues from the tap. It is an unknown. Will it go on or will she soon turn the taps for gas or water and find nothing forthcoming?

For this meal Adriane Gerst seats herself at the dining table. The man has books. It is now obvious that no woman shares the premises. The books are to do with engineering. There are some on science and a number on avionics. Also a collection of fiction by German authors and others. Even a little philosophy. The man, it appears, is a learned fellow. There is a copy of Mein Kampf but it looks untouched.

Adriane takes out a large volume on airships to look through as she eats. Spills a bit of her porridge on a page and wipes it off with just a touch of guilt. The book contains many pictures of the great German machines that for a while plied the globe. There are pictures of the crews and the happy passengers relaxing around wicker tables and chairs, drinking and being served meals.

Other information about the airship's construction and complex engineering. Grand statements about their future as a mass transit system for people and freight.

After her meal Adriane looks for the first time out the apartment windows. She blinks. There is little to see below. The tops of undamaged buildings several streets away are in view. To the right there is the balcony door near the curtains. It is locked. Staring at this outside area, she remembers the key. A practical owner may decide that one key is sufficient for all their locks. Once again, that satisfying click.
Outside the balcony is sparse. A large pot with a sur-prisingly live green plant and a single wooden, foldback chair tucked in close the wall, out of the weather.
The area is enclosed with three arches on the outside. It is now, seeing the exterior, that the layout makes sense. This balcony provides a pleasant, though protect-ed, outdoor area, accessible from both the lounge and the main front bedroom. It is the sort of apartment that would suit a very private person.

Adriane is cautious in her approach to the balcony edge. It is possible to look through the balustrades without the need to put an all too visible head over the edge. On her hands and knees Adriane can look at her domain. The floors below also have balconies, though not as grand or secluded as hers. How could she not have noticed on her journey to the top? The centre apartments must share them in some way.
Despite the cacophony of last night's battle the area now shows no sign of life. Motors and voices, mechan-

ical sounds, some wisps of steam or smoke. All very
faint. Whoever is down there is not being obvious.
The balcony feels a little too exposed. She decides to
stay inside in the safety of walls and doors.

For Adriane it is time to consolidate. Her clothes still lay
in the bath. For some moments she stands looking down
at them all. Memories of the monster Brunek hover in
her mind. Deeply hidden is the possibility that he may
have impregnated her. It is far too horrible to comprehend or accept, so it stays beneath the surface.
Ever there. A moment away.
She has no choice with her clothes. They are the only
garments that will go near to fitting her. Whoever the
occupier of this apartment is or was, he was a tall man.
With her clothes now hung to dry on improviscd strings
and doors Adriane must wait.
She returns to the man's bedroom, interested in seeking
out clues to the person's existence. A further inspection reveals nothing of note. There are the shirts, suits,
heavy jackets and coats, nice ties, cuff links and studs
she had noticed before. This man dressed well and had
access to money. His shoes are so polished. It is his city
apartment. Nothing suggests this is his permanent residence. One coat pocket has a small wad of Reichsmarks.
The girl holds them. Quite an amount of money. Are they
now worthless? She decides to keep them anyway.
It is now that Adriane remembers the desk in the
loungeroom.

The top of the desk is quite neat. It has a dark green
leather inlay.

A marble and brass writing set is all that sits on the surface. She seats herself in the heavy chair. It has studded matching green leather. It moves. There are wheels on the legs and it tilts back. There is one central drawer and three drawers down each side. The central drawer is locked. The drawers on the left contain papers and files. One file right on top is full of accounts and invoices. They all bear the same name. Adriane has an apartment owner. Herr Dr. Antek Beck. Not a medical doctor? Some other type that has such a title. He has dealings with the Luftwaffe and is paid good money it seems. A lot of dealings with the Luftwaffe.

Adriane's impatience puts further analysis aside.

She turns her attention to the right-hand side-drawers. As she opens the top drawer she is certain that Dr Beck is right-handed and had some regard for his safety. Sitting alone and uncluttered, thus affording quick and easy access for a right hand is a black, shiny pistol. The only other occupants of the drawer are several boxes of ammunition with the winged eagle and swastika symbol of the Luftwaffe.

The gun is heavy in the hand of the girl. It has the markings of Walther on the side of the barrel and on the grip. The find is both fretful and satisfying at once. It is a reminder of the war and death all about and at the same time reassuring. Adriane Gerst is armed with spare ammunition.

She sits holding and examining the gun. She has used a rifle in the past but never seen a pistol. How does it load? Is it loaded? What makes it fire? Does it have to be cocked? There seems to be a safety mechanism on the side. It is too dangerous to risk firing a shot. Taking time

and thinking it through, eventually the gun gives up its
secrets. Simple once it is understood. And it is loaded.
The owner possibly expected to have need of it at short
notice.
She finally lays the gun down on the leather desktop and
opens the other two right-hand drawers.
They contain large bound volumes of what appear to be
plans and schematics for some sort of high towers. Dr
Beck's name appears with others on the first few pages
of each. In the bottom drawer there is a silver hip flask
with an eagle engraved on the side, containing what
appears to be whisky. There are some other boxes of
ammunition with the Luftwaffe insignia. They are larger
bullets but there is no gun.

By afternoon the clothes left drying are at a point where
they can be worn, even if they are still cold from the
moisture left in the cloth. Adriane decides that her body
heat will finish them off.
It is oddly quiet. A time to be alert. Silence hides stealth.
The phrase stops Adriane. It was often used by her
mother. She stands with her head bowed, just remembering.

When she is dressed, the girl sits down with one of the
Dr's books. It is called 'Last of the Mohicans' and
appears to be about American Indians. For over an hour
she struggles to become interested in the story then
cheats by turning ten pages at a time, then goes to the
end and reads the last page. It is not for her. It is a man's
book she decides.
Lying on the lounge once more she sleeps a nervous

sleep. Not deep but fitful. The sleep of the wild animal where survival is an awareness even when resting.
A noise!
An annoying aspect of the human condition. Was the noise in her dream or was it in the building. Heart racing she strains to hear. The room is the same. The light is the same. Nothing has changed. The door is closed as before. It is latched. Nobody could have entered. For a half hour she lays still and alert then annoyingly, against her plans, she falls into sleep once more.

Now she wakes slowly. From a deeper sleep. Everything is as it was. There is a certain comfort in normality.
She breaths deeply enjoying the peace.
Sitting up and stretching, Adriane stands and goes to the window. Carefully from the side she can see the empty battered streets.
Nobody moves about. It is deserted. Just rubble.
No smoke or mist.

By the time the light is beginning to fade Adriane has returned to the kitchen to scan the shelves of food and play the game of what to eat. Perhaps she will be more adventurous and create something with ham and the powdered egg. If only there was bread. It is the one commodity that is lacking. Mentally feeling ungrateful doesn't dull the wish.
She begins laying out the items for the meal. A tin of beef fat. A tin of powdered egg. A plate for the cut ham. There are several boxes on a lower shelf. Peering in the girl can make out a label.
Kreigsbrot. Army rations!

"My God …. bread." Is this room listening?

Adriane pulls the box out. It looks old. The packs inside
are sealed. They are heavy. When sliced open, the bread
is hard. It is dark and dry but not beyond use. Perhaps
fried in the fat?

It is difficult to cut. Eventually there are two rough pieces on the plate.

While standing, admiring the collection on the kitchen
bench there is a half heard, muffled noise from somewhere. Adriane is immediately alert. Nothing more.

She waits, her eyes flicking about.

She moves to the front room. Listening, her face twisted,
there is no hint of where or how the noise arrived.

Then it all happens. A cry. A voice yelling. Thump-
ing and the sound of an argument. It is not outside
the building. It is not in the distance. It feels as if it is
outside the door. Frozen for some moments while she
listens, the girl hears a high voice and a low voice.

The higher voice is distressed. Suddenly, wracked
by both fear and anger the episode with the monster
Brunek is foremost. Is this a rape?

Adriane is fumbling at the desk drawer, then realises the
gun is in front of her on the desktop. She thanks herself
for taking the time to understand the weapon.

At the door she realises the sounds are further away
than she thought. Perhaps a floor below. The higher
voice is pleading. "A girl, dragged in, to be defiled?"

In the corridor the sounds are quite distinct. "From two
floors below? How did they get in? Was the girl dragged
or coaxed up into the building?"

The words are not clear but the girl is distressed, pleading. "Nein, nein."

On the stairs it is still further away. On the seventh floor landing the sound is coming up the stairs. Creeping down, the gun ready. At the sixth floor corridor.

The door to one of the rooms is open. The voices are coming from that room.

Then a higher voice cries out.

"Nein, nein, würde ich nicht das Vaterland verlassen."

There is the sound of a slap or punch.

"I would not forsake the Fatherland. What can that mean?"

Now groaning, crying. Moaning.

"Schwein. Sie sind ein Verräter."

"Traitor?" Adriane mouths the word.

Despite all her fears and instincts Adriane advances along the carpeted hallway to the door. Perhaps sheer curiosity makes her move. Emboldened by the gun in her hand she stands at the door and looks in.

There are two occupants. Neither notice her presence. In the centre of the room is a soldier. Immediately identifiable by the twin SS on his collar and the totenkopf insignia. He is in a rage. On the old dining table is a small figure. It is a small soldier.

No, it is a boy. His uniform hangs from his shoulders. He has a cord around his neck. It goes over a roof beam and into the hands of the soldier. It is taught, pulling up, choking the boy.

The soldier is yelling at the boy.

"You are a traitor to the Fatherland. If you will not fight and die for the Fatherland then you will die at my hands. All traitors are to die. You are a pig. Not fit to be in the uniform of the glorious Reich. Hanging is all you are deserve." The man pauses. Takes an extra turn of the rope in his hand. "Goodbye. You disgust me."

He wrenches on the rope. The boy is lifted onto his toes. At this moment of imminent death with his head tilted by the rope, his eyes turn and rest on the person in the doorway.

Across the room set up by the window is a rifle. A rifle on a small tripod. It has a scope fixed to the top.

A sniper's rifle.

So many things are to be assessed at once. The soldier's head turns. He is killing a boy. He is planning to shoot people from this room. It will attract attention to the building. This cannot happen. This must be stopped.

The soldier is already dropping the rope and reaching for his side arm. A snarl of absolute rage escapes his lips. Spittle flies from his mouth. His eyes are fixed.

In his mind he sees another small person in a uniform. Another traitor. He must stop this outrage.

As he swings and hurls himself towards Adriane his gun is already out of its holster. He is unaware that the figure in the doorway has lifted its arm and pointed it at his head. Then everything is black.

The light haired, blue-eyed, devoted Arian soldier with a sabre cut scar on his cheek crashes at Adriane's feet. Only one eye is still there. The other has a hole where the bullet entered his brain.

For a long time in the room there is no sound. The figure in the doorway is shaking and white, her eyes wide, her mouth open. She cannot look away from the body at her feet. This is the second person she has killed. She begins to feel weak. She is struggling to breath. Her chest is shuddering.

It is now that the small figure standing on the table crumples in an untidy imitation of a marionette and flops first onto the table and then, with a thump, onto the floor.

Chapter 14

'Then Two'

He is lying on the bed in the main bedroom, somewhat
dwarfed by the large bed. He has a blanket over him and
a soft pillow under his head. Adriane has laid a wet cloth
on the raw red mark round his throat. He cannot speak.
She sits and holds his hand. He has tears in his eyes and
on his cheeks. One eye is bloodshot and bruised.
He gives regular sniffs and looks at his saviour.
Periodically his body stiffens, his eyes widen and he
shakes uncontrollably. She strokes his forehead and the
shaking subsides for a time. All she can do is smile reas-
suringly, her head to one side, at this undersized soldier.
He is another boy. He is her brothers at the farm. As the
memory wells up inside her Adriane realises, she too is
about to cry. It would not be fitting. She retreats hurriedly to the kitchen and stands holding the bench, wrench-
ing sobs wracking her body. This world is so hateful, so
vile, she cannot ignore all that has happened. She has
now killed two people. Yes, to survive but is this what
the world has become, where girls from a farm now
routinely kill to exist.

At her bravest moment she has crumbled. Can there be an end to it? Everything has been taken away. Putting her hand to her mouth she realises it is shaking. Why is everything so bad? She must endure, search for calm. She lowers her head and clenches her fists. She takes a deep breath, holds it and then breaths out slowly, raising her head and opening her eyes.

He is standing at the door looking at her. He lifts his arm. Does he want to be comforted or is he offering comfort? For some seconds they both stand with their arms half-lifted. He looks pathetic in his socks. They are both crying. What a situation. Then they move and embrace. It will not be spoken but both need somebody, something to hold. It is so incredibly comforting to feel another human being who means them no harm.
The squeeze goes on. She bends down and kisses the top of his head and closes her eyes.
Finally, with some effort, the boy makes some rasping noises and speaks. His tiny voice says, "Can I have some water?"

Sitting at the kitchen table sipping his water the boy smiles a little at Adriane. He is hunched under his blanket but his eyes move about. He has noticed things.
His first whispered words are, "There is food here?"
He is a survivor after all.
"Yes, there is quite a good supply. Would you like some soup? There is chicken or tomato or I think beef broth."
A light comes on in the boy's face. He has not heard such words for a long time.

A half hour later the two occupants of Apartment A on the eighth floor are seated with their bowls of soup, dipping hard bread into the warm mix. It is painful for the boy to swallow but hunger beats pain. He is stripped to his singlet to get the rubbing collar of his uniform away from the neck wound. His neck has been dabbed with antiseptic and a lint bandage applied to the broken skin. The blanket stays draped over his shoulders.

Adriane speaks. "I don't know your name. What is your name my young soldier?"

"Hauke," he rasps, "My name is Hauke Kluge. I'm a Berliner. Are you a Berliner? What is *your* name?"

Adriane paused. The boy was staring at her intently as if he had an urgent need to know.

"I'm Adriane Gerst. And no, I'm not a Berliner. I'm from the country. You shouldn't talk too much if your throat hurts but tell me Hauke aren't your parents nearby or at least in the area?"

The sadness in the boy's eyes tells her the answer before he speaks.

He swallows with some effort. Looks down at his fingers twisting on his lap. He waits a while, then whispers, "They died in the bombing over a year ago."

Conversation lapses after this information.

"Are we safe here?" Hauke asks finally.

"I thought so, until today. How long have you been here?"

"I climbed in last night. I was asleep in the room when that soldier arrived. He didn't even notice me at first. I was pleased to see him. I thought he would save me but he went crazy and called me a traitor. I'm not a traitor   ... but I don't want to die."

Hauke's voice fades. As if there is more to say but he is
not sure how to express his thoughts.

After a minute, Adriane asks, "How exactly did you get
up. You know, to the first level."

"There was a ladder."

The two people seated at the table are looking into each
other's eyes. Finally the boy asks the question.

"There was no ladder when you climbed in?"

"No."

"Oh."

Suddenly they are both alert. Outside the light is failing.
Something needs to be done.

Working their way down slowly, room by room, floor by
floor, they take twenty minutes to ascertain that there
is currently nobody else in the building. After a frantic
search they have located the Dr's other gun. A heavy
Mauser pistol in the small chest of drawers beside his
bed. Adriane has the larger pistol and the boy has the
Walther.

Down on the landing of the shattered floor they can see
the wooden rungs of a ladder shadowed across the floor
as it pokes its head above the concrete.

There is a rope ladder hanging down the wall that Adriane had climbed so carefully. How much easier it would
have been with such a device.

"That soldier must have made more than one trip."

"I'll go," says Hauke, "You have no shoes."

He lays down his gun and teetering and stretching
reaches over to the rope ladder. Then swaying about
makes his way, slowly, down to the floor below.

It is then that Adriane calls out.

"My boots. Can you get down and bring them back. I hid them so I could climb. There's other things."

Once he is on the ground level she directs him to the hiding place. He looks up, smiling at the find.

After bringing the items up to the first landing, it takes him a while with a great deal of grunting until he manages to haul the ladder up onto the floor and then drag it well away from the edge and out of view. Then two trips up and down the rope ladder. Once he is back up with Adriane they unhook the rope ladder and carry it up the stairs to hide in an empty room.

Back at the sixth floor Hauke baulks at the next task Adriane has set.

"We must do this," she explains.

"I can't, I can't go there. What if we're seen?"

"I thought you were brave."

"I've never been brave. I'm too scared to be brave."

It is the closest they come to being amused but it does break Hauke's uncooperative resolve.

The soldier's head wound has bled a lot. A heavy red-black pool surrounds his body.

It is at this moment as they stand viewing the dead man with the missing eye, that the remaining soldiers of two large Waffen SS groups in the area, launch a screaming, rushing, roaring all out assault on the nearby Russian division.

The building goes from silent to shaking, lit up and terrifying. There are screams and shouting. Rapid repeated gunfire and the sound of heavy machinery roaring.

The boy and the girl lay flat in the corridor, clutched together in the dark for joint consolement and protection. After perhaps fifteen minutes Adriane lifts her head. The battle is still loud but it is not close. It is happening streets away, not at their doorstep. She climbs to her feet and drags the boy up after her.

"C'mon Hauke, there'll never be a better time than now."

The soldier is heavy. They remove some ammunition from his pockets but it makes little difference. Holding one dead hand each they drag him along the corridor in small bursts of effort, to the back of the building.

It leaves a rough smear on the carpet that Adriane brushes away as they proceed.

"When I first saw this carpet it didn't occur to me that it's an ideal colour for hiding blood."

Hauke simply looks and says, "Yes ..... blood carpet." With the corridor window open they place first his hands, then his head, then shoulders on the sill as they inch him up. It takes several attempts to heave the heavy man to a tipping point and out the window. Eventually there is a moment where there is greater weight outside than in. As if gifted by some strange brief touch of life, the man slides forward and launches from the window. He lands with a thud on his back in the laneway. He stares one-eyed back at them. Just another victim of war.

As the last remnants of Hitler's extreme, elite soldiers fight and die outside. Adriane and her new companion carry the sniper's rifle and his kit back to the apartment. They find a block of chocolate in the sniper's bag. His

only food. They share it, greedily finishing the whole
bar. Finally they return to survey the room. Adriane
pushes the boy soldier forward.
"Go on. Take it down."
He approaches the table hesitantly, reaches up and pulls
the rope back over the beam. It flops to the floor like a
disturbed snake.
The boy stands transfixed, looking at the rope, not mov-
ing, his head bowed.
Adriane watches. "Hauke?"
After a pause, still looking down, the boy speaks, softly.
"They got Otte and Joseph. Just in the street. Alone.
I saw them, hanging from a pole, side by side."
"Oh Jesus."
"My best friends. My only friends. We were separated.
I was looking for them."
"That's a terrible thing."
"I could only just touch their boots. I wanted to get them
down. I tried for ages. I got angry. It was hopeless. In the
end I sat under the pole and cried and cried. I ran away
from them. I didn't want to look at my friends again.
Then it was my turn. Right here."
"Hauke, it seems these horrible things happen in war.
I don't know what to say."
"Why did they want us all to die? What's the point of
that?"
Adriane walked to the boy. She took his shoulders and
steered him away.
"I can't undo this world Hauke but let's close this door
and leave it closed."

By the time they are back in the apartment and locked

in, the fighting has died down considerably. They cannot
know that Russians have claimed a quick and decisive
victory by appearing to retreat in disarray then surrounding the SS soldiers. The same Russian tactic used
days previous but this time with much greater planning
and execution.

Still the Russians are perplexed that these hardened and
clever enemy troops have been so sure of their superior-
ity that they have continued to pursue what is an inher-
ently dangerous plan of action until they are trapped.
As these hard-core, original German SS will all die rather
than surrender, the Russians must now go through the
tiresome and dangerous task of granting the wish of
each and every one of their foes by hunting them out
until none are left.

So the crack of rifles, occasional bursts of fire, last
grenades and in some cases, without ammunition, a
rush of desperation with a bayonet goes on sporadically
through the night.

Adriane and Hauke can only grope their way along the
black apartment hallway to the bedroom. For a moment
the girl considers pushing the boy into the second
bedroom until a plaintive voice beside her asks, "Can I
sleep with you tonight?"

Stripped down to their underwear and exhausted they
both crawl into the crisp sheets of the soft bed and lay
their heads on the feather pillows. After some hesitation
their fingers find each other. The girl reaches out to find
the boy and draws his back to her. He becomes the large
doll she owned as a child. Her arms wrap him tight and
close. Curled together in the comfort of companionship

they both take a shuddering deep breath and in the warmth, almost in unison, fall into a deep sleep.

Chapter 15

'The Complications of Victory'

It has been a very long night. Even in the brightness of morning the men must be ever vigilant, unsure if all the SS remnants have been accounted for in the various sweeps of the area.

At 4am when every cleanup seemed at an end Captain Chaban had shot an SS Commandant on the stairs.
He had climbed the outer wall, past the guards and slipped in a window onto the stair landing. Fortunately his entry had been noisy. Captain Chaban had watched. As the man crept up, presumably with an heroic desire to take out his opposing commander, the Captain had stepped out from the corner of the second floor doorway and waited till the man saw his boots.
As he started and looked up Captain Chaban fired his pistol until it was empty.

He did not like to admit the feeling of complete satisfaction he gained from this act. He hoped he had restored some balance and that the man he had dispatched was

somehow connected to the atrocities in his homeland.
There was little time to savour the moment before several guards rushed in to bear witness to their Captain's handiwork.
It was a chance for the officer to berate his men for allowing such a thing to happen but he chose not to say anything of a negative nature. The scene spoke for itself. Besides they all faced danger at every moment.
He instead inquired whether they could, 'Clear away the body so that nobody might trip on the stairs and injure themselves.'
He liked to think they found this statement amusing and fair, once they were out of his presence.

As the morning progressed Captain Chaban, in spite of his will, let his head tilt back and closed his eyes.
He awoke with a start perhaps half an hour later, to find Comrade Kozuch standing next to him holding a tray.
The Captain blinked and smiled.
"Lucky you're not a German, Comrade. I was watching you the whole time. At no time was my guard down."
Kozuch smiled that smile of his and laid the tray down.
It was a miracle to behold. Fried sausage, potato and real eggs. And coffee? A mug of steaming milky brown substance . The Captain picked up the mug and drifted it under his nose.
"This is real and quite strong. You are a truly gifted fellow. Have you had some yourself?"
"Yes Sir," replied the adjutant.
"Good," replied the Captain. "We must share in the spoils." He paused. "Wherever and however they come."
He sipped the coffee slowly and picked at pieces of the

meal with the fork, savouring the taste.

"Now, I have something for you, Comrade."

The Captain reached down into the well of the desk and lifted out a brown hessian bag. It clinked as he placed it on the desk. He nodded toward the bag.

"Take them. Enjoy. But don't share. I want you to reward only yourself."

Sergey Kozuch removed the bag's contents. First one then a second bottle of what appeared to be very fine French brandy. Also a package of about ten packets of Lucky Strike cigarettes.

"Two bottles, Sir?"

"I had them all the time. So promising you a bottle was within my powers to fulfill. You might as well have both. Your plan worked. I didn't think we could use the same tactics twice but maybe I haven't had as much close experience of the enemy as you. And your advice on selling the idea to the men also worked."

Sergey Kozuch stood holding one bottle in each hand.

"Can I perhaps share some with you, Captain?"

Captain Chaban leaned back from his meal.

"Oh thank God. I was rather hoping you would suggest such a plan of action. Been keen to try them for a while. Consider my previous request voided for the moment."

The two men talked easily. They were not so very different, in background, knowledge and nature. Only their army ranking drew a line between them.

Captain Chaban was pleased. He was not officer material. He knew he lacked the bull-headed sense of purpose and the lack of interest in the wellbeing of his fellow humans to ever be a decisive, ruthless army man.

Also he liked friendship and company and interesting conversation. So, considering his many limitations, he had commanded a decisive victory over the desperate German opposition. Sergey Kozuch had provided most of the intelligence on the enemy and suggested the plan. It was not any breakthrough in warfare strategy but its execution was quite clever. To repeat a strategy they had employed days before would seem illogical even inept, therefore it could not be happening.

They had to draw the SS troops into a trap. These men were not fools. If they put up light resistance the SS would sense the situation and not advance into their net. So they relied on the arrogance of the German fighting men who they were sure, considered themselves vastly superior soldiers to the Russian forces. Chaban's men made dummy troops and put them in windows and doorways. Further down the two main streets they went about the distasteful task of finding a number of bodies and laying them about the area in Russian uniforms. They then created a series of staging posts and safe retreats from which the men could slip away. They lay explosives and grenades in series. All of these preparations were to give the impression of resolute resistance.
Sergey Kozuch was convinced the SS attack would be narrow. The Germans did not have a great number of fighting men. The aim, he said would be to punch a hole through the Russian lines, to reach the rail yards and station. Something they could maintain. He was also sure that the Germans were not aware how light the Russian numbers were on either side of Captain Chaban's

command. Kozuch thought the Germans would use local knowledge and try to slip through underground service tunnels. He hoped he knew where they were located. It was a serious risk. Two thirds of Chaban's troops would be shipped in trucks well to each side of the fighting as soon as it began. A circuitous route to take them back and around the area so that they could not be seen. It was hoped the SS would put all their men into the push and leave their flanks unguarded.

The Captain had decided to join the fighting rather than wait in his 'office.'

Each hour of the night came and went while expectations were raised then relaxed. At 10.17pm the men posted listening at street manholes, heard sounds of movement below. As arranged they fired off a series of charges with petroleum gel. The tunnels roared and exploded.

Thinking their advance parties had successfully fired explosives under the Russians, the SS troops poured down the streets. Every man on duty fired back in an apparent fearsome resistance. They screamed and indicated confusion and injury. Then they retreated as if in a rout. Some further explosives were set off to indicate successful German firepower. The Russians ran back past the bodies in the street. They set off oil fires to hide the smell of old corpses.

Perhaps none of this badly staged show would have been successful had it not been for the limitless optimism of the SS troops. Blinded by a belief in the righteousness of their cause and some supreme hope of ultimate victory, they rushed their advance. In the dark streets lit only by fires they saw burning bodies and were sure they had broken the Russian line.

They pulled in their rear guard, bunching in the streets, buoyed by success. The first Russian tank killed six in the opening salvo. The SS brought up their Panzerfaust anti-tank weapons and knocked out two of the Russian T34s. They deployed them effectively against the lightly armoured machines But now there were tanks at the side of them as well. The Russian fire went from sporadic to merciless. Men were being cut down from different directions. The Panzerfaust units were lost and the tanks were relentless.

Perhaps the clatter of their line being broken and wiped away behind them made them realise that they were trapped. How could this be so? The truckloads of Russian soldiers quickly took away their path back into their part of the city. Now they were here to die.

It was the part that Captain Chaban feared. With all hope gone the SS troops fought without reason, determined to eliminate as many Russians as they could before they met their end. None would surrender.
Each had to die completely to finalise their threat.
They ran into the Russian fire with hand grenades unpinned, attempted a rush at a tank to try to overpower the metal beast, even wrapped Russian coats over their own and feigned injury in the hope of drawing Russians close enough to attack.
Captain Chaban helped hold down one crazed soldier of the Reich while he roared and having emptied his gun, drew a knife in order to inflict more carnage.

His strength was such that they could not let his arms go to reach for their own weapons. As quickly as it started, one of the Captain's men saw the situation and walked over, placed the muzzle of his rifle against the man's forehead and pulled the trigger.

The Captain saw the man's eye flick from rage to realisation as he felt the steel touch his skin. Then they faded to a fixed stare as his life was extinguished. It was an image the Russian would keep in his mind and never mention to anyone, until his own peaceful death many decades later.

As the fighting ebbed, a general enlistment soldier came with a message from one of the field officers. He stepped in front of the Captain and saluted. His mouth opened to speak then a part of his skull shattered. Chaban and Kozuch both leapt onto the ground and twisted about in an effort to find the sniper's position.

"That was aimed at you, Captain."

"I know that, Comrade. Where the hell is he?"

It was hard to shelter from an unseen enemy. They scanned about, searching the windows and doorways nearby. Then in a moment of calm Captain Chaban decided to use logic.

"If I were a sniper, where would I position myself for the best possible effect?"

The two men looked again.

"There," said Kozuch, indicating with a finger across his body to a building in the distance. It commanded a view of the whole street. "It must be there. It's perfect."

The soldiers nearby were all crouched, having seen the fate of the messenger. The Captain called to the nearest soldier.

"Get tank fire into the upper floor of that building.
Go now."

The man looked terrified but obeyed orders. He waited
for a moment as if preparing for a possible end to his
life, then jumped up and bolted back toward the nearest
tank. He weaved as he ran.

The Captain took a chance to look over their shelter. He
saw a tiny flash from the building's top window. A bullet
whipped into the masonry behind the running soldier.
It was doubtful he was aware of it. The next hit his back-
pack. Then he was clear, sheltered on the far side of the
tank. He finally got the attention of the crew inside and
could be seen waving his arms about and yelling up to
the tank commander.

When the tank moved it swung out of the side street
from which it had been firing and lined itself up with the
whole thoroughfare.

The sniper was no doubt already retreating once he
saw the menace appearing in front of his vantage point.
Their tank commander was smart enough to allow for
such contingencies and directed his fire about two
floors below the sniper's last position.

He landed shell after shell on the old building's facade
until it fell away and a large part front of the building
crumpled onto the street.

Perhaps he imagined this moment as more significant
than it was in the overall thrust and parry of the battle
but in his mind, Captain Chaban felt the turning point
had been reached. The noise, the cries of the victorious
and vanquished, the clatter, chack chack of small arms,

the blast of the tank guns and numerous other parts of
the cacophony of warfare, all seemed to lessen and a
degree of calm or perhaps control came upon the area.

So, at the end of it all, the Captain sat with his 'Comrade'
and together they drank a large part of one bottle of this
fine French brandy letting the numbing effect drag the
tension from their bodies.
They talked of their homeland, their families, their love
of their country and its landscape and what they might
return to after the war.
Both found similarities in their upbringing, their education and status and their view of the world. With similar
families and income it went unsaid that one had risen
higher in the army than the other. Such were the oddi-
ties or fortunes of war.
It occurred to them that they could finally talk of a time
'after' the war when some form of a normal life could
be resumed or commenced. There seemed little enthusiasm to discuss the battle or their possible demise.
They had lived with such possibilities for some time.
If a dream was to be had or a thought shared it would be
one of optimism and a future with hope. Tentative steps
in the conversation could map a future for each man.
Comrade Stalin showed some promise they agreed.
In the new Russia he would provide a bright future.
It would be a fine place to live.

Chapter 16

'Another Morning'

After several hours of exhausted sleep, the two occupants of the bed in the main bedroom of the top floor apartment, had been woken suddenly by relentless noise of warfare right outside their building. One particular blast had cut through their unconscious state and brought them back into the world with the wide-eyed uncertainty that surrounds a rude awakening.
They had lain the rest of the night, listening, holding each other and waiting. Neither of the bed's occupants had suggested moving from the bed. It was a safe place. Looking outside would make the noises real. Here they were covered by bedclothes and had an excuse to continue being in each other's arms.

By the first hint of morning light the noise abated.
A strong smell of expended gunpowder seeped into the room. The tension in their bodies ebbed away.
They returned to sleep.
At nine o'clock Adriane woke. She stayed still while her mind again adjusted to her situation. A short distance

from her face wrapped in the gentle peace of sleep was
the face of Hauke. She lay watching him breathe, his
mouth slightly open. His face was pale, his eye sockets
were dark, beneath his eyelids his eyes flicked occasionally. At one stage he gave a short whimper.
It made the girl smile. She felt a degree of affection for
this lost child soldier. It gave her a purpose. To see them
both through whatever the days ahead would bring.

In the kitchen, Adriane stood once again and marvelled
at the contents of the pantry. It was an ongoing joy to
see so much and know it was hers, at least for the moment. This followed a small ritual in which she checked
the water supply and the gas and even tried the light
switch. All remained the same.
While she idled in front of the packed shelves, the
pantry door swung slowly closed and for a moment left
its occupant in darkness. In that moment, the figure of
Brunek reared up and took over the girl's mind.
She pushed the door back open and stood for while
shaking and calming herself. She bit her thumb and tried
not to cry, not to give in. In one final shudder that went
through her whole body, she overcame the demon and
was suddenly back in the kitchen pantry, focused once
again. "Ich haben ein leben," she said softly, "Ich haben
ein leben."
Now the choosing began.

Perhaps the sizzle of the pan, perhaps the smell of
frying, perhaps he had just woken and decided to rise.
Hauke stood in the kitchen doorway, small and blinking.
He looked at the pan and then at the cook. He smiled.

A weak smile. A mix of comfort, safety and hunger.
A boy. So much like Adriane's brothers at the farm.
Briefly her whole life welled up and reappeared, right
through to the moment of watching her beloved family
slaughtered. She stopped, everything froze. She let out a
shuddering breath. Hauke watched her. She returned his
weak smile.

The fare for breakfast had turned into potato cakes.
A mix of dried potato, milk powder, egg powder and real
ham, dusted with flour and cooked in pork fat.
Before they ate they took turns in surveying the streets
from the windows. They did not dare go too close nor
risk the balcony. Despite not being overlooked, they
feared a simple glance from someone below could reveal
their presence. The day at least was bright, almost
cheerful. A clear sky let sunshine filter the air.
Except for two sources of black smoke that seemed near
spent, the view was uninterrupted. It was extensive.
Adriane now realised why the sniper had chosen this
building.
There seemed little doubt of the outcome of the night's
battle. There were a lot of Russian soldiers about.
No sign of the German army. The Furhrer's city was
no longer his to control. A road block had been established. There were tanks and halftracks on the street
corners and groups of soldiers who seemed to be eating
and drinking. Some civilians were timidly making their
way along. Hauke noticed that they were all old people.
Nearly all were harassed by the soldiers. Some seemed
to be begging.
Perhaps for food, perhaps for their lives. Best not to

watch anymore.

They sat at the dining table, both still dressed in only army issue undershorts and singlets.

Hauke asked, "Why are you wearing army clothes, anyway? There's no insignia." The boy touched his throat unconsciously and winced. The rope burns were still red.

Adriane paused, her spoon in mid air. A long pause. Finally she said, "My dress was torn. I found some army clothes in a warehouse. Why did you just ask now?"

"It hadn't occurred to me before."

As they ate Hauke looked up again. He was puzzled.

"I think a lot of people died last night. Why are there now only old people about? Where are the others?"

Adriane paused again, then decided to be honest.

"Hauke, maybe there's not a lot of younger men left. Five years of war after all. And the women and children would obviously not venture out."

Hauke stayed silent and chewed his food, then held up his spoon as if to make a point.

He asked. "Why?"

"Why what?

"Why would the women and children stay inside?"

"Because they're scared of being molested, of being raped, Hauke."

"Oh, of course."

At the end of the meal, Adriane leant down to pick up Hauke's plate. She straightened up and looked at the seated figure. The boy glanced up, his face enquiring.

"Hauke, you smell   ..... odd. Not bad. Sort of ..... musty."

"What does 'musty' mean?"
"Well, I don't know. I think all the gunpowder smell masked it before. It's a bit like a room that has been closed up and needs fresh air. Does that make sense?"
"Ummm, no."
"When was the last time you washed?"
Hauke screwed up his face. "A fair few weeks I think."
"Right, I'll boil some water. Nice and hot. You can have a good wash in the bath. I'll wash your clothes. You'll feel much better."
"Umm, oh … okay." Hauke looked slightly alarmed.
"What will I do while they dry?"
"Same as me, you'll wear a very large dressing gown."

While not enthusiastic, Hauke removed himself to the bathroom, sitting on a chair with a dogged look while he waited for the hot water.
When the water arrived Adriane found some soap and even a bottle of Koln Wasser.
"Now," she said, "we're getting somewhere." She left and went to the cupboard to get a towel. She paused, the towel was a pale yellow. Perhaps her guest would prefer something more robust. She hunted through the pile and chose a large dark blue towel. Then she retrieved the big dressing gown from the bedroom. She returned to the bathroom, expecting to find Hauke still seated on the chair awaiting his fate.
He stood in the bath, his eyes closed as he sponged water over his head with a cloth. His slight hairless body glistened as the water ran down his chest and legs. Adriane hesitated, caught by the charming sight of the boy. She tried to put the towel down and retreat but he

opened his eyes, gave a small gasp and turned away.

"I brought your towel. And the gown. Here's the soap as well."

"Thank you."

"I'll go now. Enjoy. Scrub hard, eh."

She put the Koln Wasser on the tiled floor. She then glanced once more at Hauke's back. Frowned and left.

In the lounge Adriane sat and considered the situation. Yes, it was something she had to know. It was important. Hauke eventually emerged from his wash. He looks different. His face is softer, perhaps because it is clean. His dark blonde hair is much lighter and fluffed up by the washing. She notices his golden eyes. They seem more piercing. All in all the effect is to make the boy almost angelic. A thought she will keep to herself, imagining the bruising to his ego that such a revelation could produce. He also has one of those perpetually sad faces. A look she remembered from a dog on the farm. A lovely animal but always with a look of slight unsureness.

"You look much better. Handsome. Very handsome."

He has overused the Koln Wasser but the effect will fade. He sits on a lounge chair opposite, wrapping the large gown around his body as best he can.

"I'll get your clothes and uniform and give them a good cleaning."

"Thank you."

"Well not too clean. A too clean soldier will be suspicious." They are not sure what the comment means. Hauke is silent. He is awkward. His head is down. Could it be simply Adriane seeing him unclothed?

She has always been a direct person. Not necessarily a

socially rewarding trait but it is her way. She decides to ask the question she wants so much to have answered. "I'm sorry I came in while you where washing. I didn't know you'd started. I should have knocked. But we're friends, right? We shared a bed last night."
"That's okay," said Hauke, not meeting her gaze nor understanding the significance of 'sharing a bed'.
"Hauke, look at me." The boy lifted his eyes, looking at the girl sideways, like that guilty dog.
"Hauke, why are you circumcised?"

It is a long sorrowful tale. Told with determination once the floodgates of explanation are opened. Though it is not quite what Adriane had expected.
Hauke is a Berliner he says. He lived with his parents and Felix his older brother, in an apartment. His father was the manager of a large boot factory. He had a small interest in the business as well. They had contracts with the Wehrmacht and he thinks they were 'comfortable'. There is a brief moment of humour while he explains that the boots were also comfortable then he reverts to his hunched, quiet story-telling.
His mother worked for a doctor. The man had a practice on the ground floor of their apartment building and lived next door to the Kluges. They were good friends with the doctor and his family. The adults often played cards and had meals together and Felix liked the doctor's daughter.
Hauke's Uncle, his Father's brother, was a member of the Nazi party and when the war began he tried to talk Hauke's father into joining the army. He kept on and on but his father said no because he was needed in the

boot factory. They had a big argument in front of the family. Hauke's brother stormed out. He is five years older than Hauke and liked what he heard from the uncle. He joined the Hitler Youth and as soon as he was able he joined the Army.

Hauke was talking fast.

His Mother and Father died when the factory was bombed about a year ago.

At this point Hauke stopped as if realising the gravity of what he had just said. He blinked quite a lot and then continued in a lower tone.

After his parents were gone his Uncle took him in and put him into the Army. They were accepting old men and boys without discretion at this stage. His brother died about a week after the landings at Normandy. That's the story. Hauke stops.

There is silence. Adriane is trying to adjust to the mix of information and create a timeline. "Hauke, you didn't answer my question."

Hauke looks at the floor. His fingers are twisting nervously.

"I'm not a Jew." He pauses. "It was Dr Epstein. He was my Father's good friend. When my brother was born he delivered him and told my father that circumcision was not just some Jewish rubbish, it was a good healthy thing to do. To stop disease and be clean. They were friends. My father agreed. When I was born they did the same thing. That's all. I'm not a Jew."

"Alright," said Adriane, "I believe you."

"When all the Jewish trouble started, my Mother and Father both said I must never tell anybody or show them my penis."

"Yes. Probably wise."

"Dr Epstein killed my Mother."

"What?"

"When the war started Dr Epstein decided to leave.
He went to Britain I think. That was really mean. Germany needed doctors but he just suddenly took his family and went away. My parents really missed their friends. So my Mother lost her job. We didn't have as much money so in the end she had to work with my Father. She wouldn't have been at the factory if Dr Epstein had stayed."

"Surely you can locate your Uncle. He'd look after you. Do you know where he is?"

Hauke shrugged. "When we heard about Felix , my Uncle flew into a rage. He did that a lot. He was always blaming different people for what was happening. He would tell me what he would have done and how that would have been better. He screamed that he had an agreement with the local commander that none of the
brigade that Felix was in would be shipped out of Berlin. My Uncle considered himself a high ranking official. He stormed out of the house. He wanted the commander shot for disobedience."

"Did that happen?"

"The soldiers were sick of party officials. They shot my Uncle. The report or whatever they did said it was an accident. But somebody pointed out that the war had reached a turning point and we couldn't trust the army any more. I was returned to the barracks."

Adriane sat in the silence. With so many things to say, she said nothing for a while and then finally stated, "So,

you're twelve years old and you've got nobody?"
Another silence follows then Hauke with his head bowed
said something.
"Pardon?"
He spoke a little louder, his voice husky.
"Just you."

Chapter 17

'Refuge'

War has no winners. If we search deep into the piles of
burnt timber, rubble, broken pipes, furniture and mayhem that represents all that is left of the once fine house
that stood on this corner of this ruined street, we may
be able to make out a pair of eyes looking back from the
darkness.
A somewhat emaciated figure hunched into what was
once the brick surround of a hallway linen cupboard.
He wears the uniform of a Wehrmacht soldier.
All about, in the streets, there are Russian soldiers,
drunk with power and success and just drunk. He could
surrender. They may not shoot. He would be added to
the thousands of other German soldiers now being hu-
miliated and starved in the Russian holding camps.
But there is some fierce pride left in this man. Not love
of country or some silly notion to carry on the conflict,
just an almost academic interest in outsmarting the
victors and slipping through their enveloping presence
to a better place.

The better place has no geographical location, it is an imaginary goal that may or may not exist.

It is however all that Dieter Falke has left to maintain a will to live. He has not eaten more than some rubbish in days and he is very thirsty. Tonight must be the time to move. The initial alertness of the Russians has settled down as they realise that their enemy is well and truly finished. It may be possible to move through the streets. The soldier has been unable to find any other clothing so he chooses to remain in his uniform.

He is sleeping when at 2pm he is jerked awake by the closeness of voices. After a pause, while his heart beats rapidly, he notes that the language, though he does not understand a word, is Russian.

Squeezing his eyes to rid them of sleep he peers out from his hole in the wall in the corridor of this house wreck. There is a narrow view of the street. It shows mainly sky and one tall pile of brick that was a two sto-rey chimney. Then they pass by. One, two, four, no five of them. Talking loudly, slurred speech, drunk, happy, making silly jokes, laughing, bravado. Then a change. Perhaps a challenge, just out of view, an exchange of words.

Falke knows nothing of the conversation but the timbre of the voices tells much. A mild disagreement at first. A heated discourse. An exchange of unpleasantries. Further chiding, an excuse perhaps, a gruff reply then a dismissal. A pause, perhaps to give somebody a chance to retract. Then the voices start to move away. Fading more. One calls out. A voice quite close, startlingly close, replies. An insult, a jibe, a last chance at some face saving.

There is somebody quite near, just outside. Falke guesses he is leaning against the wall. He mutters for a minute, discussing with himself some wrong that has befallen him. Suddenly he calls out. A last curse at his departing comrades. There is no reply. They have moved on.

Silence. What is happening? Falke can only bow his head and listen and wait. Then the light goes out. He looks up. Blocking the light from outside is a very large figure, silhouetted, standing in the break in the wall. It mumbles and curses, raising and lowering it's voice as a stream of hurt and fury run through its mind.

The man is not on patrol, not seeking the enemy. Despite standing drunk in a ruined and conquered city he has allowed convention and a nice upbringing to dictate that he should hide so that he can urinate.

His stumbling path leads him into the corridor. He is holding the wall, looking about, commenting on the structure. Perhaps he envies the remnants of such a nice building. One, the like of which, he may never own.

When Dieter Falke emerges some time later he feels odd and exposed. The Russian's rifle is leaning against the wall its bayonet fixed.

By clasping the man's mouth with his right hand and driving the knife into his heart with his left he has despatched him silently and managed to keep the bloodstains to a minimum under the left arm.

The man was big and Falke, although possessing a tall and strong body does not have the girth to fill out the uniform. He wears a simple pilotka with its red star, a loose smock rubaha shirt, khaki pants with a webbing belt with two pouches. The boots are too big and the puttees hot and uncomfortable. Inside the building, in the corridor, lies a dead soldier, squeezed into a German uniform. It has taken some time to complete the swap of identities and clothes.

Walking the street as a basic private, Dieter Falke decides, is probably the safest option. Just another of the thousands of idle soldiers roaming about. As far as he can tell, the uniform does not even have divisional or brigade markings. He could, he hopes, be any Russian who crossed the border some months ago.
Inside the first of two belt pouches Falke finds a spare clip of ammunition. "Can't have been expecting any trouble," he says quietly.
Inside the second is a somewhat crushed photo of a large woman, smiling and blowing a kiss to the camera. Also a letter. The text is meaningless but it ends with clearly a woman's name and XX. Four year's ago the German felt guilt when he saw the personal effects of a dead British soldier lying awkwardly beside a tree, the contents of his pockets blowing about. Now he feels nothing.
He looks about. The street is deserted.
Trucked into this city that he had never seen, late at night, in blackout conditions, he has no idea where he is or where he must go. The Russians are heaviest around the railway, so best to avoid that area. Should he try to find refuge, wait out the war's end and hope he is over-looked, does not starve, is not shot or captured? Or should he make for the lines of some other invader in

the hope of a better outcome? Why are there only Russians in Berlin? Is it their prize? So that they might have revenge on the city and the people?

He has a vague idea that the city centre, the Reichstag, the main elements of the Nazi command is to the left, far off in a smoky distance. He will move right.

A voice shakes him from his pondering. Two Russian soldiers passing across the road have called out. What can he do? Move off in the opposite direction. Not too fast. They call again. It does not seem threatening.

A question perhaps? He takes a chance. He shrugs his shoulders as he walks, waves a dismissive hand and says, "Dah". Yes is perhaps better than 'no'. The only other word of Russian he knows.

The two soldiers burst out laughing and wave as they walk away.

One word can elicit such a response? Perhaps it was his body language.

Falke has kept his German watch. He could have looted it after all. Not speaking the Russian language is a serious issue. He stops and looks about to ensure he is alone, then punches his neck as hard as he dare.

He scrapes at the skin with his fingernails. Grabs and digs his fingers in until it hurts. Perhaps, in a one on one confrontation he can point at his throat and indicate an injury that prevents speech. Nothing, of course, will overcome his total lack of understanding of their language.

There are no more Russian soldiers in the area. A group in the distance give him reassurance about his ill-fitting uniform. He notes that most of the Russians have ill-fitting uniforms. Some too big, others too small. It must have been a lottery when the army was being fitted out. No time for matching the frame of the new recruit to his battle-dress. Whatever was on top of the pile became yours to fit as best you could.

One minor encounter occurs when an old man peers out from a doorway at the distant group of soldiers. Such is his caution and concentration that he fails to notice Dieter Falke approaching from the opposite direction. When he does, he stumbles back in horror, his arms raised. A whimper escapes his mouth. He is quite well dressed in a suit that must have been stylish pre-war but now shows the trauma of its owner. His face is a mixture of pleading and resignation as if he expects to die. Falke is tempted to say something reassuring in German but there are too many risks in such a revelation. Instead he points his gun at the man and motions him back into the building with a snarl. Possibly he did the man a favour.

He leaves the confrontation at that and moves on. The street is sloping upward toward another more main road that heads to the railway. He will reach that and then turn away. There seems to be a number of intact buildings further on. They may offer some refuge.

At the top of the rising road, pretend Russian Falke pauses at the corner of the building. He leans casually while he inspects the surroundings. Perhaps 60 or 70 metres down this main road, which once again has no street sign, there are two Russian trucks near a burnt out tank. The soldiers seem idle. Some are in the back of the truck, others are laying against the wall of a former office building.

Further away, barely visible, there are a more trucks that seem busier, as if moving goods or perhaps rations and ammunition.

To the left the road is empty, although it curves away so the view is restricted. Falke waits as long as he dares without attracting interest.

No activity, no movement. Time to be gone.

Along the road as he rounds the curve, Falke can see more Russians in the distance. Two civilians are coming toward him. They are carrying a small bag. Almost certainly food. One appears in his sixties, the other much younger, say thirty-five. They are obviously concerned by his appearance and probably considering running away.

There must be others, that they have taken the risk to go out on the streets.

Their faces show panic.

Falke smiles and nods, touching his fingers to his cap as he advances.

They stare but keep advancing. As they pass, Falke mutters, "Guten Tag."

He can feel their eyes upon his back as he continues.

Is he German or just the first nice Russian they have encountered?

Now there is nothing ahead. The soldiers in the distance have moved on. Three side streets to the left and four to the right are all possibilities although the buildings in the streets to the left seem more whole, less damaged. This street has a degree of normality as if only brushed by the war.

From one of the higher structures Falke may be able to
ascertain where he is and where he might be able to go.
He has not been looking behind, so is caught by surprise at the sound of a truck. It rumbles past with about
ten Russians in the back. Some are singing. They call
a greeting, to which he waves. The truck continues for
over one hundred and fifty metres into a wide street
with a flagstone square before suddenly stopping at the
curb with someone pointing at a doorway. The men in
the back give a cry and leap from their vehicle. Their
calls are not those of war but glee and stupidity.
They all rush to the building kicking furiously at a door
until it gives way and breaks open. Then they stumble
into the building, the men from the trucks cab joining in.
There are cries and screams. from within.
For about a minute various roars and yells emanate.
Falke is frozen, looking at the empty truck, listening to
the muffled chaos.
Then there is another yell. A man in trousers and a
white shirt is catapulted backwards from the doorway
into the street, landing hard on the road. Two Russian
soldiers emerge after him, their rifles pointed at his
midriff. The man, obviously in pain, raises himself to his
knees. He is pleading, crying to the soldiers in German
which they obviously do not understand, although the
intent is enough.
"Please, have decency, the war is over. You must have
families, think of them. You can't do this. Let us be. Take
anything. I beg ...."
Falke jumps as the shots echo in the street. The man
flops forward onto his face, his white shirt already red-
dened.

A ripping scream comes now and a collection of bodies stumble and crash through the doorway. A mixture of people and soldiers. Another man is fighting. A soldier rams his bayonet into the man's back. He is then shot on the ground. There are women and children. The women scream.

A young girl breaks away, running toward Falke. One of the Russians calls out to him. When Falke does not respond he shrugs his shoulders, brings the rifle up to his eye, there is a crack sound and the girl spins sideways and skids to the pavement. She has pigtails with red ribbons. Eight years old perhaps.

Now the Russians have the others surrounded. The women are sobbing and screaming, the Russians are screaming back.

Falke can see two women, a teen aged girl, two younger girls maybe ten or eleven. There are two boys who look a similar age.

The Russians corral the younger ones and drag the two women aside. Next to the truck they are held by their hair while their clothes are systematically ripped off until they are completely naked. They are dragged around and draped over the back of the truck, their legs are spread and the two Russians from the trucks cab drop their trousers and lean over them.

Something happens. A spit? A scratch? The officer stands back holding his face. He roars, leaning onto the woman he beats her face, slapping it first one way then the other. Finally he stands and yells down at her. It is some sort of threat. He is going to make a point. None of this is necessary but principles and stupid dignity demand absurd reaction.

He turns to the soldiers with the others and calls out.
The men let out a cheer and descend on the children.
They too are stripped. Screaming or numbly submitting.
All are brought round to stand in front of their bloodied
mother. Then the soldiers start to take turns with the
children. Even the boys are not immune. They all whimper as they are attacked.
Falke is now in tears. He still stands where he stopped.
His hands shake. His mouth hangs open. What can he
do?
The beaten mother looks on, too shocked, too injured
to say any more. A big Russian with a mean narrow red
face laughs as he grabs at one of the boys. The boy
cries out and drags himself away, fighting and punching
feebly. It is too much for the Russian officer. He secures
the boy by the neck, pulls out his pistol puts it behind
the boys ear and pulls the trigger. This act elicits an
unearthly groan of horror from the mother. The officer
turns to her to continue from his interruption as if it
were a minor nuisance. Others are already working on
the other woman on the truck.

Soldier Falke raises his rifle, advancing as he does.
He aims and squeezes the trigger. There is a click but
nothing happens. He is too committed. He keeps walking, fiddling with the unfamiliar weapon, then raises it
again, stopping this time to steady his aim.
The officer's head jumps upwards and he slides off the
woman and flops to the road behind the truck as the
bullet finds its target. The action initially draws no attention from the miscreants. Falke is able to fire off three
more rounds before the soldiers can take their minds

from their deeds and begin to respond. Two are dead
and one wounded from the German's fire. The Russians
have their trousers down or off and their rifles are not
at their sides. Falke hits another who cries out. He fires
again before realising that this time the click signifies an
empty magazine. He fumbles out the second clip from
his belt pouch. He is about to die. Why did he do this?
The Russian soldiers are now yelling and pointing in his
direction. As he fires once more bringing another down
he is aware of the first bullets hitting the wall near his
head. He fires again but the shot is wide.
A dreadful pain shatters his mind. It comes from his
head. He feels faint. The ground revolves.
As his shoulders contact the wall behind and he begins
to slide down, he is aware that the family being attacked
have all but disappeared. Just the last pale naked figure
of the injured woman is limping away in the distance
behind the men shooting at him.

He is not dead. People are yelling. He is being roughly
dragged between two soldiers along the street. His eyes
are blurred. They are loading the wounded and dead
onto the truck. Why is he still alive? A soldier, possibly
of some rank, is dancing along in front of him, gesticulat-
ing wildly, yelling and punching the air in anger.
Now he is at the truck. He is lifted and thrown into the
cab beside the driver. The man with rank climbs in beside him and again launches a torrent of abuse.
'They still think I'm Russian.' Falke keeps his head down.
It is wet and aching. There is blood all down his tunic,
on his pants and on his boots. The truck starts.
The driver is given instructions. It involves turning to

head back. It must be that they are taking him to a command post as a renegade or insane person, to be dealt with by a higher rank. Perhaps he has killed somebody of authority in the little skirmish. It is wartime. There will not be time for rest and recuperation. Besides he speaks no Russian.

How many chances can he have left?

The driver is young and having trouble with the gears but now they are rolling.

Once again the man beside him curses in anger. Then he grabs Falke's hair and pulls his head back so that he can look him in the face. The pain shoots through behind Falke's eyes. The Russian speaks again. It is a question. Falke indicates to his throat, touching it. The man peers at Falke and at his throat. His eyes narrow. He asks a different question, possibly one that does not require a spoken reply. Falke makes gagging noises and touches throat one more time. The Russian now turns his head away and then swings and pushes his face up to his captive. His words are more deliberate, slower and more to a point.

Falke knows the Russian word for German and it is in the sentence he has heard. The man's face is close and he is glaring into his Falke's eyes.

The next action is so insane, it could only come from a man who knows he is going to die and has lost all hope, all sense of personal safety and reason.

Falke pushes up from the seat and takes hold of the truck's steering wheel. Fortunately the young soldier who is driving let's go and leans back away from the madman. Instinctively his foot rams down seeking the brakes but finding the accelerator. The engine screams as truck mounts the footpath and lurches over the two-brick high remains of a front wall. It hovers for a second over the vast bomb crater that sits beyond then gives a suicidal jump and launches over the edge. As it topples over, the truck slews sideways and rolls. The men and bodies and wounded in the back are hurled out and away in all directions as the machine, its engine roaring, crashes to the bottom.

After the chaos of the drop, there is suddenly silence. For a second time in a very short period Dieter Falke discovers he is not dead. The truck, its back broken, sits upright in a muddy pool. Through the shattered window some way off, one of the soldiers from the back is trying to stand. It is obvious he has not looked down at his leg or he would realise the task is pointless. Somewhere behind another is groaning. The call is quite feeble. Inside the cab Falke leans up and looks at his tormentor. His skull is shattered. It has hit the frame of the door. The man still retains the accusative stare he employed at the moment of the truck's change of direction. Falke slowly turns his head to the young driver. He is alive. His eyes are wide. His mouth is turned down in what can only be a fight against terrible pain. He is not a threat. It occurs to Falke that he too may be terribly injured, unaware of his plight due to shock. The examination begins. His legs seem intact. His arms work when tested. Upon trying to close his fist however he notes that the bones in his left hand must be broken. He can almost see the hand swelling. The bodies of the two other men in the truck's cab have taken the force of the crash and left him largely uninjured.

With a considerable shove the dead man beside him is toppled out of the open truck doorway to land face down in the mud. Falke inches away from the driver and using his one functioning hand lowers himself down from the truck. The soldiers lay scattered. There is no way of telling which were previously dead and which were killed in the crash. The two that are moving are not interested in the man from the truck.

Some heavy bombers rumble overhead quite low. They are probably American. Falke does not know their name but they are shining, glinting in the light. He remembers that it was the American planes that always glinted brightly before they rained down destruction on his lines and the German armaments when he was in the columns retreating toward Berlin. Now they just pass by. Their work is done.

Nobody has come to investigate the crash and the noise but doubtless they will. At the back of the crater the earth has been blasted into a much gentler slope. It should provide an exit route.

As Falke is about to head away, he notices the man in the mud beside the truck has a side arm.

He retrieves it and pushes it into his belt. A rifle and a pistol. He even retrieves some more ammunition for his rifle although it is doubtful he could summon the will or the strength to fight anybody at the moment.

There is the sound of a vehicle approaching. It is time to be gone from this mess.

At the top of the crater Falke turns briefly to look back. Two scout cars are coming to a halt at the gap on the road through which minutes before he had plunged into this pit.

"Well Herr Falke," he says out loud, "Your head is still on your shoulders. If there is a God he is either on my side or he's out to lunch today."

Chapter 18

'Good Life'

"Das ist ein Magischer Raum."
Hauke is in an expansive mood. He is lying on the lounge
in his shorts and singlet and the owner's giant dressing
gown. He has not changed since his bath. His uniform is
clean and dry awaiting its owner. But he is not interested in becoming a soldier once more.
"And what a beautiful ceiling. Look, there are little draw-
ings." He is pointing to the corners above his head.
Indeed, there are odd little blue cherubs adorning each
corner of the ornate plaster. They have gold leaf out-
lines. Nobody had thought to look up until now.
"That is something we did not have."

In their time together Adriane has extracted pieces of
information about her guest. His life was fairly privileged. Though he still does not notice. He was somewhat protected, physically and mentally, from the war
going on outside his parents narrow world. His naivety
runs well beyond the problem of his youth. Only the end
of the war for Germany has caught him up in its tenta-

cles. And, not unreasonably, he does not like it.

"A Magic Room indeed. Oh you poor thing," says Adriane, seated at the table. "Who could grow up without fat little babies on their ceiling?"

The boy is not terribly good with sarcasm either but he picks up on this one.

"I cannot help it if we had nice ceilings ..." He looks briefly across at Adriane and pauses, "Farm girl."

It takes Adriane quite some time and patience to wait out Hauke's alertness. He is aware of his remark. Perhaps he should have apologised. He is not sure of the finer points of such protocol. When there is no reaction he suspects the worst. Either the woman is insulted or she is angry or she is both. He cannot see how she will not react in some way.

Yet she continues with idle conversation about the early spring weather, the Russian presence, how much she enjoys the soup they made.

Perhaps she saw it as it was intended. Just a joke. Fun, like brother and sister.

Time passes. She goes to the kitchen for a glass of water. Stands near the window, sipping. Sits again.

"You know," she says, standing again, "I am still thirsty. It must be that salted pork."

This time she returns with a pitcher of water.

Hauke is gazing again at the ceiling. He points once more.

"Each little baby is different. I hadn't noticed. They are hand painted ...."

Adriane empties the entire jug over the boy. He jumps up and she pushes him back. Sits on him and massages his wet face roughly, poking her fingers in his eyes and then cuffing him half-gently across the ears, again and again.

"Farm girls can look after themselves boy." Cuff. "We eat city folk like you." Cuff. "You are cheeky and ungrateful, my little soldier." She pauses. Cuffs him again. "Aren't you?" Cuff.

Hauke is silent. His eyes wide, staring up at his attacker. Now she is concerned she has hurt the kid. Has a line been crossed. He doesn't understand? Has she hurt him?

Then he starts laughing. He shakes with mirth. Wriggling about like a five-year-old. Looking up and laughing again.

When she does not join in, his laugh dies a little. Just a solemn face. Could it be he has misjudged the situation yet again, even though he finds it so funny?

While he stares up waiting for some sign, some reaction, she smiles. It is a tender smile. A type of smile he has almost forgotten. She looks away for a moment, strokes his forehead and then bends down and kisses him on the lips.

"You're not a great soldier, you're not even a good one. And you're not a hero. But for now you're my soldier and you're all I've got. I can teach you manners. It will take time but I am patient. Little fellow."

She steps off the boy and wipes her hand on her pants. "And you're very wet."

Hauke stares at her. "Umm, yes, well so is my gown and our lounge. Very wet. You've ruined our lounge."

There are gunshots. In the distance but quite distinct.

Some conflict has broken out. Sobering, taking away their mood and quietening the room. Treachery is still out there.

More shots, distant voices. Some quite close. Other soldiers discussing the noise? The temptation to look from their windows is great but must be ignored.

Both occupants of the apartment are frozen in their position, eyes slightly skyward, heads turned, listening. More noise then there is a crashing sound.

Any further aural information is drowned by the roar of some planes passing over the city. High but still noisy. When they have gone there is silence. More complete than before. As if the neighborhood had all stopped to listen.

Hauke moves off to the bathroom to get a towel. He walks bow-legged, water dripping down onto his feet. When he emerges he is reduced to a pair of damp shorts.

Adriane, seated at the table looks at this slim, drain-pipe boy. His flat stomach, small shoulders. He is quite pretty. She stores that thought for a time when he might once again need some cutting reprimand.

He flops on the lounge, arms folded, then realises it is wet and quietly stands, retaining a modicum of dignity and joins Adriane at the table, arms folded.

"Aren't you cold?"

"No, I'm fine."

"Would you like some warm cocoa?"

After a pause, "Yes, I would ..... Sir."

There is renewed activity outside. Trucks and light ar-

moured vehicles are travelling up and down the streets.
They are laden with troops. They seem be searching.
It is not a time to be seen at a window. Adriane and
Hauke are particularly careful. Aware that while a casual
glance may not spot them, a closer inspection by someone with binoculars may detect their presence.
They venture down the stairs, far enough to hear the
motors revving up the street. One stops and they fear
that the Russians are going to look more closely at their
building. A lot of chatter, then the sound of two motors
moving away.
"Must have been passing on some information." Hauke
is kneeling on the stairs in front of Adriane. He is positioned so that he can peek round the corner of the
landing's wall. His bare back and slender fingers, hooked
on the corner, make him seem quite vulnerable.
"I think we should go back up, Hauke. I don't like all this
.... whatever it is. If we're found it will be nasty.
Even if we're not who they're looking for."
Now she has the boy worried. He hops back from the
corner and sits beside her.
"What do we do?"
"We don't do anything. We remain invisible. We don't
exist. It's just that if they are looking about, searching
for people, we might be an accidental find. Angry men
do bad things."
Hauke looks round. His eyes bigger than usual.
"Like rape?"
The statement or question sends a stab of memory
through the girl. One that she could do without. But she
won't let it haunt her..
"Yes, like rape. People die in war, too. It's all so easy.

No judge, no policeman. It just happens and they move
on.."
Adriane puts her arm around the boy's shoulders.
"I'll protect you. Will you protect me?"
"Well of course, Fraulein. It is a soldier's duty to protect
women and girls."
This is the contradiction that is Hauke Kluge. Is he just
a child who stumbles through his predicaments as they
present themselves, occasionally, by the law of averag-
es, getting something right? Or could it be he is more
enigmatic than he appears? A cunning young person
with wit and judgement and a sense of irony?

Back in the apartment the two occupants set about
ignoring the dangers lurking below and prepare some
food. The initial delight at having the larder and the
means to survive and even cook, have dulled. Now the
building is a haven and a prison. It gives them a degree
of safety but takes their freedom. And an unspoken nagging question floats in their minds. When will this end,
as end it must? What then, what will the future hold?

At the table they have another concoction. Hauke has
discovered the owner's shirts and is resplendent in a
pure white cotton garment of high quality. It has long
cuffs to fold over and hold expensive cuff links.
Neither Adriane or Hauke understand this concept so
the sleeves are rolled up. Still the boy is swamped by
the floating white cloth that surrounds him.
On the plates this time they have the contents of a can
of pork with a strange sauce being a boiled up mix of
dried apple, sultanas, currants and sugar. They have

some pickled red cabbage and haricot beans to complete the plate. Each has a glass of water.

As Adriane sits she places a bottle and two glasses on the table.

"What's that?" Hauke eyes the new item with suspicion.

"It's Plum Brandy. It will warm us up and add some comfort against the noise outside."

Hauke examines the bottle, his finger running over the label. "Will it really do all that?"

Adriane pats his hand. "If we drink enough, the whole world will go away."

It takes several attempts for the boy to be convinced of the joys of brandy consumption. His cautious sips and screwed up face and gasping give the impression he may never master the art.

However, he is persistent, perhaps to save face or perhaps because the first drops have made their way down his throat and are now doing their job.

His sips become more frequent and his enthusiasm grows as the warmth flows through his body.

Adriane proposes a toast. Another new concept for the young guest.

As they touch glasses she says, "May our futures be bright and may we both find happiness and peace wherever our paths lead us"

Hauke sips and then pauses.

"Together .... we'll be together, won't we ....?

It can't be anything else. You're all I have."

In the silence that follows Adriane considers the proposal. It is not something she had imagined, nor had she rejected the idea.

"Yes, of course," she says.

They eat their meal and sip their drink. There occurs much smiling. The girl out of amusement. The boy because he is suddenly deliriously happy. No one can know what state of drunkenness will be there lot until they have reached that state. For Adriane it is quiet and reflective. Hauke however appears to be a two-phase drunk. Phase one being euphoria.
He sits grinning stupidly at his companion.
"I am so happy. We are like a married people. This is nice. Just us two people, here, now, at the table, together, just us, nicely here, at this room, this a magisch raum, it's it's .... nice."
His head rolls a little. He reaches for the bottle but Adrianc gcts thcrc first.
"Maybe we should save this."
Hauke looks puzzled, trying to take in the out of reach brandy bottle. His hand resting where it had been only moments before. He looks across the table, his eyes a little soft focused.
"There are lots of bottles. I've seen them."
Adriane, more alert, says, "We don't know how long we'll have to stay here."
It is a logic that is way beyond Hauke's ability to refute. He simply slides his hand back and sits for a while with his head slightly lowered, occasionally glancing right or left. Phase two is taking place. Slowly he lifts his head. Even Adriane who has been enjoying the show, disturbed by the change in the boy's face. He looks as if he is about to cry. His gaze falls not on her but past her to some place that only his mind can see. Then his eyes

return their focus to Adriane.

"What is it, Hauke? Are you remembering things? Look here ...." The girl reaches across to her companion's face, takes his chin and turns his head to her. What can I do to help?"

For a while the situation is frozen. As if Hauke is processing his new found concerns through the newly acquired fuzz of alcohol. Finally, reaching some point of acquiescence he leans forward and speaks.

"I have questions. Nobody will ever answer my questions." His voice rises. "Not now boy, go away boy, where do you get these silly notions, oh Hauke don't concern yourself." He leans forward. His words are more distinct, as if the use of his remaining mental faculties has partially cleansed his senses.

"Will you answer my questions?"

Adriane is wary. Then she looks again at the immensely sad face opposite. What harm can there be? Besides, she is intrigued to know what the questions might be.

"I'll do my best. How many are there?"

Hauke looks to the ceiling for guidance. It takes a while. Finally he makes up his mind. Holds out his hand with a number of fingers pointing up.

"Three. There's three. Well three big ones."

"Alright."

"Can I start?"

"Whenever you're ready."

Hauke Kluge straightens up, takes a breath. He blinks. Wipes his mouth as if clearing any debris that may hinder his utterance.

"Question one. I need to know. What is death?"

Is he serious? Yes, he is. His eyes are intense. He is waiting for an answer. As if he had asked, can you remember
the name of the Furher's dog. No hint of sarcasm or
some agenda.
The flippant answer is 'the absence of life' but it is not
appropriate. If only he'd been on the farm. Death is no
mystery to children on a farm.
There are so many possible answers. Which one is he
seeking? What will satisfy him?
"I mean, what's next?"
Adriane looks up.
"Oh ……. so you understand death. You'd like to know if
there's something after that?"
"There must be, right? Things can't just stop. All that
waste. So what is after?"
Adriane tries a new tack. "Are you religious? Did your
family go to church?"
"My father said, it was a great shame that so much energy was wasted by so many people praying to imaginary
beings of their own creation." Hauke looks quite proud
of this statement.
"My parents and those neighbours. You know Dr Snip,
Snip." Hauke points at his crotch. "They would have
dinner together and then spend hours arguing about
religion. The doctor and his wife sort of defended the
Jewish stuff a bit and my parents would argue that it
was all just a human need for understanding the unknown. They would all finish up laughing. It was just an
exercise of their minds. Other nights they would talk
about nature, or art or music or national socialism.
Ummm."
Adriane leaned back, surreptitiously placing the bottle

of brandy on the floor as she moved her hands onto her lap.

"It seems you've just answered your question. It's all imaginary. There is nothing else."

The boy's reaction is quite startling. He half stands, then unsteadily falls back as he shouts, "No, that cannot be. We must go somewhere. I want you to tell me. Where ? It can't just ...... end. That's not right. That can't be it. What comes next?"

Hauke's head bows. Then his shoulders shake.

"Are you crying?"

"No."

"I think you are."

" What if I am. Everybody is dead. I want to see my parents again and my brother. War is so stupid. Nobody wins. Everybody loses" He shakes again, his head still bowed.

"You are a bad drunk, my soldier. Some people are happy, some are at least comfortable. You, are a sad one. It happens."

Adriane lifts the bottle off the floor. "How about one more?"

Hauke is an eager drunk. He drains the new offering quite fast.

"At least you haven't been sick. You're tough."

The boy seems quite taken by this description and its manly implications. He brightens in his blurry, unfocused world. Not wishing to have more sobbing, Adriane presses on.

"What's your second question?"

Once again Hauke hesitates. Either the import of the

question requires some preparation or he needs time with the phrasing. He fiddles about with his own fingers, concentrating on tying them into digital knots. Running them together and pulling the result apart.

"Well .... ?"

He seems awkward.

"People keep talking about it. I pretend to know but I don't. It must be something bad. Something that gets done to you if you're caught. They laugh and use it as a threat. The Commandant said it would happen to me. I think he despised me."

Adriane reaches across the table and takes the boy's hand.

"Hauke, I can't help if I don't know what you're talking about."

"Rape," he states loudly. Hauke is looking into her eyes, unblinking. "What the hell is rape? What happens when you get raped? How is it done and who does it? And why?"

Involuntarily withdrawing her hand Adriane gives a short cry. Hauke sits back, startled by her reaction. She is returned to the dark room with the monster Brunek. Just as the memories had been suppressed, now they are back, raw and brutal. She closes her eyes and tries to force the thoughts away. She feels nauseous. His blows across her head, his manic insults are in her mind once more.

And facing her is a wary boy who knows none of this and it appears, not even the basics of human reproduction. If only he was one of the farm boys. This conversation would not be unnecessary. Time for a break, perhaps some coffee.

After she has made coffee and they put some blankets on the large lounge which is still a little damp, they sit together and Adriane considers her options. While she stares over the steam from her cup, Hauke asks anxiously.

"Are you upset? Did I say something bad?"

"No, nothing wrong. I just need to think of the best answer for you."

After a minute Hauke again enquires. "So it is bad?"

"Yes, Hauke it is bad. It is very bad. It is horrible. I want to give you the correct answer. Please, let me think."

Option one. Make up a story. It is a euphemism for a beating or face slap or some minor discomfort.

Option two. Explain reproduction. Use science and farm metaphors to paint a picture in which rape is the action. Difficult.

Option three. Tell the truth and hope he understands enough about the act of sex or love to recognise that having it forced upon you is terrible.

Option four. Show him? They are alone. Should she be the one to introduce this child to a new phase of his life. Would it work? Would he be embarrassed, glad, impressed, delighted or horrified? What is she thinking? He's only a boy.

Now to consider these each in turn.

It would be an easy path to take. Make up a plausible story of ritual and harsh treatment. Brutal but not life threatening. A form of punishment, well known to all sides. No, it is not fair to mislead this earnest young man. He seeks an answer. He must have an answer.

Besides, he must already realise that there is more to
the term than mere punishment. Dismiss the first option..
"Are you thinking?" Hauke is watching Adriane's face,
his head tilted.
"Yes. Please be patient. I need some time to explain.
Wait, relax, you've waited this long to ask."
The science of reproduction. Male, female. Lust for
humans and urges for animals. Only humans have com-
plicated the first two by adding love to the mix. It may
work but it is so clinical. The boy needs hope, even from
this he needs to understand that the same thing can be
horrible and beautiful.
Always a practical girl. Known through the village for
her intellect, Adriane is less confident than she has been
for many years. She had only ever known two men.
One bright young man who found his way into her skirts
in the woods. Both seventeen they had considered it
terribly romantic. A mere three months later he and his
family had moved away. Then came Ernst at nineteen.
He studied chemistry. To what end she was not sure.
They were deliriously happy. Despite warnings of not
being charmed and giving up her prized possession
(little did they know) she gave it readily when asked.
By amazing luck she did not become pregnant. War took
Ernst away. He was 'needed' was all he would tell her.
He wrote for a while then the letters stopped.
Then there was Brunek. It did not count.

Perhaps three. The cold facts. Herein lies a possible
road block. If Hauke is a complete innocent when it
comes to sexual matters, where does she start and how

can it proceed. With diagrams? It is almost amusing.
"It's raining."
"Pardon?"
"Look." Hauke is pointing to the windows. "It is raining. Now I feel more privileged, to be safe in this warm
house." The boy smiles disarmingly. "We can't go out
walking. I'll just have to sit and wait for your answer."
"Yes," Adriane says, "And ...." She looks at the
rain hitting and running down the window glass. After a
pause she says, "I think my answer is to ask 'you' some
questions."

Hauke is a reluctant witness. Even his short time in the
Hitler Jungend has left an entrenched air of suspicion
when it comes to being questioned.
"Do you know that boys have a penis and girls have a
vagina?" Adriane begins.
"Yes, of course," Hauke replies brightly.
Adriane secretly sighs. "Of course." That is a good sign.
"Do you know how babies are created?" she continues.
Now Hauke is out of his depth. He reddens and looks at
Adriane before a stumbling reply.
Perhaps if he is wrong it will be considered in incredibly
bad taste. Even if he is right. It is something he has con-
sidered in boyish dreams. And heard from older Jugend
members. But always on the fringe. That A might possi-
bly fit into B and be the source of many mysteries.
He did not understand and was certainly not going to
ask. Still he plunges in after more twisting of his fingers.
"Does it have something to do with a penis being put
into the vagina?"
"Yes, that's how it is done."

Hauke looks both mystified and relieved. As if he had stumbled onto the correct answer in a maths class. Now he is concerned that he may be asked how he arrived at the correct answer.

It takes an hour of slow extraction and reveal, as the rain falls solidly outside, to walk this soldier of the Reich through the intricacies of human emotion, coming of age and the changes that occur, love, lust, passion, semen, eggs, birth and associated conditions to finally arrive at rape and its consequences. Then another fifteen minutes to walk through the concept of male rape.

It is the latter that scares and horrifies Hauke the most. It seems the boy is hovering on that incredible borderline between childhood and puberty. Staring across the frontier into a wild untamed land.

Adriane too is on the edge of her knowledge of such details. If Hauke was a girl she could speak from experience but a boy's passage to adulthood is not an area of which she can voice opinions with any degree of confidence. It is only thanks to the expansive world of Ernst and endless hours spent lying in his arms listening to his thoughts on just about everything, that Adriane has a store of information that would not normally be the lot of a twenty-one year old farm girl.

No subject was off limits for Ernst.

At one stage of the proceedings Adriane does consider that removing all their clothes would prove a lot simpler than trying to paint word pictures.

But no, he is like a little brother. It is not something she could do. She remembers their first night in the apartment when they huddled together, half naked, with only the wish for comfort, warmth and the touch of another

human.
They have a bond but is it one of necessity or genuine affection?

She leaves Hauke sitting on the lounge, plumbing the depths of the information he has taken in. He has his nose resting on his hands. His stare is into an area in the centre of the room.
Adriane looks back, as she walks to the kitchen.
A flicker of light is resting on his blonde locks. He looks fragile. Bony shoulders sticking up.
"What was question three going to be?" she wonders.

Chapter 19

'Hunting Party'

From the 'office' window the area appears even more grey, miserable and useless. A city of rubble and broken dreams. An empire taken down, taken to pieces and scattered by those who opposed it. On the desk is a plate with crumbs and an empty tea mug.
If he had not eaten the sandwich and drunk the black tea brew, Captain Chaban would have earned the disappointment of Comrade Kozuch. Not a good thing to do. The man, this Kozuch enigma, the preparer of sandwiches and finder of good tea leaves enters the room.
"I have them downstairs."
The Captain turns from the window. Kozuch never calls him 'sir'. He rather likes the friendly, cautious informality.
"Good. Let's see if we can find out what exactly is going on." He takes his aides arm. "Before we do, Comrade, do you have any information that might advantage me when I speak to them?"

Downstairs there are four Russian soldiers. Three are

seated and appear to be badly injured. The fourth is fully upright and alert. He salutes when the Captain enters. The others out of suffering or lack of care, do not. It is the able soldier who receives the first question.

"You, are you the one who found these men?"

The man stiffens. "Yes sir. Comrade Illich, sir. I am not of this division. I was riding despatch. From the northern sector. As my motorbike turned the corner in the street that runs up the hill over there, I saw one of our trucks in the distance. It was heading toward me. Suddenly it swerved, mounted the footpath and disappeared."

The man Illich stops, as if he has now said his piece.

"Yes, Illich, go on"

"I stopped sir. My bike. I paused. I was confused."

"Why did you stop, Illich? Why were you confused?"

"I thought at first that the truck had perhaps turned off, into a laneway or building. But it seemed to me more, that the truck was out of control. Then it disappeared. Very odd."

"So, what did you do, Illich?"

"I waited sir, to see if perhaps the reason for the truck's change of direction was because it had come under fire. I did not wish to rush in and suffer a similar fate, sir."

Captain Chaban nodded in an effort to keep the man on course. "That seems logical. How long did you wait?"

Encouraged by the officer's demeanor the man opens up a little.

"Some minutes, sir. I listened very intently for any sound of conflict."

"And you heard none? And you proceeded toward where you last saw the truck."

"I did, sir. When I arrived at the point where the truck

had vanished I immediately saw the truck at the bottom of a very large blast crater. There were a number of our soldiers laying about in the hole."

"Was anybody up and moving about?"

"Yes sir, just one. One of our Russian soldiers. He was away on the far side of the crater. He had made his way out. He walked away, off down the side street away from me, as some of our scout cars arrived."

"He did not acknowledge you or call out?" the Captain asked.

"I don't think he saw me sir, but no, he seemed anxious to get away. Perhaps he was injured and confused."

Comrade Kozuch now motions to a pale junior soldier propped up by some cushions but still leaning to one side of his chair.

"This young man was the driver of the truck. He can tell us of the strange events that led to the accident. Sir, he is in a lot of pain."

Before Chaban can address the soldier, he looks up, winces as he shifts his position then addresses the captain.

"It was not an accident. I can assure you of that, sir."

"Why do you say that, comrade?"

"The prisoner grabbed the wheel sir. He held it with a grip of iron and swung the truck. There was nothing I could do."

Chaban looked into the eyes of the young soldier.

The man looked desperate. He reminded the Captain of a trapped animal.

"So, what is your name comrade?"

"Bunin sir. My name is Pyoter Bunin."

"Well Pyoter Bunin, I want to tell you something. I am a
patient and understanding man. You need not fear me
or fear any repercussions from today's accident. I prefer
to deal in facts and I intend not to apportion blame.
So let us have that cleared up." Chaban gave a tiny smile
which may have helped or may have looked sinister. He
continued.
"Now, there are aspects of your story that I wish to clari-
fy. First, if there were only soldiers of the Soviet Army on
board the truck. Why was one a prisoner? Secondly, why
couldn't you simply apply the brakes when the steering
wheel was taken?

Soldier Bunin is uncomfortable. He ribs are giving him
great discomfort. The pain remedy they have given him
has had a limited effect and it has made him nauseous.
Combined with the pain and the necessity to concen-
trate, he is struggling.
He hopes the others are listening as he relates the story
he has already told to the man called Kozuch.
"We were on patrol, sir. We were conducting a random
check of identity of a number of civilians. They had been
gathered in the street for interrogation. As we spoke to
them, a man, a Russian soldier, not from our unit, approached unseen along the footpath. Without warning
sir, he started shooting at our party. He killed our officer
sir, he killed others and wounded more. We returned fire
once we ascertained what was happening. This soldier
was incapacitated by one of our shots and he was captured. We were returning with him so that the incident
could be investigated when the accident occurred."
"I see," says Chaban, looking at the truck driver who

has bowed his head once more. The Captain glances at Kozuch. He knows the story is a little untidy. It has some inconsistencies.

He calls the aide into the corridor. In the empty space he looks the man eye to eye and pulls a face, twisting his mouth and narrowing his eyes. "There is more to this story. I am not hearing it all. First of all, who went with Illich to provide assistance?"
"Some men from the engineers. They were at the rail station."
"Did you speak to them?"
"Yes, I did."
"What did they find?"
"The truck, in the crater, our men dead or injured."
"Did they look around the area?"
"No. They were concerned at returning our men to safety. Only later did we send patrols out to look for their attacker."
Chaban paused, leaning his head against the wall.
"But, nobody has examined the scene of the shooting. The place where this story all began. Not right, it's not right. I would like you to go, by yourself, back to the street were this happened. Find the scene of the shooting. See if there are any residents who may have seen the incident. Find the house of those who were being checked. I want to know what I am not being told.
Can you do this for me, Comrade?"

It is mid afternoon when Comrade Kozuch returns. He enters the Captain's room carrying two cups of coffee.

Chaban sniffs the hot mug.

"I am still at a loss to know how you do it Comrade.
I am afraid to ask any more for fear it will all go away."
He sips. "With real milk. Astounding." He motions his
aide to a seat. "I assume that a serving of hot coffee
means that you have some information to impart?"

Kozuch leans forward.

"I went to the bomb crater first. Rode a bicycle so as to
appear more of an interested lone soldier.

It seems to match the story. The truck is there. The
marks where it went over. Footprints of our men as they
went backwards and forwards. And upon examining the
other side of the hole there are in fact a single line of
boot prints leading up and over the top, into the street.
I lost them after this point."

Kozuch stops to take a gulp of his coffee.

"It took me a while to locate the place where the shooting occurred. I considered the fact that the truck was
moving downhill and had gained enough speed to ensure the accident could happen. I was looking for blood.
There was none. The rain had washed it away. But I
found bullet marks on the wall."

Chaban queried. "Rather ambitious Comrade. There is
little of Berlin that has not seen the impact of a bullet or
two."

"True. Strangely or perhaps fortuitously this particular
street is largely undamaged. The houses are intact and
there is little sign of war on the facades."

Chaban apologised. "I'm sorry Comrade. Obviously your
method worked. Please continue."

"Once I had the bullet marks I could align where the
truck must have stopped. I found blood. The rain had

removed much of it but there was still as substantial amount, once I had ascertained the spot.

I knocked on the door of the house. The houses are all three storey in this part of the street. It was very quiet. I gained the impression that any residents nearby were keeping away. The door was not locked so I entered. Very tragic. In the sitting room in the front of the house I found the bodies of two men. Both had been shot. Head shots. Executions. One had been bayoneted in the back. There was also the body of a young girl. She had been shot in the back. Finally there was the body of young boy. He had been shot in the side of the head. They were all laid side by side and were covered with a large rug. It seemed to be a clumsy effort to hide evidence of some behaviour. Something that would be difficult to explain when we are trying to create a stable situation in the occupation."

Captain Chaban looked away and then back to Kozuch. "The bodies were recently dead? What are you implying? What behaviour?"

Kozuch shrugged. "The boy. He was naked. He had been obviously molested."

"Oh," said Chaban. "Our truck driver Bunin?"

"It seems a fair guess," said Kozuch

"Did you find any witnesses?"

"No. Anybody who was involved or saw the whole thing has moved on. Wisely it would seem."

At the Field Hospital near the rail terminus Captain Chaban and his aide Comrade Kozuch have come to visit private soldier Bunin.

On the way, in the staff car Kozoch has filled in details

of the unit in the truck. They are a transport group led by a sergeant who has a reputation of being a ruthless fool who has a string of bad reports involving behavior, discipline, following orders and morality. He and his men were more like a gang. They looted and abused all they met.

Chaban nodded. "Well now the man is dead. Is the world a better place? It's war. Not all soldiers are noble beasts. I hate what many of the soldiers of Mother Russia have done including mine but I have to balance their actions against the slaughter we have seen at the hands of these people we have now defeated. From reports I have received I conclude that my family are safe and I believe yours too are unharmed. We cry for our millions who were not so fortunate, our murdered comrades, their raped and battered wives and children. How can I condemn the actions of our troops when revenge is at hand?"

Kozuch turned briefly from the steering of the car. "Of course we can't. But are we savages like them or are we of a nobler race?"

Captain Chaban remained silent for a while then said, "You are right of course Comrade but greater minds than ours have fallen prey to righteous causes."

Bunin is in a cot. He watches the two men approach with wary eyes. They draw up chairs and sit beside him. "Well Comrade Bunin, you indeed are a lucky man. Your sergeant is dead. Of the fifteen men under his command only three are alive." Chaban waited.

"Four sir, you mean four are alive."

"No three. One more of your colleagues has just died."

Chaban waits again then continues.

"Your injuries are quite severe Comrade. Ribs, a punctured lung. Who is to say if you may soon be joining the dead. Perhaps, and I mention this only as an idea to be considered, you would like to unburden yourself, in case things turn worse. Which can sometimes happen quite suddenly.

The young boys and girls you molested, the people you murdered, the children, the mothers ...... All at your hands. Witnesses have come forward Comrade ...."

Now Bunin has the Captain's arm. "They're wrong. I did none of this. I was against such things. I had to appear to join in their actions or I would have been in danger. The boy struggled. One of the others shot him. It was the Sergeant's idea to go to the house. He had seen the families go in there as he passed earlier in the day.

He said they had some nice daughters. I had only been posted to the unit a week ago. I didn't want to be involved."

Kozuch can only watch in awe as his Captain, with only a scrap of information can extract a full story from this worried soldier.

They leave Pyoter Bunin sometime later with a complete detailed recreation of the attack, rapes, murders and the strange events that followed.

"What is to become of me?" Bunin asks as they leave.

"Nothing for now," Chaban answers. "Perhaps in years to come you may wake from your sleep in a terrible frame of mind and remember the 'actions' you took. Perhaps you will continue to sleep fitfully as you recall it all and see the faces of your victims. The soldiers of

Mother Russia should be better than this."

In the car once more Chaban turns to his driver. "Kozuch, I want us to be better. If not for Russia then perhaps as a sign that humanity can survive. I have heard stories of our enemy. Of their death camps, set up to exterminate whole races and human types. Of levels of vile brutality that the most hardened human would find distressing. I can give you a small example. At some camps apparently the guards played games with the new arrivals. If it was a quieter day and they had less of the unfortunate masses to process, they would take larger families aside. First they would march the husband away then they would say to the mother, 'We have decided to let one of your, say four children live. You can choose which one. If you don't choose we will shoot them all. You have thirty seconds.' Imagine Comrade, the horror, the agony of placing a mother in such a position. To make such a choice."

"Was the chosen child saved?"

"No, of course not. They shot them or gassed them all anyway. So, we must find this rogue soldier who would murder his own. It is Russian pride at stake here. I want my sector to be an ordered and respected area. Not one that allows a man like this to roam free despite the circumstances."

"Could he be German?"

Chaban is gazing ahead. "Yes, he could. Which worries me more. Is he a renegade out for final revenge or just a soldier who decided not to be rounded up? So many questions.

Chapter 20

'Reunion'

It is Adriane who finally breaks into the reverie surrounding Hauke Kluge. It is becoming dark outside.
He is still seated on the large lounge chair idling away the time in the room, looking vaguely about as if some momentous task needed completion.
"There are more Russians in the streets. They are driving about, looking in buildings."
Hauke turns his head up as if searching for the voice. "What? Who's looking?"
"The Russian soldiers are in the streets. A lot of them. They seem to be searching."
"Oh. Are we safe? Would they come in here?"
Adriane looks at the door. "I suppose it depends on how much they want to find somebody or something. Perhaps there are still some Germans who feel they should keep the war going. We must be careful. Stay away from the windows. No light or noise."
Hauke brightens slightly. "We could block the stairs. With wreckage. Make it impossible to pass."
"It's a good idea Hauke but a sudden blockage in an

otherwise tidy stairwell would only aid their suspicion.
Best just to look deserted."
Adriane is pleased with the reply. Let him down lightly.
Not to stifle enthusiasm.
The routine of the room settles in again. In their gilded
cage, life for the two tenants finds different paths in
bearing the boredom. Creating new ways to mix the food
supplies to present a fresh plate at their table. Often to
no avail. They are all variations on a limited palette.
The water still flows and the gas still cooks and the
lights continue to not come on.

In their idle searchings of the apartment the two have
built a profile of its owner. Though there is not a lot to
find. He seems to be a civilian. He has papers from a university. He has Nazi Party membership cards and a pin.
There are photos of a woman and some small children
in front of a big house. They are seated on the steps.
It appears to be in the country. Then the same children
sitting on ponies. The reins are held by the woman and a
tall man with a thin moustache.
On the back of the first photo are the names Geli, Anna,
Felix - August 1938. There is nothing on the back of the
second photo.
They decide the tall man is Dr Antek Beck, owner of
their abode. There is little evidence to confirm this opinion but then there is little to the contrary.
Apart from the clothes, food, books and basics of
cleanliness and comfort there is scant else in personal
effects. It is from this limited collection that Adriane
slowly forms an opinion or theory.
"There are no trinkets," she utters after one of their

exploratory circuits. "If this was a home there would be more personal items. More of those little things that people collect around them. It's what makes a home. I think this man just used this place to stay in Berlin. His work must have required that he had to be here part of the time. After it was bombed he probably didn't bother anymore."

Hauke is intrigued by the theory. "So he could still be alive and might come back?"

Adriane, always aware of the need to stay calm says, "It's quite unlikely now. Who would want to come to Berlin?"

"You did."

"Yes, but I had Russians chasing me and I'm quite mad."

"Then why couldn't the Russians be chasing the man with the thin moustache?"

"Don't spoil my theory Hauke. It can be dangerous to be too logical. If they were after him, he wouldn't go back to his address in Berlin. At least that's what I think."

It is Hauke however who finds a further clue a day later when he goes through the pockets of the man's suits hanging in the bedroom wardrobe. He finds a handsome silver cigarette lighter in one. It has the initials AB engraved on the side. In another, tucked into the inside pocket of the coat, he finds a map. The map is of Northern Germany. On it in blue pencil somebody has traced a route from Berlin to a little town on the Baltic Sea. The town is called 'Peenemunde.' It is interesting but means nothing to the two squatters.

The boy also decides that the locked, top central drawer of the man's desk may hold further secrets. He pops it open quite easily with a kitchen knife.

"It's just a notebook," he says.

"A handsome one, just the same," adds Adriane, examining the find. "Leather bound. For important notes."

The notes consist of formulas, small rough diagrams of odd pieces of machinery and a series of sketches with variations on something called a gyroscope.

"I'll keep this for my important notes." Hauke clutches the book in his folded arms. "There's still lots of pages."

A little later Hauke asks, "I still don't understand why this man here has so much food?"

"Perhaps he had little dinner parties, or lots of colleagues calling in for long discussions about their work. He may have wanted to keep on the right side of party officials by giving them a good meal. I suspect he used a cook or maid. I doubt he planned to stay here if Berlin was under siege. This was just a place for him to stay while visiting the city."

Hauke seems satisfied with Adriane's answer.

"Okay. That makes sense."

Is he being patronising? It is hard to tell with Hauke.

Before it is too dark to see, the evening meal is eaten and then the long empty night begins. They dare not use even a match light. So they simply sit about in the darkness until this becomes unbearable then they retire to bed. Despite the dark they are now familiar enough with the surroundings to navigate quite well. On nearly all the nights Hauke decides to join Adriane in the big bed. Despite his enlightenment on the ways of the flesh, nothing changes. Beneath the bravado and his Hitler Youth

facade he is still a boy who needs his mother. Adriane
is the only substitute he has and on occasions she finds
herself cuddling the boy as you would a child.

This night however there is something to do. The noise
in the streets is quite intense. Skulking by the curtains
they are able to glimpse Russian trucks stopping periodically and disgorging troops who begin systematically
searching houses and buildings. Lights flash about and
scour the walls and streetscape. German citizens are
dragged out of their houses but then after some minutes
are allowed to return.

Eventually, inevitably they hear their own street being
examined. They go out into the corridor to listen down
the stairwell. Suddenly voices rush up from below.

They are inside. The voices are loud. Even in Russian
they can deduce that there is a discussion taking place
in the bombed out street level. Could those whom they
seek have managed to get into this building and should
they try to do the same?

It takes a while then a voice of greater authority is
heard. After feeble protestation the greater authority
wins the discussion and the voices fade. It is doubtful
the soldiers had much interest in trying to gain
entrance anyway.

After waiting with hardly a breath Adriane and Hauke
return to the apartment and go to bed.

It is at about 7am the next day as the coffee on the stove
begins to boil that events move along. Hauke has decided to wash and is standing in the bathtub soaping
himself down. Adriane is laying out cups for the coffee.
Their familiarity has reached a point where neither seek

privacy. Hauke stands with his bucket of water in the
bath tub. The door is open. He is singing and humming
quietly as he lathers. Adriane listens for some time, trying to remember the song. It takes her back to the farm
kitchen. Perhaps a folk song. What is it?
She leans across the hallway door, smiling at the back of
the glistening body in the bath.
"You're good. Maybe you'll be a singer one day."
As with so many bathroom performances the revelation
that they are being heard makes Hauke fall silent.
Despite coaxing he will not resume.
She is aware that Hauke has taken to observing her
when she washes. He finds reasons to come into the
bathroom. On one occasion seating himself for a chat,
until she shooed him out. A little disturbed at first she
concludes that he is only curious, especially after the
'talk.'

Adriane retrieves a pot of porridge from the stove and
pours it into two bowls. She tops the mix with a little
sugar and salt. She puts the bowls and two cups and
the coffee pot onto a timber tray with a detailed forest
scene inlaid on the surface. Carefully carrying the load
she walks out into the hallway and into the lounge.
For her first few steps she does not notice, then some
primeval instinct clicks in and she freezes. Lifting and
turning her head she is a short distance from a Russian
soldier. He is standing just inside their doorway. His rifle
is pointed at her stomach. For a moment they stare.
He has blood on the side of his head. It is dried in lumps
and matted in his hair. She is aware of the sound of her
breathing. He then takes one hand off his rifle and raises

it in a gesture that says 'do not move.' This changes to just the index finger as if he is saying 'wait - I am listening.'

They stay frozen. Adriane is shaking. The cups rattle a little. She grips the tray with whitened knuckles. After all they have been through, are they about to die? She swallows. It is all she can do to speak.

"Please, do you understand? We are harmless. There is nobody here of any importance. I ...."

The Russian raises his hand again, somewhat angrily. He is being very cautious. Are there others coming? Is this the end of their freedom, their lives, their magic room?

"Please, don't harm us ......" The soldiers attention moves back to Adriane's face. As their eyes meet, his eyes suddenly widen. He is staring past her to another part of the room. What is happening? Adriane turns her head. Standing to her left is Hauke Kluge. He has a vile, dangerous look on his face. The little boy has gone. He is wrapped in just a towel about his waist. In his hands, steady and menacing is Dr Beck's Walther pistol. It is aimed at the Russian's eyes. From the menace in Hauke's posture he is about to fire.

The Russian is strangely not reacting. His eye are fixed. The stand-off ticks away. The Russian moves his head forward and peers, not at Adriane but at the boy.

His eyes narrow as he leans.

"Hauke?" he says. "Is that you?"

"Was dieses ist?" says Hauke, tilting his head slightly.

Now Adriane's head moves like some sporting spectator between the two. The Russian speaks German? And with no accent.

It is Hauke's turn to stare. His eyes widen and his mouth
opens and hangs.
Finally he says, with some enquiry in his voice, "Herr
Falke?"
The Russian lowers his rifle. "Remember I said to call
me Dieter."
Hauke's gun wavers a little as he stares, then looks
away, then back. He analyses what is happening.
Perhaps the Russian uniform has him confused.
The terrifying confrontation ends abruptly when
Hauke's towel lets go and drops to the floor.
"Scheisse," he says.

Chapter 21

'Settling In'

Now there are three. Dieter Falke is an agreeable house guest. His head wrapped in a padded bandage from their host's quite extensive medicine chest.
It takes several hours after his arrival for him to stare at Adriane and exclaim, "My God, you're that girl who visited our defence post."
From eating his first bowl of porridge and savouring in almost dreamlike delight his cup of black coffee, he is all of appreciative, helpful, friendly, knowledgeable, clever, resourceful but most of all he is an adult male and a soldier as well. His hand is bruised not broken which pleases him.

He will be occupying the second bedroom. A room that Hauke implies he will reluctantly forgo for his friend. Adriane plays along saying that she is happy to share the large main bed and bedroom with the boy.
The man looks at them when this is first proposed, considering the second bedroom has two beds. He smiles slightly. "Just be sure to behave yourself Hauke Kluge.

Honour is at stake here."

The boy looks awkward. Adriane hugs him from behind and kisses his cheek. "We'll be just fine," she says. And now he blushes.

Dieter finds the previous tenant had nice clothes and even shoes that match his own frame quite satisfactorily. So he is transformed into a civilian.

The water he explains is coming from a giant water tank in the roof. It is gravity fed. On examination he reports that the cistern arm still produces a trickle of water when activated but the new water may be contaminated. He suggests cutting off the tank inlet. It is a big tank. It will still last them quite a while.

The gas, he says, is a mystery. The pressure is low but it is continuous. Somehow there's a supply trapped in the street pipes and it must be sufficiently sealed to maintain a flow.

They show him Antek Beck's belongings and papers, his guns and his map.

"I think he's a scientist," says Hauke.

"It's a good guess. Good as any." Dieter lifts up the map for a closer look. "Peenemunde? There was some talk in the field. All our battles were down south. Not much information. We knew the war was over long before the officers. Walked backwards on the way to Berlin while talking of the final victory. I hoped that the young soldiers would just get out of there when that last stupid stand took place. Well one of them listened."

He gives Hauke a pretend punch to the side of his jaw. For the rest of the day the three rest and eat. In the afternoon Dieter Falke shuts the door to the bathroom and spends a while washing and shaving. When he emerges he is quite transformed.

"I didn't feel right dressing in the clean clothes when I was covered in mud, sweat and dust."

"And blood," adds Hauke.

It is Adriane who cuts to the core of their new relationship. "It's been a surprising day, I want to know your story. Why were you in a Russian uniform? We can share. I have a story too. And Hauke here, he got away and all the way here." She holds out her hand. "Do we agree?"

Soldier Falke hesitates, looks down at the girl's hand, then at her. He takes her hand.

"Yes, sure, we should tell our stories. I assume none are pretty. Can we do it tomorrow? I'd like to rest."

In the morning, after breakfast Adriane can wait no longer. She makes a hot drink and brings out some almond biscuits. She seats all three round the dining room table. "Now, it's story time she says."

"Whoever Herr Beck was, he ate well and had contacts," Dieter holds up the biscuit with dusted icing and takes another bite.

"Alright," says Adriane, "You first. Why was a large section of the Russian Army looking for you? Are you more important than you appear to be or did you do something to anger them?"

Dieter looks at his cup. "The latter," he says. Then, as if unburdening himself, he shrugs and begins, gathering substance as he proceeds telling them his whole story, starting with his enlistment in Dresden and his farewell kiss for his mother and father.

His battles, his near misses, the deaths of all around him. Seeing fellow soldiers blown apart by US Army artillery. Their vehicles exploding and being strafed by American Mustangs. Passing abandoned detention centres with stinking corpses. No food, no ammunition and party officials calling for them to regroup and win on orders of high command and special orders of the Fuhrer.

An older soldier shot the official who gave them these last orders. An officer raised his pistol at the soldier and the men all raised their rifles at the officer. In the end they all walked away.

In one epic stand the Americans drove them out of the forest they were sheltering in and across a marshland. They were caught on both sides and mown down. Falke abandoned his gear and swam underwater, hiding for a breath in the reeds.

From there his luck changed. He pauses at this point and laughs. "Did I say luck?"

A transport unit takes pity on the twenty men still alive from his regiment and 'transports' them all the way to Berlin. They are to defend the city until the massive reinforcements, that have been organised by the Fuhrer, arrive to push the allies back out of Germany.

The SS and officials believe this to be the case.

The Wermacht regulars do not. It is time to think of survival rather than dying for no reason.

"I was a proud German soldier at the start of this mess. Four years, I have seen what we did and heard much more. There's little glory in any of our activities.

We've brought incredible misery on most of Europe.
When it was just Austria, Poland and the Czechs I
thought that maybe we might stop. We'd doubled our
size. The world may have let us keep these lands and
it could have been a greater Germany. Hitler is insane.
Why did he continue? Didn't he ever hear of Napoleon?
What madness, to attack Russia."
"I've heard that before," Adriane smiles.
Hauke looks crestfallen. "The Fatherland is still our
land."
"I wonder how proud you'll be when all our deeds are
revealed? Tell me that again in the future. You think the
Russians are barbarians. A lot of them are. But by God,
they have justification."
Adriane lays her hand on the man's arm and turns her
head to look him in the eye.
"Why were you in a Russian uniform?" she asks slowly.
As the story unfolds Dieter Falke spares no detail
despite his young audience. Hauke Kluge and Adriane
Gerst both have tears in their eyes. The reasons may
have varied but no part of the story brought them any
peace.
It finished with Dieter Falke's desperate climb up into
their building. He, like them, had hoped that the difficulty of gaining entry would dissuade any pursuers or just
the curious that nobody was within. His damaged hand
had made the climb painful and difficult. The discovery
of a ladder hidden on the first level made him wary but
as he saw the empty or damaged apartments on each
floor he doubted anybody would be left.
When he entered their apartment he was as surprised as
they were by meeting in such a way.

"As for the future. Hopefully they won't remember me too well. If I'm a civilian then I have a chance of just being another German."

"Why?" said Hauke urgently. "You're not planning on going out or leaving are you?"

"I don't know what I want to do. The Russians have just arrived. They are disorganised, prone to shoot, in search of revenge and still very angry. Raping and looting are their main interests for the time being. Have you two thought about the future? This is a truly, what did you call it, a Magisch Raum but eventually the world will settle and everybody will have to take a chance at life once more. I know two things. First, I am alone.

I have heard about Dresden. There's no point going back to a city that no longer exists and a past that isn't there. Secondly, the best direction out of Berlin is west.

To Braunschweig perhaps and beyond. Then turn south. Anywhere away from the Russians. None of the occupying forces will be going home in a hurry. I'd rather be in the hands of some force whose lands we didn't occupy and whose people we didn't brutalise."

"So, the Americans or the British?" Adriane asks.

"Seems the safest bet. Now my girl, let me hear your story and then we will hear the life and times of Herr Kluge. How did we all meet in this time and place."

An hour of listening with an occasional query and they are finished. At the end of the two stories, Dieter looks away and sighs.

"Good God. We're all orphans. I assumed you had something to return to, some past that could be taken up again." He hugs them both and kisses Adriane on the cheek.

In the silence that ensues Hauke asks the question he needs to know most.

"Will you take us with you?" His eyes are wide. He has an encouraging half-smile.

Dieter frowns. He hesitates, then he looks away and in a low voice says, "I travel best alone, Hauke. It is safer. You two people will be okay."

But the answer is not enough.

"How can you say that!" Adriane has urgency in her voice. It stops Dieter Falke abruptly.

"Alone," she continues, "You're a soldier trying to escape and worthy of investigation. With a wife and child, you're a family man returning home or going to stay with relatives or something."

Dieter chooses his words. He has survived until now by making his own decisions. Before him are two scared and frail people. Looking into his eyes for some hope.

"I hadn't realised you were considering this option. You've thought about it? I'm thirty one, you're twenty or near and Hauke is twelve. The figures don't add up."

Adriane does not give up.

"They could. So you have a young wife. Hauke is my cousin then, recently orphaned."

Dieter pushes the girl and boy's heads together and looks at them.

"Ah, of course, I can see the family resemblance."

"Then," says Adriane, her voice husky, "He is your son. Those figures add up. And I am your new wife. You can be rid of us if you wish. Once we're away from here. If you find us so burdensome."

The man looks afresh at the two people before him,

their eyes damp. He has walked past so many scared and shattered people over the past few years he has forgotten how to become involved. Fear, cunning and a need to survive have driven compassion to the back of his mind. For some seconds he says nothing. Looking away he puts his hand to his mouth and tries to think as a person who will inhabit the new Germany. A person who will need a life to live. He looks back.

"Well, we're not going anywhere for a while. The situation must improve quite a lot."

He notices a slight brightening in their faces. It is a hint of hope, he concludes.

Adriane grabs his arm once more. She is frowning.

"You were still living at home at the age of thirty?"

"I didn't say that. I said that I kissed my parents goodbye."

"Then you lived elsewhere?"

"Yes."

"With your wife and children?"

"At the University, studying to be an engineer. I have had relationships but never been married. I made a late decision to do something with my life."

"Oh."

"You ask very odd questions, Adriane Gerst. I arrived but yesterday." The girl looks down realising the transparency of her query.

"She's very clever," interjects Hauke, "she told me all about penises, babies and farming."

Now Adriane's eyes widen and her face reddens.

"Then she is indeed a woman of substance. I must check some of the facts in those subjects myself, to ensure I have them right."

How quickly a situation can change. Now Dieter Falke can look at the girl and once more feel like the adult in the room.

Chapter 22

'Orders'

It is in its way, a piece of very good news. Directly from Marshall Zhokov's office. The German Furher Adolf Hitler had been found. His charred body and that of his mistress Braun were at the bunker complex. Thcy had suicided.
German forces had now surrendered, though the Russian Army should remain at full alert in case there were any who might wish to fight on or perhaps end their life in some dramatic fashion.

All occupying divisions should hold their current positions and set up more permanent arrangements for the soldiers under their command. They should establish check points on their perimeters and be on the lookout for senior Nazi and SS personnel trying to evade capture. Photos of wanted war criminals would be forthcoming. In the meantime any males should be thoroughly interrogated and if any doubts as to their authenticity are encountered, they should be handed over to Russian Military Police or Army Counter-Intelligence for further investigation.

Captain Chaban leaned back in his chair. The leather of his uniform creaked. He lifted the communique and read it once more. Then he smiled. He looked up at Comrade Kozuch.

"I assume you have read this Kozuch. You know, I think, if we're sensible we may both survive this war."

Kozuch relaxed a little and stroked the side of his face.

"I suppose it was a forlorn hope that we might capture Hitler."

"And no more rape and looting."

"Yes, I saw that."

"I wasn't aware it was policy."

"Well, if it was, now it isn't."

As a man of some learning Captain Chaban was respected by his junior officers. Some of the more cynical thought he was a little naive. Although they could not be sure he was perhaps being wise and letting the men get away with small things while controlling the large.

They sat about enjoying several good sized glasses of Vodka while their commander outlined the plans for controlling and managing their sector.

He chose older, less impulsive men to take charge of the checkpoints. He chose younger, more eager men to look into what services might be repaired. Cleverly he

challenged them to show how Russian ingenuity could
be used to reinstate German made infrastructure.
Two more complete kitchens were to be set up in order
to give the troops better quality food and assist the
population of the city. Troops can be housed in empty
buildings where available. Local inhabitants should not
be evicted.
Confiscating property and looting is to cease. Troops
accused of rape or brutality will be severely dealt with.
The practice of trading cigarettes and food for 'favours'
from desperate local inhabitants is also to cease under
threat of punishment.
The Russian soldier is to prove that he is a better
human being than the armed forces of the German
Reich.
As Captain Chaban finished he noted general satisfaction from the men in the room. They looked from one to
another perhaps curious about their assigned roles or
perhaps just glad that the hostilities had ended.
One young officer spoke. "Are any SS captured to be
treated in a special way, sir? They shouldn't be hard to
find. There's the tattoo for a start. They will no doubt be
trying to leave the city. I would happily execute every
last one of them." He waved his side-arm about to emphasise his desire to murder Germans.
"Put that thing away comrade, before you execute somebody in this room."

Chaban looked into the faces of the men. For a time
he took in their various worn beaten features, then he
spoke softly.
"I lost my Mother," he said, "She starved to death. My

Father is alone and distraught. Nobody has heard from my brother in the Russian Army." He paused. "Many of you have lost much more. I believe in some cases everything you knew and held dear has gone. And the reason for the suffering we have endured is right outside these windows. The German people deserve our loathing, our hatred and our revenge. But then ...... "He paused again. "Where does it end? You shoot one, you shoot one hundred. You rape the woman and daughters, you take away their possessions. Beat them and curse them. When do you stop? Will it bring any of the past undone? Reinstate your dead families? Rebuild your homes? Revenge never ends. Only the future is a path we can

follow. The past is a path that brought us to this point. If honour is something we can cling to then let that be your objective. Give no quarter but take no more. The world has suffered enough. We are red army soldiers and we have overcome this evil. Now we must show how we are not of the same mould as the enemy we have defeated. We are greater than they can ever be."

The men before Captain Chaban sat in silence. The questioner, his head bowed, reholstered his gun. One of the more senior men at the back touched his eye with a finger as if annoyed by emotion. Then one by one, starting with the young questioner, they slowly clapped until the whole room rang with the steady beat of their hands. Just as quickly it stopped, as if the participants were embarrassed by their show of emotion.
The senior man at the back stood. He took his cap from under his arm placed it on his head. He then nodded to Captain Chaban and said simply, "Thank you, Comrade."

Others followed, nodding and vaguely saluting as they filed out.

When they had all gone Comrade Kozuch looked at the Captain, his eyebrows raised. He too said, "Thank you, Captain. That was ....." He held his arms out in a gesture of uncertainty. "Something we all needed to hear."
"How is your family Comrade? I should know but I keep having other thoughts when I think to ask."
"My wife and two daughters are all accounted for. I had the news confirmed yesterday. War seems to eliminate pleasantries. I meant to tell you. I'm sorry to hear of your mother. I thought they were well. Do you think your brother is lost?"
Chaban glanced at his companion.
"I like to think that my brother is simply lost in the army records rather than physically. Time will reveal all I hope. My mother is well. I took the liberty of embellishing the story to make my point."
Kozuch sniffed. "It's a fair tactic. I think your talk to the men should help all those 'lost'."
"Well," said Chaban, "they probably won't shoot the SS now but I doubt many will get past."

Chapter 23

'Decisions'

In the many days that followed his arrival Dieter kept a
respectful watch on the activity around their building.
"There's a lot happening down there."
Hauke looked up. "I'm not allowed near the windows or
the balcony. I'm too 'obvious.'"
Dieter half-smiled. "Well it's probably easier if there's
only one of us doing the watching. Anyway, the Russians
seem to be quite active. I don't know if there's a new
German offensive imminent or they're consolidating."
"Will you join them?" Hauke asked brightly.
Dieter looked at the boy. "Hauke, it's over. If some idealistic remnants of this ruined Reich want to die, I won't
be joining them. From here on in, survival is the key to
any future we might have. All of us could have a future,
providing we can survive the present."
The girl appeared from the kitchen with coffee and tea
and food.
"If we stay here and keep quiet, surely some order will
be restored. People will start to work on the city. It
will come back to life. There's enough food here for six

months perhaps a lot more if used sparingly. If we wait, time will save us."

Dieter Falke sat at the table, facing his two companions. He took a sip of the coffee.

"You know, you have this coffee just right. It's really excellent. I wonder how many people nearby are sitting down at the moment drinking a cup of hot freshly ground coffee? Or even tea."

He inclined his head to Hauke who had suddenly discovered the 'British' drink. "Even the Russians. We're incredibly lucky."

He paused, drinking slowly, looking about,

"It's so tempting but I fear we have too much to lose. You can stay, it's your decision. Each of us must decide what is best for them. I don't trust the situation. I will be going when the opportunity presents itself."

"There it is again," thought Adriane. "First the inclusion of us all in his plans and speech and then he talks of running off alone."

Hauke will not let the subject close.

"Why should we go? Help us, tell us the reasons."

Dieter is arranging the food on his plate with his knife. Idly moving it about.

"To stay," he said at last, "is a comfortable thought, however ...." He raised his knife to point out and emphasise his words.

"Consider this. We are in a very fortunate position. Down there, all around us, people are desperate and starving. This building is largely undamaged and full of quite nice apartments. Even the water and gas seem to work ...."

"Undamaged?" blurted out Hauke. "There is a huge hole in the side."

"Yes, and that has kept others from gaining access. The building is sound. Only an outer wall section and the stairwell have been removed. Once the streets are quiet and the population start exploring they will inevitably investigate this place and the more adventurous will realise that there could be good reasons to look further. It will happen Hauke. This building is fairly new and it is one of the highest in the area. We are noticeable. And it doesn't belong to us. Owners may wish to return. Now ....."

Dieter paused again, waving his knife about.

"People will get in here. Oh, they will say, there are already some occupants. How have you survived so well, trapped in a tall inaccessible building? You will not be able to keep this .... this giant larder we have here a secret. But the consequences of it becoming known can only be bad. Desperate people don't use reason. They will fight and kill to survive. And a food supply such as this is worth any cost. Now, accepting all those issues we then ...."

Hauke interrupted again. "There's more?"

"Yes, there's much more. Berlin is a ruin. It's also a prize. It's full of intrigue. It will be the centre of a lot of turmoil. The Russians are not going to give it up. The German population may get in the way and be expendable. It's also a large, ruined city. Hard to supply and difficult to control."

Now Adriane cut in.

"If we leave here and manage to get away, with only a vague notion of which way to go, how do we survive?"

She used the word 'we' in the hope of instilling it in the mind of the soldier.

"There will be thousands of refugees on every road. Farmers will not be friendly nor will fellow travellers. There's no law. Is it worth the risk? Are the Americans or the British going to be any better than the Russians? And why aren't they here in Berlin?"

After sitting for a while in silence staring ahead, Dieter Falke refocused and said simply, "Yes."

"Yes?" said Adriane.

"They are better."

Before any more of the pros and cons of their alternate plans could be exercised, a roar came from out side. From the windows Dieter reported large numbers of trucks and a few tanks moving past on the two main roads he could see. A lot of soldiers on trucks.

"Something new is going on," he said. "I don't think it's fighting."

This was followed by a sound that for some reason reminded the soldier of a football match. A hum and clicking noise. It was distant but distinct. As if something had come alive. At once he realised it was an amplified human voice.

Adriane and Hauke moved closer. "What is it saying? I can't hear."

"Wait, it's coming closer."

The voice floated in the wind, tantalisingly close but still hard to interpret."I think they must be stopping every few streets and repeating the message. It's in German, not Russian."

"Could we have won?" asked Hauke.

"Not from the amount of Russian armour I just saw go past, my friend."

The voice had stopped. They waited. Then it boomed out again.

"I can see it." Dieter pointed to the far street corner. "It's a van. There's Russians and a German soldier. I'll open the balcony door. Listen."

The mechanical voice floated up.

"Citizens of Berlin, please listen carefully. The war is over. The war is over. General Wilding has signed documents of surrender for the city of Berlin. Also Field Marshall Keitel has signed a surrender on behalf of the German nation. All German armed forces must immediately lay down their arms and cease conflict. Failure to do so will not be tolerated. Marshall Zhukov of the Army of the Soviet Union assures all citizens they will be treated fairly. You have nothing to fear. Checkpoints have been established in all areas to begin a transition to a peaceful existence."

"Citizens of Berlin, please listen carefully. The war is over.

....

"It's just repeating."

The three residents of the apartment stood and looked at each other. They were all smiling broadly. Dieter held out his arms and hugged Adriane. He lifted her off the ground. She tilted her head and he kissed her. A kiss that lingered a little longer than that of a congratulatory nature. They parted and dragged Hauke into their hug. Dieter tousled his hair. Adriane leaned down and kissed him on the lips.

"For my other soldier," she said, while Hauke blushed.

There they stayed. Holding each other and enjoying,
not only the news of peace but some genuine human
contact. It was quite some time before they let go. Even
then they lay together on the lounge while they talked.
The conversation took up from where it paused before
the loudspeaker announcement. But now varied by the
input of the new information.
Would it be better to go or stay? What would the next
few months be like? What would the next few years be
like? Would the Red Army be good house guests? How
much longer could they stay undiscovered? Would their
water and/or gas run out? What if it did? How could they
go? Where could they go? What direction would each of
them prefer to take? How would they know a direction?
Protection? Murdered on the road? When would be the
best time to go? What if they leave it too late and are
trapped?

Hauke said at last. "I am really scared? Would one of you
take me with you? Pleeaase?"
Dieter Falke roughly pushed the two others aside and
stood up from the lounge. He walked to the mantle and
placed his hands on the edge. He stood for a time with
his head bowed, as if considering some impossible puz-
zle. Finally, he took a deep breath and turned to face the
girl and boy sitting waiting on the lounge.
"Okay," he said, "okay." He grimaced, as if the words
were difficult. "First of all, the time to go is now. While
everything is still disorganised. Before the Russians
establish themselves and settle in. I have been thinking
of various options for a while. As you know I prefer not
to have 'passengers'." He held up two hands, each with

a raised finger, to emphasise the implied burden of having others with him on any journey.

"You may think my next idea rather callous but it seems to give me the best chance to get out of here. The thought of travelling in a group concerns me because it increases the chances of somebody in the group forgetting their story and unravelling the whole creation.

The Russians will be looking for any odd sounding information or people who can't get their facts right. One slip and we'd all be in trouble."

Hauke interrupted. "We're just ordinary people. We haven't done anything wrong."

"If life was normal, you'd have a case Hauke. You're German Army so am I. Not important I know. There's thousands of ex-soldiers. But I've murdered a lot of their men. We're trying to leave Berlin. Why? They haven't gained their prize to have everybody leave. Yes, we're of no consequence but they'll be looking for important people and if they think we could be of interest we'll just get swept up in their net. That's the bit that worries me. So I've made a decision."

"No ...." said Hauke.

However .... it's a chance I'd prefer to take."

Falke looked steadily at the two listening from the lounge. They seemed unsure of the meaning of his words.

"My son, my mistress. Why not? I was just a soldier but as a soldier who murdered Russian Troops I am no doubt on a few of their lists. As Dr Antek Beck, dressed in a suit, with an appropriate attache case containing some of the more subtle, obscure pieces of identification we might just get through. Heading for my home

in some town. I don't think this guy was of much consequence. Just a minor technician. Besides, they won't
know what sort of doctor I am. Something that is of no
use to them. Perhaps a doctor of philosophy."
"Of course you are, Father." Hauke was smiling from
the lounge, "we have often sat at night, discussing the
futility of war."
Falke gazed at the boy. He looked away and back.
"Where did that come from?"
The answer of course was the Jewish doctor and Herr
Kluge senior as they sipped brandy and the young boy
listened. But it was not the time to explain.
"The only danger will be if Dr Antek Beck is known and
wanted. Perhaps for things he has done or perhaps his
knowledge," said the girl. As she spoke Adriane regret-
ted what she said, in fear that it may discourage the
soldier from following through on his plan.
Dieter shrugged.
"German bureaucracy is or was very big. Lots of minor
players and officials. A lot with many privileges. I hope
he is one of those. Also, the Russians will take a long
time to work out who is who once they get below the
top men. It's a chance we'll have to take. Are you two
willing to take the chance with me?"

While the light of the day remained the three began
work on their plan and the instruments of it's fulfillment.
Laying out a suit, shirt, tie, socks and shoes, Dieter Falke
tried each item. Though fractionally tight they fitted
sufficiently so as not to appear out of place. "For once,
I am not the problem," he said. "You two cannot play
your parts dressed in even parts of a uniform. A woman

in a Wehrmacht troopers clothing and a Hitlerjugend boy. The only idea I have is that when we leave we go from house to house until we find some clothing. We're surrounded by deserted houses. Surely there will be something suitable for you both."

"Can we take food? Perhaps some of the meat and cheese? Biscuits?" Adriane stood with her hands out in posing the question.

"They may confiscate such things, out of spite. Or fellow travellers may trouble us. I suppose if it's not too much and not too obvious. I really don't know."

"Could my pregnancy help?"

"Pardon?"

"I could put some padding in a dress. It may gain us some sympathy."

Dieter looked at the girl. The thought of pregnancy, of a baby, briefly warmed in his mind, then he said, "If I were a Russian soldier I would be highly suspicious of any supposedly pregnant woman. It's an obvious place to hide valuable items that I might souvenir for my trip home."

Antek Beck had two small cases that would be suitable for carrying some items. One was a slightly military looking shoulder bag with a flap. The second was a leather briefcase with two front straps. It seemed quite expensive and had the initials AB gold blocked onto the centre of the flap.

The military bag was a bit larger and more practical while the briefcase looked a little too luxurious. After considering both for a while the soldier decided to use the briefcase. It was not an item that would be of great

use to anybody else and it fitted the persona of a doctor.
Next he sat at Beck's desk and sorted through the man's
papers. Most were of no use. They carried swastikas,
Nazi alliances or information that indicated the Dr was
working on some war project.
The final collection consisted of a letter from a university asking for the Dr to speak at their dinner. It gave
no hint of the dinner's purpose or the Dr's profession.
There was several pages of correspondence regarding a
proposed book that Beck wished to submit to a publish-
er. They were pre-war but harmless. Some certificates
for training in first-aid and fire-fighting. A membership
letter to a cafe's 'special guest' monthly dinners and
finally a three page piece of personal correspondence in
an envelope that after several readings seemed perfect
for the role the threesome were about to attempt.
It was from some people who could easily be friends
or relatives. It did not indicate who they were. It was a
pleasant update on the local town. Although over twelve
months old it had one great attribute. It was postmarked
from southern Germany and it contained a photo.
A picture of four people, leaning against a stone wall. An
older man and woman and another pair, perhaps in their
thirties.
The perfect parents and brother and his wife.
The trio spent a few minutes giving them names and
personalities for their upcoming act.

Adriane found a white shirt, that when bunched at the
waist with a belt looked slightly feminine.
Dieter quietly admired her from across the room. Having
white around her face suddenly gave her a level of beau-

ty he had completely missed.

"As long as you can hold their gaze and they don't notice your army trousers and boots," he said. "You have quite lovely eyes. It may work ..... if we can't find other clothes."

A small silence ensued, as all three digested what appeared to have been a compliment. Hauke, his mouth slightly ajar, glanced furtively at the other two as they went about pretending that nothing new had happened. Hauke had found two cotton flour sacks. He scoured the apartment looking for items for his journey.

"Souvenirs of your days in the Hitler Jungend are best left behind," Dieter advised. "Perhaps it's best that you put that part of your life behind you as well." He placated Hauke with a handsome penknife he'd found in the Dr's desk. "More practical than the Jugend knife and no 'Blut und Ehre' on the shaft. Look it has several blades and other fittings."

Steadily the pile of potential travel items grew on the large loungeroom table. It soon became obvious that most of it could not go.

Adriane picked at the edges. "Such a shame but yes, we have to be practical. Only useful things that stand a low chance of being stolen or confiscated."

Dieter looked at the collection. "Then your need for pipe and a tin of tobacco will have to be foregone."

"I thought they might make good items for bartering."

"Maybe just take the tobacco. That will be like gold. I notice nobody has brought out any food. That and a supply of water will be what adds to the weight. Carrying water was a burden when we were fighting."

By 4pm the table held three distinct groups of what was considered either practical or useful.

They all had an identical collection of food. Sausage, hard biscuits, dried fish, cheese, some caramel sweets and chocolate, dried apple and prunes. A diet carefully evaluated to offer the best chance of transport, longevity and nourishment.

Dieter Falke was to carry his briefcase and another small suitcase into which he placed items that might give the impression of a man carrying clothes and some momentos. In the mix he included a number of 'trinkets', that he hoped would interest any checkpoint guards and distract them from their true purpose. With some string he surreptitiously secured a knife to the underneath of the briefcase. The thought of being out in the world without a weapon, in the chaotic post war, was not something he wished to undertake.

Adriane Gerst also had a small suitcase. It was an odd and expensive looking piece made of solid leather. It's appearance concerned her, as it could give the impression of privilege to the Russian soldiers. But, no other suitable article presented itself, the pillowslips were too flimsy and Hauke guarded his flour sacks with some determination.

Hauke Kluge took some time to give up the amount of 'goods' he wished to transport. He was convinced when asked to stand in the centre of the room for ten minutes with the sacks hanging from his shoulders. This operation convinced him that walking for any extended period with such weights would render him unfit for further travel.

Counselling, strong argument and threats brought the contents down to a fair compromise, then they forcibly halved it again to arrive at two much less bloated sacks.

Now they felt ready. The choice of a date and time was the next point to reach on their acceptance that they must move on.

As they sat in the late afternoon light, Dieter watched the streets below.

"I'm going down," he suddenly announced. 'There's quite a few people in the streets now. It would be better to find some clothes for you two before we leave than chance that we might locate some when we walk out of here."

"I'll come with you," said Hauke.

"No, it will be easier by myself." Dieter hesitated.

He looked at the boy. "No, wait. A father and son would be a good combination. After some 'adjustments'."

Fifteen minutes later Hauke stood disgusted but re-signed to a new look. His trousers had been reduced to shorts. Scissors had also been applied to a grey shirt from the Dr. Beck's wardrobe. If not examined too close-ly with the cut away sides tucked in, the shirt appeared to fit.

With no alternate shoes he would go barefoot.

"You look suitably miserable," Adriane said encourag-ingly. "And you," she turned to Dieter, "look too well dressed. I suppose you have no choice. I don't think Antek Beck ever wore old clothes."

For a while at the bombed out basement the man and boy watched to make sure the area was clear. They climbed down, Hauke tentatively walking across the rubble at the bottom.

Peering out into the street Dieter looked from building to building.

"That one there. The front is burnt but the back is still in fair condition. They crossed the road and walked as casually as possible along the roadway. It took time to arrive with Hauke grimacing as he hobbled over the rubble on bare feet. At the building they found the entrance hopelessly blocked with metal and masonry.

They made their way up a small side pathway to a wooden gate. At the back of the building there was a yard with grass, a timber garden shed and steps leading up to a doorway. The windows were all greyed out from smoke but it seemed the back was not fire-damaged.

The door at the top of the stairs was very solid and jammed shut.

"Can you lift me?" asked Hauke. He pointed to a window to the right of the doorway.

At the side of the steps the boy climbed up onto Dieter's shoulders. He struggled with the window sash, pried the tiny gap with his penknife then gave a little gasp of triumph as the window slid up. One more hoist and he stepped up onto Dieter's head.

"Sorry," he said and wriggled up over the sill and dropped inside.

"Be careful, there could be glass. Don't cut your feet," Dieter called softly, up at the empty space.

He waited for the boy's head to appear. It did not.

The sky was darkening and still he waited.

Slowly as time passed he began to imagine the possible mishaps that could have befallen his small companion.

He dared not shout. Not sure of the situation or the consequences of being discovered. He stood back, hoping
to gain a clearer view of the window opening. Climbing
the steps he was able to see a little of the room. All
inside seemed soiled by smoke and some debris. It was
not very encouraging. He paced about unsure of what
to do. If the boy had injured himself it could all be very
difficult. Not a sound. He couldn't just leave him. He'd
have to get in. He went back to the door at the top of the
stairs. Then there was a sound.
It seemed to come from the inside. A scraping noise,
then a click. The door in front of him opened.
Hauke stood before him, smiling triumphantly. He wore
a black jacket and cream shirt, shorts, socks and brown
boots. Draped over his arm were several print frocks.
On his head was a woman's hat with feathers.
"The hat is not your colour," suggested Dieter, "but the
rest is okay."
"The door was just locked. I turned the key. That room,
where I climbed in, it's a boy's room. Well two boys. A
bit dirty but not burnt. Just a lot of smoke I think. The
room next door is the parent's room. Lot's of clothes
in drawers and closets. They smell of the smoke but
they're all clean and tidy. We're in luck again, Dieter ar-
en't we?" He paused then added softly. "Luck is a funny
thing."
"How did you know it was a boy's room?" asked the
soldier.
"They're all still there," replied Hauke, "I suppose they
couldn't breath and couldn't find there way out. Early in
the bombings." Hauke looked at the man, blinking.
He tried to smile then looked away.

"It's okay." The man patted the boy's shoulder then hugged him for a moment.

Back at the apartment Adriane eyed the ladies selection spread on the lounge. They had searched the rooms for more items and chosen the clothes on practical terms and for a purpose.

Their return was decidedly faster with Hauke now wearing socks and boots.

As they crossed the road, Dieter looked at the boy beside him. He had an odd gait. It made him look as if he secretly wanted to break into a run.

"So this is what it's like to have a son," he thought.

Adriane raised her eyebrows. "I may have chosen differently but thcy'll do I supposc."

Dieter looked at the girl.

"We were dealing with the clothes of a middle-aged housewife with children. They, the adults and the children had all suffocated. Besides the clothes are part of our charade. We're all playing parts."

Adriane paused, then put her hand on the man's arm.

"I'm sorry. Of course. I feel ashamed. Those poor people, so many ways to die."

Then Hauke said something of note.

"I think we should wash them all. To remove the smoke smell." Then he paused and looked at the two adults adding, "Or should the people of Berlin smell of smoke?"

Chapter 24

'Checkpoints'

The soldiers snap to attention and await the next move by their commanding officer. His sudden appearance at their checkpoint is unnerving.
"At ease Comrades, I'm merely calling in to see that you are okay. If you have any problems I would naturally like to hear them and possibly help."
Chaban touches the shoulder of the nearest man.
"Have you slept, are you being fed, have you caught any Germans who require further scrutiny?"
The soldier answers guardedly. "No sir, it has been quiet. Perhaps the people in this area are all Berliners. I mean they may not wish to leave."
Chaban looks at the man and nods respectfully.
"You could be right comrade. The locals may wish to stay with their city no matter how bad the outlook seems but a quiet checkpoint could also be the place where a war criminal might choose to exit Russian territory. I simply ask that you remain alert and don't assume anybody is above suspicion."

Back at the staff car Chaban turns to Comrade Kozuch.

"That's odd. I would have assumed this last checkpoint to be the busiest. It is in a direct line to the American Forces. There is no secret that many are trying to reach the Americans. They are considered more reasonable in their dealings with German prisoners and their commanders."

"If I was a German trying to get out of Berlin I would think carefully about my options," said Kozuch. The most direct route, the shortest route, the least suspicious, the quietest area to traverse, the busiest, even the most obvious because it would be an insane option. Which they choose will vary from one individual to another. I think all exits have potential for different reasons."

Chaban looked at Kozuch.

"Of course you are right again. None of our checkpoints can become complacent. It would not be favourable for any of us if some important catch was able to pass through our sector."

On the drive back through the streets of the destroyed city, Captain Chaban noted that the citizens were beginning to trust their surroundings enough to venture out. Light was fading, a woman wheeled a cart along with a small mattress attached. No doubt for a child. A man carried a loaf of bread. A sign that some life was emerging. At one corner four children were chasing each other about. Six or seven years old. Too young to take note of their surroundings.

Up one side street in the distance a man and boy were carrying armsful of clothing across the road.

Overall, Chaban was pleased. He wanted this whole terrible war to slip away and be replaced by some energetic rebirth of the population so that he and his troops could go home and let the human race get on with existence once more.

He wanted so much to hate the Germans for their aggression, their vile invasions, their destruction, their evil and the suffering and death, yet in the end all he saw were other humans. He wondered why and how people could become so devoid of their basic humanity, yet he could not hate the ones that remained. It left him feeling as though he was at fault and that he should feel more rage in his gut than he could muster.

"I am not a very good soldier," he thought.

Back at the odd little building they called their base, he slumped into his chair and looked at the ever present, ever wise Comrade Kozuch. The man was smiling oddly.

"What of our situation brings forth amusement, Comrade?"

"I have discovered something." Kozuch walked to the corner of the room and with some aplomb, pulled back a blanket covering a small table.

"Good God," said Chaban, "Does it work?"

Kozuch wound the handle and lowered the needle onto the disk. Music, scratched and vaguely tortured issued from the horn of the old gramophone.

"It was in the basement. I'm afraid there's only a choice of Brahms or Beethoven," Kozuch commented. "I chose Brahms. I always thought he should have been a Russian anyway."

"How much we are alike, Comrade. I must admit a fondness for Brahms."

They settled in two comfortable chairs and talked. The music bringing a faint degree of civility to the situation, interrupted by the frequent need to turn or change the record.

"Our checkpoints are not going to catch the masterminds you know. If we're lucky we might be able to obtain the services of a number of their scientists or inventors before the damned Americans or British mop them all up, but as for the Nazi operatives .... only the lower level swill who carried out their orders will be caught. The smart ones have either suicided or have arranged well in advance their exit from this whole sorry mess. We'll finish up with a compound full of fanatical, dangerous minions who worc the death's head insignia and carried out atrocities like blind automatons. What is the point I ask you? Is it better they don't reach our compounds? Of course such action could kill an innocent."

Kozuch watched his Captain's musings then took a bottle and presented the man with a glass of some confiscated German wine.
"It's all we can do. Life is grossly unfair. More evil lives than ever dies by the sword of righteousness"
"Are you quoting something there, Comrade?"
"No Captain, it just came to mind."
"Then," said Chaban, "Well done. Summed up most eloquently. Perhaps after this war you could make a fair living as a writer for the theatre."
Chaban raised his glass. "Come on, you must obviously

drink with me. By the way you know you are a cliche."
Kozuch looked up at this new description.
"I mean the standard fictional assistant who can acquire
the unobtainable, as if by magic. And, provide wise
counsel. And, yet still appear unrushed, untroubled and
the model of a fine soldier. They do not really exist. It is
just a trick by authors and playrights for the amusement
of their audience. Yet here you are. All of those things
and more."
Chaban gestured, "Here, please sit back down. That
was my attempt at a compliment. Perhaps lacking your
eloquence."
"Well it was a pleasure to receive such praise sir. I assure it is appreciated. You have previously mentioned
my ability to acquire items."
"I probably have," said Chaban. "But it can stand repeating."
Kozuch shrugged. "The magic I wield could probably be
called implied danger. The men all know I work for you.
If I ask for something. More often than not it appears.
Simple really."

The two men sat and conversed quietly through the
whole bottle of their drink.
They talked of home and the Russia they hoped to return to once their duty was done. They cautiously spoke
of Joseph Stalin once more until it was clear that neither
man trusted or particularly respected their leader. This
discovery made them jointly caution each other about
voicing such feelings elsewhere.
Finally Chaban said, "I'm tired. I think I might sleep well
tonight. Help me Comrade, have I overlooked anything?

Is our sector, secure and at peace?"
Kozuch considered the question.
"I think it is. Which makes me consider bad luck and the unexpected."
"How so, Comrade."
"A mine, a bomb we missed, a fanatical German who wishes to end his life with some grand gesture, desperate locals, poison, a building falling unexpectedly, trouble with our own men ...."
Chaban held up his hand. Both men grinned.
"Damn you Comrade, I'm still going to sleep well."
But he did not.

Chapter 25

'The Move'

The night had a hint of genuine warmth. An early sample
of the Spring to come.
It was Adriane who heard them first. Muffled, far off,
breaking into her sleep. Woken she sat up, turning her
head and straining. Voices, floating about. A bump, then
another. A door?
She moved to swing her legs from under the covers.
Hauke lay sleeping beside her. She felt his face and
body to be sure. Despite moves to have him sleep in the
other bedroom, it was his habit if he woke scared or had
dreamed, to creep into her bed so that he could sleep
again.
Even after Dieter's arrival and his careful manipulation
of the arrangements, Hauke was almost a permanent fix-
ture in her bed. It was something she found quaint and
sweet. It seemed he was quite happy with permanency
as well.
Adriane's stirring did not wake him.
Standing in the hallway the sounds were more obvious.
They were coming from below. She listened again, comfortable in the darkness. Another quite distinct bump.

Her hand went to her mouth, more in puzzlement than fear.

She turned to go to Dieter's room. He stood behind her. "I heard them too," he whispered.

"If it were Russians they'd be going from room to room or some similar manoeuvre wouldn't they?"

"Yes."

"Maybe, it's just some people wanting a place to stay."

"At 2am. I doubt it's that simple."

Dieter slid past Adriane out into the main room. She could see his shape outlined by the meagre light that entered the windows. He moved to the front door of the apartment. She heard him open the door. He did not go any further.

She waited, not sure whether to join him at the door or stay waiting. Eventually he closed the door and beckoned her over to the lounge.

"They're German. I couldn't make out what they were saying but it was definitely German. Perhaps they are just scared people looking for a place to stay. Though why they would choose this building I'm not sure?"

"We chose this building." Adriane countered, "All three of us."

"We were escaping. Looking for a hiding place. We all chose this building because it was the least likely in the area, to house anybody. The war is over. Unless you're somebody of note the Russians are not all that interested in the population."

"Then perhaps they are somebody 'of note."

"Which is not what we want. I've locked our door. Hopefully they will stay quiet and not disturb us. Sometimes decisions are made for you. I think this might be a sign."

"A sign of what?" asked Adriane.

"That it's time for us to go."

The two figures crept back to their respective beds agreeing there was little they could do in the night. Tomorrow they would plan their departure. In the meantime they would keep very quiet.

Back in her bed Adriane put her arms round the sleeping boy. He half-stirred and twitched in his slumber. She held him close, feeling a genuine warmth and love for the lost soul that was Hauke Kluge. He responded with a sigh.

As she drifted into sleep once more she smiled at the tentative embrace she had received from Dieter in the hallway. Surprisingly he had also kissed her forehead.

"Stay safe," he had said.

When Adriane woke again the room was light. Hauke sat on the side of the bed. He looked more like a boy in an undershirt and shorts that actually fitted him. He was staring at her.

"What happened?" he said.

"Happened?"

"You were frowning in your sleep. You never frown. Has something happened?"

Uncanny, thought Adriane. She took Hauke's hand and sat beside him.

"Yes, something happened last night."

"I knew it," confirmed Hauke.

She told him of the noises and the possibility that the presence of others could be detrimental to their own plans.

"Dieter thinks we should leave soon."
Sitting at the table eating quietly, all three listened for
any more sounds. Finally Hauke spoke.
"They're going to hear us. You know that. What happens
when we flush the toilet or bathe? Or drop something.
They may be friendly." He looked at Dieter. "We may
worry for nothing."
Dieter spread his hands.
"I know Hauke but my instincts tell me to think otherwise. There's something odd about crawling up into a
building like this when there are no more hostilities and
other much more accessible choices in the streets.
I'd prefer to take no chances. We must leave today.
This afternoon, I would say. The soldiers at the checkpoints will be tired and we will have enough light to get
along our way before night."
Hauke wanted to talk.
"Tell me again why we are better going to the Americans?"
"Because we invaded Russia, betrayed them, murdered
their people and laid waste to a large part of their
country. Russians are much like us. They are a war-like
nation. They will not treat us kindly after what we did.
Now or in the future. I would rather face the Americans.
I fought them all the way back to Berlin.
Perhaps I should have surrendered. The Americans will
move on, go home. The Russians will not. Here, we are
likely to trapped. If we leave we may find sanctuary and
a life somewhere else."
"Alright," said Hauke emphatically. "Why have you
grown a moustache?"
"Because I want to look less like Dieter Falke, Wermacht

soldier and I suspect, wanted man, and more like a man called Dr Antek Beck. An academic type."

Through the day Adriane, Dieter and Hauke checked their luggage then pulled all of it apart and checked it again. Dieter sat and read through the doctor's papers, trying to create the character in his mind. All three went over their story of Dieter and his son Hauke, together with his second wife Adriane. The girl and boy practiced the idea of their new surname. Saying over and over to themselves. "Adriane Beck, Adriane Beck." "Hauke Beck, Hauke Beck."

They ate lunch. They moved about quietly. Dieter talked them into the idea of not clearing the toilet. It would not matter once they were gone, he argued.

Adriane slipped her arm through Dieter's arm. "I'm practicing being a wife," she said, with a weak smile. "Do you have an idea where the checkpoints might be?"

"Not really. But thinking of the area I'd say there will be one somewhere along the main road to the south-west. It's the shortest and most direct line to the American or British Armies. I think we should go that way. I am chancing that nobody who is on the Russian lists would be so obvious. Just a lot of genuine refugees. Hopefully we can mingle."

"How far away are these Americans?" Hauke asked.

"I'd say they've halted just outside the city. To allow Russia to take the city. Some sort of prize."

"Then once we're through we won't have far to go?"

"I hope not."

In the early afternoon the three potential refugees were

all dressed in the clothes they had chosen.

Dieter put on a suit and tie with a clean white shirt and shiny shoes. After inspecting the result in a mirror, he removed them and found a much older worn suit.

He crushed and dirtied a shirt. Spilt some food on a tie and scuffed up some worn down shoes until he was suitably shabby.

Adriane dressed in a long, unflattering grey frock and flat black shoes. She looked in the mirror and was happy with the tired, older woman that she perceived.

Hauke dressed in thick cream woollen socks and boots, old dark brown shorts and a cream cotton shirt. He rolled the sleeves up past his elbows. Finally he put on a black cloth cap that was oversize but fitted well enough.

Each participant packed a jacket or coat to stay warm at night.

It was still only 1.30pm. Now they waited. The decision was that they would leave at 4pm.

They had heard no sound from the new occupants downstairs and had managed to carry out their preparations with none of the three inadvertently making a noise.

Nervous and apprehensive, they sat about and counted off the minutes, not knowing what else to do.

Dieter stood by the window watching the streets below and winding his wristwatch. People where in the streets. They moved cautiously, still unsure of their safety.

Russian soldiers could be seen patrolling the streets but they appeared generally at ease.

From the window it was possible to just glimpse a lot of activity at the end of the street.

The window was too high to obtain a clear view. It appeared to be a Russian canteen. Soldiers milled about but Dieter could not clearly see what they were doing. He watched for while. He looked at the building next door blocking his view. Then he turned and looked at the two people sitting on the lounge. He walked over to them and leaned forward.

"Tell me again. Tell me the story of how you rescued Hauke. What floor was it?"

As the two related the story Dieter felt a shiver run up his back. They noticed the look on his face. "What is it?" asked Adriane.

"I think our guests might be on a suicide mission. That floor has a clear view of the Russian canteen. I'd say they're waiting for some officers. I think we should leave now. We have to get out of this building and away from here." He noted the fear on the faces of his companions. "I'll take the doctor's pistol. Hopefully we can get past on the stairs without them hearing us. We have to go. This is all going to be very bad."

They gathered up their bags. Hauke slung his sacks across his shoulders. Dieter retrieved the pistol and checked that it was fully loaded.

"Okay, my family," he said, "let's be on our way. Say good bye to our Magisch Raum."

He opened the door and looked out into the corridor then motioned them forward. After Hauke and then Adriane had requested one last look, they closed the door gently behind them. They carefully made their way to the first flight of stairs. Adriane and Hauke both looked back again at the door to their sanctuary. They smiled briefly at each other.

On the stairs they prayed that there would be no creak in the woodwork that would give them away. There was no noise. Each step remained firm.

On the next landing they waited and listened. At one stage a few short words were spoken from below.

"What did they say?"

"I don't know. Come on, keep moving," whispered Dieter. The second step of the next stairs gave a loud creak.

They froze, waiting for a query from below.

Somebody did speak. It was louder than the faint voices they had been hearing. The phrase was repeated.

"Dort sind sie."

"There who are?" asked Hauke, next to Dieter's sleeve.

"Damn, not now. Just another few minutes," Dieter muttered.

Then the screams rang out.

"Ruhm zum Vaterland! Ruhm zum Vaterland!"

A roar of rifles shattered the silence.

They were screaming out their cry as they fired round after round.

The three on the stairs stumbled back. They forgot being silent, there was little point. Running up all the way to their room they fell inside as the firing continued.

"Should we have run past?" asked Adriane.

Dieter shook his head. "The noise was too loud. Their door must have been open. They want to die and they'd have killed us the moment they saw us."

He went to the window. The firing continued making no attempt to conceal the source of the onslaught. Almost out of sight, Dieter made out the nose of a Russian Army truck stop at the corner of the building. He glimpsed a few of the soldiers alighting.

Still the firing went on.

"There are Russians here already. Help me," he said. They locked the door and dragged the table across to create some sort of barrier.

"If they die quickly," said Dieter, "maybe the Russians won't investigate any further."

They waited. The rifle fire continued for minutes, though not as intensely. Suddenly there was another crescendo of screaming and firing. This time automatic weapons and perhaps a pistol.

Now they were behind the lounge, crouching, holding each other. Adriane and Hauke were crying, as much in despair as fear.

A lot of shouting followed. The crashing noises moved closer. More firing. It was obvious without any exchange of words that the Germans were retreating up the stairs. A loud explosion shook the building.

"That was a grenade," said Dieter. "Whose, I don't know." Now the yelling reached their level. German voices.

"Hold your ground. Take as many as you can. We can ambush them. They are at the disadvantage here. Stay back ....."

The sound of boots along the corridor. The crash of timber being splintered. Then the smash as somebody tried to break open their door. The sound kept up. Another joined in. The door finally shattered. The table was quickly pushed aside. Two SS soldiers stood peering about.

"Somebody lives here?"

Dieter shot the nearest through his forehead. The other man spun about, his gun blasted into the ceiling as he fell with a bullet in the chest and another in his neck. Adriane held Hauke behind the lounge. They whimpered together.

"Damned insane SS brigade," muttered Dieter. "I'm killing fellow Germans. Our very own madmen."

Now Russian voices and German.

A cacophony of gunfire followed. The smell of the gunpowder wafted in through the open door. Screams followed. Single shots. Finishing off shots.

Only Russian voices now. Two or three. Footsteps along the corridor. Dieter slipped out from the lounge and retrieved the nearest soldier's automatic rifle.

They entered the room.

The voices sounded confused. Looking at the bodies on the floor. Germans they had not killed.

Dieter fired. He brought down the first two, then the gun stopped firing. One of the Russians seemed dead or unconscious. The other groaned and rolled about on the floor. The third, untouched advanced on Dieter, his rifle and bayonet glinting. As he lifted the gun to shoot, Hauke Kluge, soldier of the Reich, flew at the man from the other end of the lounge, his penknife raised, the blade open.

The soldier turned and caught the boy in mid-flight, folding him up on the end of his bayonet like a soft rag toy.

Hauke let out a horrible gasp as his eyes widened.

The distraction gave Dieter the moment he needed.

He swung his empty gun at the man's leg, crumpling it and bringing him down. He beat the man with the handle of his knife. The knife from the bottom of his briefcase. He beat the man until exhausted. Then there was silence. He looked for some seconds at the knife blade, then put it down breathing heavily, his eyes still crazed.

They lifted Hauke and placed him on the lounge.
His lovely new boy's shorts and shirt were covered in his blood. Adriane lifted the shirt. The horrible slit in his stomach was just below his ribs. Blood oozed out.
"Oh hell, boy," said Dieter, "what have you done?"
Hauke looked with eyes that did not entirely focus.
"Don't leave me. Please don't leave me," he implored.
"Wait for me." Adriane held his hand tightly. It was all she could do.
They sat beside their little hero. Dieter Falke who had stoically battled across Europe to this day and seen untold horrors, found that his eyes watered and could not speak.
Hauke gave a slight shudder. His eyes opened wide again. "I don't want to go there alone."
Then he closed his eyes again.
After a moment Dieter placed his fingers on the boy's throat. His voice was husky. "Oh God. There's no pulse, Adriane. We only have one chance. We must go now."
Adriane looked down again at this little boy.
"I can't leave him. I can't."
Dieter grabbed her shoulder.
"Please Adriane. It's our only chance. He'd understand."
He choked and lowered his head. "He's my boy too. He'd understand," he repeated slowly.

They stood, reluctant and guilty. About to desert this idealistic child.

Dieter spoke again. "He gave me hope you know. I thought if we could get him away and give him a chance .... perhaps Germany might overcome these times and they could grow again together. Silly idea."
In turn they bent down and kissed their small friend. They tucked him in with a blanket as if asleep, unable to cover the pale face.
As they turned to leave they realised that the wounded Russian soldier was watching them.
Dieter bent down and patted the man's hand. He had been hit in the groin and shoulder. He was obviously in pain. They quickly wrapped some cloth around his wounds to apply pressure. In the end he was just a fellow soldier. They placed cushions under the man's head, quickly checked the others and then they fled.

Chapter 26

'To Pass'

There were rumours of a disturbance near the canteen.
It made the men edgy. By late afternoon they were all
tired. Virtually nobody wanted to enter their sector but
a great number of people wanted to leave. The red flag
of Russia hung limply on a makeshift pole. The soldiers
had used the gutted shell of one of their T70 tanks, it's
walls had been pierced by two German Jagdpanther
shells. It formed a solid barrier in the narrow street.
By funneling the line of people into this area, they were
much easier to watch and control. Behind the crossed
wooden poles and barbed wire stood another of their
tanks intact, along with a scout car. A machine gun was
mounted on the back of the scout car.
The sun had been quite warm today and the crossing
had little shelter. Another two hours before a change of
personnel for the night. Very few crossed at night.
Their officer was dealing with a man and woman he had
pulled out of a few coming in. He thought he recognised
the pair. After some discussion and some stern words
they agreed to their bags being searched. The man angrily threw his bag down. Now their officer drew his side

arm. The woman calmed the man down.

The bag was full of American cigarettes. Also false papers. Lots of false papers for crossing and recrossing and profiteering.

Now the pleading began. Communication was imperfect. The Germans spoke no Russian but the officer seemed to have a fair knowledge of the German language.

The soldier waved through a family heading out. They had a great deal of proof that they were headed to their parents home in Leipzig. The man had an eyesight issue. He could not have been any useful part of the Nazi effort.

Now an old man stood before him. The soldier's partner said, "Yes, Grandpa. What do you want?"

The man trembled. With the use of a few Russian words he tried to explain that he wished to go to his house. He pointed ahead and indicated with fingers that the place he sought was three kilometres past the checkpoint.

His jaw stuck out in a display of independence and resolution.

The soldier looked at the man with doubt. He didn't like his attitude.

A request for papers brought a dumb look. The soldier in exasperation did a pantomime of getting out some identification.

In the background the confrontation with the officer was becoming quite heated. Raised voices rang out. One of the spare soldiers unshouldered his rifle.

The old man now stood with his arms folded. The soldier considered how tired he felt and how he didn't want to deal with this man. A rifle butt to his head would quickly resolve the issue.

"How would you like to go to hell, Grandpa?" said the soldier's partner.

"Vas ist?" yelled the old man. His face was in the soldier's face.

From behind the old man a young woman stepped up. She took the old man's arm and in bits and pieces of Russian explained that he was known to her. He was a little mentally unwell. She would take the man as she went on her way and drop him off as they passed his house. It was five hundred metres not three kilometres

"Who are 'they'?" said the second Russian.

"I am Dr Beck," said a man stepping up next to the woman. "This is my wife."

The soldier looked from the man to the woman and back again. He smirked. This tired man in a suit and a young woman or 'wife'.

"I am not mad," said the old man. His eyes were wide. His face a snarl of indignity.

Adriane tried to signal the man to be silent but he continued to demand that the soldiers get out of his way. Dieter tried to explain in a mix of languages and gestures.

"Naturally the mental condition of a patient does not allow them to recognise their own disorientated state. Mental illness must be recognised by others rather than the patient."

He had no idea how much of this information was being understood by Russians.

Another voice joined in.

"This man is your patient then." The officer had finished with the racketeers who were being led away. "Who are you?"

Dieter Falke knew that they had reached that critical point where they would have their day or lose it all. "I am Dr Antek Beck. We, my wife and I, wish to travel to Halle. My elderly parents will accommodate us at their house."

"I see," said the officer. "Beck, Dr Beck? Wait here."

The officer stepped back and retrieved a collection of sheets of paper from his bag. He began leafing through them, running his finger down lists on each page. He glanced up at one stage then continued.

Dieter noticed that the rifles of the two soldiers in front of him were slowly being raised and pointed at his stomach.

At this point the old man exploded in a fit of abuse. He dispensed with any Russian and swore solely in German. He would not stand to be ordered about in his own country by barbarians from the land of Russia. They would stand aside and let him pass. He had his face very close to one of the soldiers when the officer nodded to the other soldier, who brought his rifle up and battered the old man in the head with the butt. The man fell sideways, groaning and crying out.

Behind in the line of people in the queue there were mutterings and discussion though nobody would step forward or offer any condemnation.

Dieter Falke and his new wife Adriane Gerst stood as humbly as possible, their heads bowed.

Finally the officer put down his papers and said to them, "Come with me."

He took the two aside and grabbed the briefcase from Dieter's hand. It clunked as he placed it on his table. He undid the straps and pulled out the contents. Dieter's

knife had begun to drop away from were he had fixed it
under the case.

The officer had the papers Dieter had selected. With one
finger to his mouth he read them one at a time. It was
unsure how much he understood. He held up the letter
and photo. The one from some friends.

"This is from Halle?" he queried.

Dieter nodded.

"And you're a doctor? Of philosophy. One who may
someday publish a book it would appear?"

Dieter nodded again.

"No doubt the war has been a great inconvenience for
you."

Dieter shrugged his shoulders and smiled weakly.

"I don't like you," said the officer. "This is too neat. You
can't have spent the war, quietly going about your business while all of this country was destroying Europe and
my homeland. I think we might have to have some longer talks with you Dr Beck. Perhaps you and your wife
have a lot more to tell me. I think we will take you to one
of our special facilities for further investigation."

There are times in the life of every human when events
take a turn that reinvents the moment.

The Russian officer stood back and drew his side arm.
He motioned to Dieter to pick up his papers and his
briefcase. All their plans, all their hopes and subterfuge were about to end in a Russian interrogation unit.
He would be found out and shot. And Adriane. Would
they believe she was just an innocent? A great burden
of sorrow and desperation swept over him. He began
collecting up his papers, thinking as rapidly as he could

if there might yet be some way to get out of their situation. He may as well die fighting rather than submitting to the methods of the conquerers.
Behind, still lying whimpering on the ground, the old man suddenly regained his faculties and his anger all at the same time. He rose to his feet, staggered and roared once more. This time he tore at his shirt, stumbling into the people now talking to the Russian soldiers. He implored them to shoot him. His wrath knew no bounds. At the back of the crowd there was a slight disturbance. The line parted as a Russian staff car nosed through the people toward the checkpoint.

Staring at the approaching car, then to the ranting old man, then to his two captives, the officer seemed to dance on the spot. He looked at his watch. He glanced about at other members of the checkpoint guard, all the time rubbing his hands together. This he continued for some seconds. Then his agitation ebbed away. He put his hand to his mouth rubbing his lips. It was at this point that he came to a decision. Still staring out at the car he said, "Okay, okay, you are an unnecessary distraction. You can you take your 'patient' Dr Beck. Silence him and leave now! If you can't I will shoot all three of you." He glared at them. "Well? Yes?"
Dieter Falke and Adriane Gerst strode forward and grabbed the old man. One on each arm.
Through gritted teeth as he gripped and frog-marched the man, Dieter said, "Shut Up. Don't stop, don't argue. None of us want to die today. You have been freed to go. Walk with us and don't look back. For all our sakes you can't make a sound. Just keep walking."

The old man looked sideways at the people who held his arms and propelled him along, away from the checkpoint.

"Ja sir," he snapped. Then in a quieter, apologetic voice. "This is all I wanted to do anyway."

At the checkpoint, the officer and his men saluted as Captain Chaban emerged from the staff car and walked up to them. They all liked their commander for his fairness and frankness. All the same, he was a man who did not enjoy incompetence and they were keen to ensure he would leave with a good opinion of their post. Standing with his officer, Chaban explained that there had been a shooting and sadly a number of Russian soldiers had lost their lives at the canteen and others in a skirmish. It seemed the incident was caused by some fanatical remnants of an SS unit. Apart from the SS soldiers there could have been others involved. Civilians or others. The situation had the same oddity to it as the killing of the men from that truck a week or so back, though there seemed no connection.

Chaban stood looking over his officer's shoulder. In the distance a man and woman were walking, almost escorting another man down the road.

"What is this?" asked Chaban, indicating to the threesome.

The officer appeared unconcerned.

"Oh just a senile old man," said the officer. His son and daughter came to collect him, after we found him wandering. He was quite a handful. His home is just down the road."

Chaban looked from the figures walking away, to the

officer. He paused for a moment tapping his finger on his belt. He looked once more at the people off down the road.

"You seemed quite anxious to have them on their way when I arrived."

"I'm sorry if it appeared that way sir. I had checked their bona-fides and I thought we would not be able to converse with the old man causing a disturbance. Also it may have continued to distract the men from checking other people."

Chaban nodded. "That's logical. Good, fine. Keep the peace, eh. So, no other incidents or disturbances?"

"No sir, completely quiet here."

"Well please remember. This city is still not safe. Be vigilant."

Back in his vehicle Chaban said to Kozuch, "Last check. Let's head back. Our man here is lying I think. He's not very astute. Just trying to keep his nose clean until he can go home. I don't blame him."

As their car proceeds slowly back along the streets, winding round rubble and the shattered remnants of the war, Chaban taps Kozuch on the shoulder and says, "Stop here, Comrade. I won't be a minute."

Walking across the road Chaban heads for three soldiers sitting on the bonnet of a burnt out car. They spring to attention when they realise it is their Captain approaching. In his usual way Kozuch notices the men relax as the Captain puts them at ease. He talks then listens, then seems to ask more questions. Finally they all salute and the Captain walks back.

"What was that all about, Comrade? I know you want to ask," says Chaban, climbing back into the car. "Turn right up here. We'll exit through a different checkpoint. One of those men was the driver of that truck that crashed with our renegade soldier. He's tough if nothing else. Last time I saw him I suspected he was about to die. I asked him to describe the man. Their prisoner. I have a hunch. Probably wildly inaccurate but indulge me. We need to find a refugee.

Communication received by all Berlin checkpoints three days after these events -
Russian Army Headquarters - Berlin
Persons of Interest - Amendment 14D
The following German nationals should be arrested on sight and brought under guard to our interrogation unit, as per previous orders.
August Feuling
Albert Staack
Elena Gaiser
Dr Antek Beck
Jorg Wertman

Chapter 27

'The Road'

They dropped the old man at a house near the railway line. They watched him go to the door, produce a key and enter. He gave them a brief backward glance and nodded, as if dismissing them from any further obligation.
"He has a green door," noted Adriane. "All the others are brown."
Dieter looked again at the now closed door. "A non-conformist and slightly mad. Perhaps too much war. He got us through the checkpoint when that staff car arrived. We have that to thank him for but I'd rather be well rid of him now."

For the first time since their hurried walk from the checkpoint, the pair could take stock of their situation and surroundings.
They were at the top of a hill. The railway line was in front of them. Russian armoured units were spread along the road. A great number of Russian troops moved about. The area showed all the signs of concentrated shelling but the line now appeared to be operational.

A trickle of civilians were heading along the road, mostly in bunches. No doubt displaying some thought to there being a little safety in numbers. None of the Russian troops seemed interested.

Dieter took Adriane's hand. "Let's sit for a moment." He led her across an open area to a stone wall with a stone seat both of which had remained intact despite all the war's best efforts.

"Well, here we are. There's no convenient street signs. I can't read the Russian army signs but they probably just say, 'This way to the fuel depot' etc. We'll have to use our instincts and wits and stay out of trouble. For instance we shouldn't sit here too long. I retreated in front of the Americans from this direction. Now I have to find my way back."

Adriane asked, "Why did you say we were going to Halle?"

Dieter sniffed. "I don't know. It's near Leipzig so it's in the right direction. It seemed less obvious if we were going to a smaller place."

"Have you ever been there?"

"No. I've only heard of the place in odd references."

For a minute they sat silently watching the activity around them. The degrees of purpose from the various people. At one stage a truck rumbled past with a load of German soldiers on board. To a man they looked grey and crushed with nothing left but the need to breathe. They watched it move away and turn a corner.

Suddenly Adriane bowed her head and began to cry. She shook and sobbed. Dieter looked at her slightly surprised then a flood the emotions took hold of him also

and he put his arms around the girl and pulled her close
to him. She lifted her head and placed it on his shoulder.
"Hauke," she said. "We should have your son with us.
Our boy. We left him. We ran away from him. Left his
little body, just lying there. He wanted comfort. He
wanted us to be with him and we left him. He was afraid
and alone." Adriane cried again. Tears slid down the
soldier's face. He bit his lip and they held each other
tightly.

When he was able to speak Dieter said, "I'm so sorry.
I'm a soldier. When your best friend dies next to you and
the enemy is about to overrun your position there is
no time to say goodbye. Hauke was a soldier after all. I
think he would understand."

"He was a little boy." Adriane lifted her head to look at
Dieter. "He was a scared little boy."

He stared back at her, blinking away his tears. "You're
right. He was. That is what we were reduced to. He was
a boy. And should have been allowed remain so."

Dieter used his thumb to wipe away some of Adriane's
tears. He took a deep breath.

"Whatever happens to us, we are together. If you want
me I am yours. I promise I will not leave you. There is no
more war. We are all we have, you and me."

Adriane looked at the man in the suit. The soldier pretending to be a doctor of letters. She could not smile but
her face had some light in it for the first time in a year.

"Thank you," she whispered. They both closed their
eyes and hugged, enjoying their pact and the genuine
touch of another human.

Neither heard the Russian staff car slide to a halt next to

them.

When they looked up, a Russian officer and another soldier were emerging from the car, looking straight at them.

"Hullo, I'm sorry to interrupt your moment here. I am hoping you can help me."

The Russian officer spoke excellent German.

"My name is Captain Chaban. This is Comrade Kozuch."

Dieter Falke felt the blood draining from his face.

"Can I ask who I am addressing?"

"I am Dr Beck. This is my wife, Adriane."

Chaban held out his hand. "Good to meet an academic."

They shook hands. The Captain wore leather gloves.

"Are you a medical doctor?"

"No, I'm a doctor of philosophy."

"Really," said Chaban. "I thought the Jewish people had that area sewn up. Though come to think of it, Germany does have a rich heritage. Perhaps the stories I have been hearing about your actions against the Jews are some plan to win back control of philosophy."

Dieter stared back dumbly. His knowledge of German or any philosophy was limited to his school days. Was this man being witty or darkly serious?

The Captain gestured. "Still, a street corner in a bombed out city is not really the place to strike up a conversation about philosophy. More of a late night brandy and cigars line of work I think."

He turned to his adjutant. "I wonder if some day I will see irony in what I just said." They both smiled.

Turning back to the bench, he continued, "No, I'm seeking information about some events in my sector whereby a number of my soldiers have died in quite odd circumstances. I know you have recently passed through a checkpoint. Can you tell me where you have been in the last few weeks? Your information may assist my enquiries."

Dieter Falke was relieved and very nervous at once. The Captain had not picked them at random. How much did he know? He was not asking about Dr Beck. Was it because he already knew that he was dealing with an impostor? In the end he would have to tell a story and hope that it worked.

He told the Russian that he and his wife had sheltered in a partly burnt house for some weeks because their apartment was in a partially destroyed building. When lying it is best to have a basis of truth so he placed himself in the building where he and Hauke had found the clothes. They had some food and water but eventually it was time to move on. They are heading to his parent's home in Halle.

The Captain was intrigued. Surely they would have heard all the shooting and fighting quite nearby and only the other night. Could it be that these actions took place in the very apartment the good doctor had vacated?

It is possible Dieter countered. When there is shooting he and his wife always hid under their bed. It is not safe to go outside to investigate the source.

The Captain revealed more. He told them that the shootings and battle had taken place in the building and partly in the rooms of Dr Beck. He told them that he found the whole situation very odd.

Dieter could only feign surprise. No amazement at the

series of events. Adriane sat dumbly, too terrified to speak.

Now the Captain added fuel to his line of questioning. He told of an incident previously in which a Russian soldier had attacked his own men on patrol and had killed a number of them before escaping. This too was in the area of Dr Beck's apartment.

Dieter Falke could feel the web of probes and deceit tightening. It was now just a matter of time before it brought him down. He decided to continue the bluff with a little truth. What after all was left?

"Captain," he said, "I am reluctant to speak of this because I fear it may offend you but I do know a little of those events."

"Really. Please go on."

"A neighbour of mine, August Haas. He was out looking for food. He witnessed an incident. I think it is the one to which you refer. He saw a group of Russian soldiers drag two German families from their homes. Men, women and a number of children. They executed the men and then proceeded to rape and kill the women and children. My neighbour saw a Russian soldier in the street take aim and begin shooting the men carrying out these deeds. At this point my neighbour ran from the scene."

Dieter stopped. He had fired his last shot in this subterfuge. The whole fabric of lies they had created was so flawed and full of implausibilities, it was now simply a matter of the Captain tearing it apart and calling over some men to arrest them. The apartment alone was full of clues. Items that would quickly destroy his case.

Captain Chaban stood back. He looked from one to the other of the two people before him.

"You've been crying," he said. "There is a great deal to be sad about these days."
They waited. They felt powerless in front of this man who seemed to know more than he revealed.
Finally, the Captain shook his head. Then he turned to Kozuch. He muttered something. He walked back to his car and with his hand resting on the door handle he said, "Thank you for your help. Good luck in Halle."

In the car heading away, Kozuch with his eyes on the road said, "Why?"
Chaban too kept his eyes front. "Oh he's the one. But he's Wehrmacht. So much a soldier. What would you do if foreign soldiers were raping and killing your country's children. He's a more honorable man than those of our people who didn't survive."
"Are you too forgiving? After all that Mother Russia has suffered from these Germans?"
"I know, but the war is over. I'd like to think it's a start on a new path. What would be the point of taking them in and destroying them. It would be a continuation of this killing. Perhaps if he had not stopped some of those SS in his apartment or had not put a cushion under the head of our wounded man in that room. Our man who observed them leave."

They drove on in silence. When nearly back to the checkpoint, Kozuch said, "You didn't ask about the boy. The boy in the apartment."
Chaban slapped the dashboard. "Damn. Of course. The crying. How could I have forgotten. Turn around, turn around."

They drove about the area and searched down many
roads until light failed but they could not find the
couple again.

Chapter 28

'Moving South'

"Who was August Haas?" Adriane asked.
"He was the friend who died next to me in battle." Dieter
looked at her. "It was the only name I could think of at
the time."
Dieter had removed his coat and tie and rolled up his
sleeves. Already on the roads so broken by the tracks of
tanks and trucks, the mud had coated the two refugees
in the same layers of dirt and blended them into the
line of people making their way to various parts of the
country.
The day was ending. They had walked as far and as
fast as they could but were still on the edges of the city
when the light began to fail.
They spent their first night in a small yard, partly concrete and partly grass. They sheltered next to a large
rusting shed. The area was full of disused machinery.
It gave them suitable cover. Well hidden, they were able
eat a little of their food unseen by any desperate or
cunning fellow travellers. While the night was only cool,
they did not attain any degree of comfort and moved
back onto the road at first light.

A short way down the road, idle Russian troops, obviously drunk, called out to them from a nearby camp. One soldier with his shirt off had spied them through the trees. They made gestures at Adriane and invited her over, clutching their crotches but were too tired or inebriated to take the situation any further.

"Drunk bored soldiers with little interest in your well-being. Not a situation I want to get into," Dieter said, as they moved on.

By late morning they were away from the centre of the city of Berlin and moving into open country. It was hard to not rest but they needed to move toward their goal while it was, in theory, attainable.

A family sitting against a stone wall watched them approach. The two youngest children walked up to meet them. A boy about six who seemed to limp and a girl of perhaps four, who took on a quite doleful look.

"Have you food, sir," he asked, his voice raspy. "We have not eaten in days." The little girl took Adriane's hand and smiled weakly up at her.

"No, we have nothing, my friend. Not a thing."

Adriane looked sharply at Dieter. Surely they could spare something. He stared back at her and shook his head slightly. Adriane raised her eyebrows but again he shook his head.

They passed the family who all watched them mournfully. The two children peeled off and flopped back down beside their parents and siblings. The father in particular eyed their packs. He had a piece of grass hanging limply from his mouth like a cigarette.

Once past they could hear the family muttering behind them.

"What just happened?" asked Adriane.

"They have plenty of food," said Dieter. "I could see it hidden behind the wall when we were still a fair way off. I've seen starving and that wasn't it. They're using their children to get what they can from others. Probably spent the whole war racketeering."

Adriane glanced back. The family were already lining up a group of people approaching in the distance.

Other travellers and refugees were about. Some with carts of their belongings, others with practically nothing. Afraid or past the ability to care, there was very little communication between different groups. They made their way along to wherever they were going in stoic silence. Eyes fixed and visage expressionless.

By early afternoon they had to stop. Dr Beck's shoes were not made for long distance walking, especially if the fit was not made for the wearer.

"My army boots would be ideal," said Dieter.

They sat for a while by the side of the road on the fallen trunk of a large broken tree, perhaps pushed aside by advancing armour. There were other trees with early spring foliage over their heads.

Russian Army trucks were moving past, heading in the their direction. One convoy contained more dispirited German soldiers.

"I don't like this," Dieter observed, "they seem to be consolidating positions. I think we should get off this main road."

"And go where?"
"Smaller villages, Any places that command less attention and aren't of strategic interest."

Later at a quiet intersection they found a road off to the right. Dieter looked about, walked down the side road a little way then motioned to Adriane to follow him.
"I know this area. We fought or more aptly retreated through here. From what I recall, this road will take us to Bruck." He stood with his hands out.
"We were fighting Americans all the way. I don't understand. Where are they now?"

Even on this lesser road there were Russian troops passing.
A man with a horse and cart gave them a lift for some distance before saying he had to turn off. He had kept his horse moving at a brisk pace, explaining that he wanted to be off the road as quickly as possible.
At Bruck, the town had a large number of Russians sitting about. They hurried through with a few other refugees. Local people seemed to be staying out of sight. Many shops and houses were boarded up.
As they passed a soldier sitting on the step of his truck, smoking, he said something and shook his head.
He gave a derisive laugh.
A little way along they heard a man behind speak to a younger man with him. "You understand a little Russian. What did he say?"
"Something about wasting our time."

They pressed on with an unknown urgency in their

stride. Dieter suffered with the expensive dress shoes.
"They have thin soles. Excellent in a carpeted room with
other scientific types but not for walking out and about."
Near the next town of Belzig he stopped. They were
alone on the road. Ahead the way led through a forest.
Trees overhung the road.
"We need to detour."
"Why?" asked Adriane, sitting for a breath.
"The Russians must be staking a claim on territory.
I fought my way through this forest. It's not very big.
The Americans were giving us hell. I came out onto
the roadway just down there, expecting to be shot.
We should have reached the Americans. They were all
through here. They must have pulled back. If we enter
the next town we might be rounded up. Let's disappear."

Dieter walked barefoot for while trying to give his feet
a chance to recover. He put his socks and shoes back
on as they made their way round Belzig. They ducked
and crept along a ditch when they saw figures in the
distance. Further off through the trees they heard a
loudspeaker suddenly begin sending out a message. It
was indistinct at first, then the message became clearer,
perhaps as they moved about. 'All German citizens may
not proceed past this point. This is the Soviet Zone.
You must go back.'
The message was repeated every minute.

Dieter squeezed Adriane's hand and then kissed it.
He smiled at his intuition.
"We can stay in the trees from here till Wiesenberg.
I think we might find Americans there.."

"If we're moving past in a forest, surely that idea would occur to others."

"I know." Dieter looked at the girl. "I hope the Russians have other problems, such as establishing their bases, feeding their troops to be bothered chasing a few refugees."

Dieter's hopes were in vain.

The ten kilometres between the two towns was made doubly difficult by Russian soldiers poking around the edges of the forest. One they saw was using binoculars to scope the forest area. Under the tree cover Adriane admitted, "I'm exhausted. We're nearly running."

They stopped and drank the last of their water.

Further on, patches of burnt, blasted trees and debris came into view. At one stage a stench of rotting German corpses caught their noses.

"We're not likely to find August Haas here are we?" asked Adriane, concerned that her companion may be traumatised by such an event.

"No," said Dieter matter-of-factly, "He died much earlier."

The centre of the forest had a shallow dip. Enough it seemed to have given about ten young Wehrmacht soldiers the idea that it might provide sufficient shelter for an ambush or to establish a position. Holding their hands over their noses they looked at the scattered bodies. Bloated and distorted. Half were blown apart. Probably a series of well directed hand grenades. Their blood had pooled to a black tarry mess amongst the leaves. Their guns and ammunition still lay about glinting in the light.

Dieter shook his head. "Perhaps I was a coward, perhaps
we all were but we just wanted to survive. There wasn't
any more talk about victory. They sent us these new
recruits. We kept as far away from them as possible.
It was obvious they had no idea of battle. Being near
them lessened your chances of living."
Dieter's eyes glistened. "It's why I wanted to help Hauke
at that redoubt. If I could have saved one it might have
helped. Just one."
Adriane took the man's hand. "C'mon. We shouldn't stop
too long."

They crouched and moved from tree to tree, still afraid
that at the other side of the very next one would be a
man with a gun.
Away from the battle zone they slowly moved into a
pretty area of pine trees and soft grass. Early spring
flowers were blooming. There were mushrooms at the
base of some the trees. It gave an impression of calm,
as if the war had not been allowed in this particular
part of the forest. Even the birds were in residence.
Light stabbed through the canopy creating contrasts of
brightness and shadow as they made their way along.
The area seemed to expand.
They sank to the ground. Lay still on their backs, staring
at the sky.
"Should we stay here for the night?"
Dieter rolled on his side and looked at Adriane. "I know
you're very tired. I'd love to sleep here. It's the first
beautiful place I've seen for some time. C'mon, stand up
before we both give in to our bodies."
Standing, Adriane asked, "How much further to Weisen-

berg? It will be dark soon."
"I don't know." Dieter looked about. "We must be half-way. We've got to get further along. I'm not sure where the Americans are anymore."
Adriane had sunk to her knees once more. Dieter looked down at his companion.
"It will get cold here."
"Then please hold me so I don't escape."
Dieter looked at Adriane's face. He saw somebody he cared for very much.

With a pine needle bed and a coat for covering they held each other through the night and woke as the first light cut through the trees.
Adriane had stirred and slept fitfully. Each time she woke, Dieter would hold her closer and do his best to make her comfortable. She was beginning to feel safe in his company.
Before they left, the two went through their baggage and took out some heavier clothes and food.
Then they moved off walking across a large open area toward more trees on the other side.

"I hope we don't regret leaving that food."
Dieter looked at Adriane. "We can't be far from the Americans. They were all through here. I'd imagine they'd feed us. They always appeared to be well sup-plied while we ...."
"What?"
Dieter stared off through the trees to their right.
He peered. Squinted, shading his eyes.
"There's a truck. Must be a road over there. Can you see

it?"
Adriane could just make out a faint shape in the distance.
"Shouldn't we avoid it?"
"I don't think it's an army truck. Wrong shape. I'm going to take a closer look."
"Why?"
Dieter held up his hands in a gesture of despair. "I have no idea where the Americans are. They should be here. If that's a local they may know the situation. If there's any danger I won't approach. Please, wait here."
He half-smiled and moved off before the girl could protest. She sat, then climbed onto her knees to watch as Dieter crept away.

The truck was certainly not army, Russian or any other nation. It was a big old beast with a flat top back. There was a small covered section attached to the cab while the rest had drop down sides. A farm truck. The covered section for taking workers to the fields, the open back for hauling produce. Even from the safety of the trees Dieter could see it was piled with something dark.
He guessed potatoes.
Sitting on the cab step a man was hunched, tapping his foot on the ground and smoking a cigarette. Dieter watched him for a while. The man twice consulted his watch. He was waiting for something or someone.
A chance to be taken.
Dieter stepped out of the treeline and made his way across the road.
"Guten Tag, mein freunde."
The man on the truck looked up. He was quite old.

He tilted his head back, the cigarette hanging from his lips.

"So you're my friend, eh."

Dieter continued to approach. "Just a figure of speech. I'm passing by and I wonder if you can give me some information?"

Again the old man tilted his head back to look at Dieter. The cigarette smoke curled up into his eye.

"What sort of information would that be?"

By now Dieter had reached the man. He held out his hand. "My name is Dieter. I was in the Wehrmacht. Now I'm just heading south."

The man looked him up and down. "You're well dressed for a soldier."

"I had the chance to change my clothes, so I did."

"And now you're heading home?"

Dieter hesitated. Should he lie? He decided to try the truth.

"No, my home was in Dresden. I thought I'd try my luck in the south."

"Oh, Dresden. I'm very sorry. Everybody knows about that situation. Why south?"

"To find the Americans. Are they nearby?"

The old man gave a laugh that turned into a cough.

He paused for a minute to finish coughing and consider his answer. "Even on our little backroad. People heading south. I'd offer you a cigarette soldier but they're a little scarce. These ones are Russian. Rather rough. In fact dreadful but they're all I can get."

He threw the butt on the ground and crushed it with his boot.

"Are you alone?"

"No," Dieter said, "I have my wife with me. She's over there in the trees. As a fellow German I thought you might be able to guide us. We'd like to find the Americans." In the back of his mind Dieter wondered about a German with Russian cigarettes.

Standing, the man held out his hand. "My name is Rolf. I'm just a local farmer. If you are Wermacht then I salute you. I have the information you require but I doubt you'll like it."

For some time Adriane watched Dieter talking to the man at the truck. She had crept closer for a better view. They seemed to be discussing things. After a handshake they were pointing down the road and motioning as if indicating areas ahead. The man had tapped his watch and pointed up the road.

Then to Adriane's surprise the man had pointed in her direction in the forest and both men nodded. Dieter seemed to be thanking the man who shrugged his shoulders in a gesture of compliance.

Dieter ran back across the road and into the trees. Adriane called out. "I'm here." She expected a reprimand but Dieter was agitated and had news.

"The Americans are nowhere near here. The Russians have Thuringa. The American zone starts at Hesse." Adriane felt a wave of despair. The distance was immense..

Dieter held up his hand. "There's a chance. If we're willing to take it." He motioned to the old man at the truck. "That's Rolf. A decent man as far as I can tell. He's a local farmer. This area, he and his neighbour's farms survived the war without damage. He has fields of pota-

toes. The Russians came and took some. Being an angry old man he complained to the local Russian commander. To his surprise the man forbade his troops from entering the farms and has instead agreed to pay for the produce from the farms. Apparently the Russians are short of food in this whole area. They don't pay much but it is an arrangement the farmers can live with for now."
Adriane touched Dieter's arm.
"That's nice for the farmers. How does this help us?"
"Well," said Dieter. "We need help and they need help. Virtually all the sons and daughters of the local farmers have been killed or captured or are missing in the fighting. Only old people left running the farms. They're too old to leave their farms so they'll take their chances with the Russians. They have to deliver the produce to various Russian barracks from here to Eisenach."
Dieter paused for effect. Adriane raised her eyebrows.
"Eisenach," Dieter explained. It's very close to the Hesse border, the American zone."
Dieter held up his finger.
"The deal is, we help load and unload the truck all the way on the trip and then at Eisenach we are on our own." He paused. "You see, the Russians refuse to help and the labour involved is very hard on the old man. We're just a couple of the man's children from the farm."
"You're wearing a suit."
"That too has been discussed. There's clothes in the truck I can use."
"And your shoes?"
"I'll cover them with dirt. Nobody looks at people's shoes."

Fifteen minutes later a small truck pulled up behind
Rolf's vehicle. The man inside was even older than Rolf.
After a quiet discussion the man came over and shook
the hands of the two new farm labourers. They then set
about transferring a load of pumpkins and beet onto
the large truck, stacking them on top of Rolf's potatoes
while the two old farmers watched with approval.
The old clothes that Dieter wore fitted him well. He suspected they had belonged to Rolf's son but chose not to
ask for fear of bringing raw and difficult memories to the
surface. Some thick socks helped pad out Herr Beck's
shoes.
Despite the cool day, both labourers were hot and tired
when the transfer job was complete.
All four people stood by the roadside and shared some
cool cider from a stoneware jar in Rolf's truck.
The neighbour bade them farewell and a safe journey.
Before he parted he snapped his heels to attention and
gave a traditional salute to Dieter. "For the real soldiers," he said.
"Three sons," Rolf whispered as he walked away.

On the road, rolling at maximum revs, the truck ambled
along clashing gears toward Weisenberg. Adriane sat
in the front with Rolf while Dieter sat in the rear. Their
cases were hidden behind the truck's bench seat. Dieter
marvelled at the empty road and lack of Russian troops.
In the town they were stopped initially but quickly ushered through once the guards saw potatoes on the back.
At the canteen, set up in a relatively intact street-side
restaurant, they unloaded potatoes and pumpkin into
large steel drums and then wheeled them to the back

of the kitchen area. Twice, Russian soldiers shouldered Dieter aside in a show of dominance. After Rolf had weighed out the prescribed quantity for the delivery the officer in charge insisted he unload another drum full ignoring his pointing to the order form.

As they drove away Rolf explained that they all took more than their allotted amount so he added sufficient load to cover their standover methods.

"The bastards won the war. They can do whatever they like. Possibly the name on my authority letter isn't a high enough rank to scare them. I think your wife is safe if she stays close to us."

Adriane felt a wave of concern. The possibility of harm had not occurred to her.

The next town was Zerbst. Once again a smaller garrison with a kitchen set up in some occupied buildings. A lot of Russian soldiers idled about. They were fed and content and even helped with the unloading. Adriane felt comparatively safe. Before leaving, the commandant had some fuel added to Rolf's truck, to 'ensure that his comrades down the line were well fed.'

"They seemed quite decent," Dieter remarked as they moved off.

Rolf looked at him askance. "Probably city soldiers. Well bred with some education. I've learnt never to trust any of them. There are no rules. Assume the worst and be occasionally surprised."

Their next stop was Harzgerode. Dieter noticed that Rolf made an effort to travel on backroads, even tracks and avoided any larger towns. Their route was not direct.

On the outskirts of Harzgerode a Russian patrol stopped them and seemed aggressive. They spoke no German and ordered everybody out of the truck. They looked over the load suspiciously until Rolf took out some papers and a badge of some sort. He showed them to the soldiers. All eight of the Russians scanned the papers. They did not seem to be convinced by what they had been given. One large angry looking man held the papers close and studied them carefully. Suddenly he lifted his head and gave a beaming smile. He walked to the truck took a potato, holding it to his mouth and making to eat.

"Ja, ja," said Rolf. He pointed at the load on the truck and then at the soldiers. The big man spoke to the others and much laughter ensued. They were ushered back into their truck with mock haste and were waved off. Once down the road Dieter hung round from his seat in the back and asked through Rolf's window, "What just happened?"

"Dumb bastards were all illiterate. I have papers from reasonably high up giving me protection and passage as long as I'm carrying a load but none of them could read the damned papers. Finally the that big fellow squeezed enough words out of the documents to understand what was going on. Like I said, the Russians are a varied lot."

In Harzgerode there was a quite small Russian contingent. Their kitchen was on the ground floor of a building. They seemed more a collection of clerks than soldiers. They took their allocated amount, did not ask for more, nodded in a matter of fact way about the whole transaction and showed them out the door, even standing aside to let Adriane proceed them to the truck then wandered away.

"Rather large town, very few troops. There's very little logic in this occupation."

Rolf looked at Dieter. "I agree. It's haphazard. And unsettling."

After long winding stretches they neared Sondershausen. Rolf was uneasy. The garrison had grown a lot since his last trip. Their camp covered both sides of the road on a large area outside the town. Suddenly they were surrounded by Russian soldiers, trucks, tanks and great amounts of activity. In the distance a fenced area held German soldiers.

These Russians looked more on edge, rough and dirty.

"They keep moving things around," said Rolf, seeking the canteen area.

After several stops the truck was directed to a field full of tents and people. The road in and the tracks within the camp were muddy from overuse. The field kitchen was a giant tent with open sides. Steaming cauldrons of food made the place drip and set the mood for the whole area.

"Stay in the truck," Rolf whispered, patting Adriane's knee. "And slip down low."

The chef was grubby and short-tempered. Most of his clients were drunk.

"I'll take the lot." The chef spoke rough German. He stood with his hands on his hips. Like a man who has spent his life making terrible food and has never washed it off. He stood outside his domain, aware that he and his food had some importance.

Rolf took out his papers and tried to explain. He pointed out the allocation he was supposed to give them.

Two soldiers came from the side and pushed Rolf to the ground into the mud. His glasses flew from his head.

They spoke some Russian.

The chef stood over Rolf nudging him with his boot.

"They said, we're really hungry. Unload the lot or we'll fucking shoot you and take the lot anyway. Do you understand that, fucking old German?"

Dieter retrieved Rolf's glasses as one of the soldiers tried to unsteadily stand on them.

He helped Rolf to his feet picking up his scattered papers.

"Okay, okay, the lot," said Rolf. All the life had abruptly drained out of him.

They were directed to the back of the tent and spent the next half hour packing all the remaining load into wooden crates. Several soldiers peered into the truck cab, making lewd gestures at Adriane, inviting her to come with them.

To Dieter's relief the threats went no further, possibly because they were so drunk or perhaps they were under orders to stop their victory mayhem.

Once finished they climbed back into their truck and headed out of the field and away from the encampment. In the hurry to leave, Dieter had squeezed in next to Adriane in the front cab.

Rolf had tears in his eyes. "I can't do this anymore," he said, his voice broken.

Dieter's heart sank. With no load and a defeated old man, their chance of getting close to the Americans had gone.

Dieter noticed their saviour was still heading south.
They skirted round Sondershausen and then Rolf turned
off onto a well maintained dirt road that led through a
forest. Here he stopped the truck and turned the engine
off.

This is it thought Dieter. He's going to say sorry and
dump us here.

Outside the truck, Rolf reached back into the cab, under
his seat. He withdrew a mid-sized bottle.

"Brandy," he said, "better than water." He took several
gulps, before wiping the top and offering it to Adriane.
"Drink, I have plenty."

Adriane drank and handed the bottle to Dieter.

Rolf looked at his two passengers. He raised his eyebrows. "You're thinking, what now? This has happened
every time but it's getting worse. Generally they want
an extra 50 kilos but not the lot. I've noticed each trip
it gets more dangerous. And the potatoes will eventually run out. Then what? This will be my last trip unless
they force me. The best Russian soldiers are in Berlin.
They've moved all their useless rabble down here. They
just need bodies on the ground to occupy this area and
keep their claim from the Americans."

Dieter asked the question he didn't want answered.

"So with no load left are you going back?"

Rolf took another large mouthful of brandy from his bottle. He looked at the ground. Kicked a few pine cones
aside.

"No," he said at last. "Despite their appearance these
Russians do communicate. I'm only paid when they all
confirm a delivery. Back at the farm I have to make a
trip to the local Army HQ. They pay me in Reichsmarks

sometimes or Russian Promissory Notes which I suspect
are also useless. Sometimes they give me supplies they
don't need. Rarely food. Once they said they had no
money for me and gave me some army cots, for God's
sake."

"Why did you do this at all?" Dieter asked.

Rolf shrugged "For my sins, I am the representative
of the Farm and Produce Society for my area. My colleagues in other areas were killed so my jurisdiction
somehow became extended. When the fighting finally
stopped here I thought it best to have some arrangement with the conquerers. You know, to stop them pil-
fering. Briefly it was the Americans. They were excellent.
A little arrogant but fair and honest. When the Russians
moved in and they started taking things I had the 'arrangement' reinstated but they insisted I do all the
deliveries down through their sector. To 'keep it simple'
they said."

Again Dieter asked.

"But you have no supplies?"

"There's a farm down this road. As a fellow German he
will overcharge me but I will be able to get enough to
complete the run to Eisenach."

Chapter 29

'Eisenach'

Rolf was in a better place. Hearing of their treatment at
the hands of the Russians at Sondershausen and being
made aware of the plight of Rolf's two passengers, the
farmer had struck a quite fair deal with his visitor.
As they pulled away Rolf put his arm around Adriane
and hugged her.
"I think it's been a while since he's seen a pretty girl.
He softened right up. Never experienced that before.
Normally he's a very unhappy man. That husband of
yours ...." he said, indicating to the back of the truck, "is
very fortunate."
Adriane blushed.
Rolf had noted that neither of his passengers wore a
wedding ring but that could be for many reasons. Lost,
traded, stolen, hidden. War is a game of chance.

"What can we expect at Eisenach?" Adriane asked.
"I wish I knew." Rolf turned his head to the girl. "Have
you noticed something? Since we left on this journey
I've seen less and less travellers on the road. Now no

refugees. I made this trip five days ago and there were some. Now, nothing. The Russians don't want Germans fleeing to the Americans or the British. So they're doing their best to stop any movement. There were quite a few Russians there in Eisenach last time. This time I feel there will be many more. I'm sorry my child, I'll do my best to get you close but it is going to be very difficult for you. Very, very difficult."

The words of the old farmer had barely left his lips when they swung off the forest track onto the road, just as two Russian trucks went past heading north. Rolf tried to speed up as he pushed his old machine through its gears but one of the Russian trucks had already turned and was coming up behind blasting its horn.
"I hope these idiots can at least read," he said as he slowed and stopped.
About a dozen Russian soldiers surrounded the truck and made them all stand aside while they searched the vehicle.
"Why don't you show them the papers, the food order?" Dieter suggested, "before they discover our cases behind the seat."
"Let them calm down. Eventually they'll ask us what we're doing. The cases are safe. It takes a genius to discover and operate the mechanism that allows access to the back of the seat."
A man in civilian clothes alighted from the Russian truck and approached. He was accompanied by a young looking Russian officer. The officer spoke to him in Russian, then he looked at the threesome.
He spoke German. "My name is Carl. I'm from Sonder-

shausen. I speak a little Russian so they grabbed me to interpret for them. I had no choice. Can you tell me why you are on the road? What is your purpose? Where are you going? If you're doing anything wrong I'll try to cover for you. This lot are none too bright. Especially this chap next to me."

Rolf did not give any hint of relief at the man's words, that might alert the earnest young Russian.

He took out the orders.

"We're simply delivering produce to the Russian kitchens in Eisenach. Here is the order. It's in Russian and some German so they will understand it. I make this run perhaps twice a week."

Carl looked decidedly pleased that he would not be put in the position of saviour. He spoke to the officer and showed him the papers. In the background two soldiers were helping themselves to the jar of cider.

Rolf raised his arms and pointed. "It's the only refreshment we have. Please."

The officer turned and snapped at the men, ordering them back to their truck. He then turned and added a new question to his interpreter. Carl nodded.

"He wants to know who these two people are?" He indicated to Adriane and Dieter.

"They are my son and his wife. Farmers like me. They do the loading and unloading. I'm an old man. The Russian soldiers are far too busy to help."

Carl passed on this information. The officer looked all three up and down. His youth made him keen to make his mark in the ranks. He tilted his head and looked at Dieter. Then he spoke to Carl once more.

"He says his father too is a farmer and that all farmers

are the salt of the earth. His question is, why is a farmer
wearing the shoes of a businessman from the city?"
Dieter felt his theory concerning shoes evaporate. He
spoke up before Rolf could think of an answer. "My
boots fell to pieces. No new ones were available. I took
these from a man on the side of the road, who no longer
needed them. It is better than being barefoot."
When Carl spoke to the officer this time the man just
stood for a some time, as if he was considering options,
looking for a trick or a way to make things difficult. He
then walked to the truck and peered at the load. Finally
he called out to Carl and began walking away.
"You may go. He says Russians like potatoes. I'm afraid
you're going to get a lot of this interruption. The area
is infested with Russians. Good luck, whatever you're
doing." He smiled at Adriane and shrugged. "Hope you
make it," he whispered.

Rolf was right. The further they drove the more Russians appeared. They were stopped twice more. It became more difficult. With no interpreters the paperwork
was all that got them past. After each holdup, Rolf came
back to the truck and climbing in muttered, "We were in
luck again, one of them could read."
As they approached Eisenach the sun was low. Shadows
hung across their road. There were no people about.
Rolf pulled to the side of the road and turned off the
motor. He called Dieter in from the back and all three sat
inside.
"There are some things to consider," he said. "Let's plan
a little. Do we pull off into some forest and sleep till
morning? The Russians will be less suspicious of a truck

in the daytime than at night. Besides only one of my headlights works. Or do we carry on to do our delivery and have the cover of darkness for you two people to make your way with some safety? I don't have a lot of fuel to drive around too much. The Russians might give me some. I don't know." He stopped and waited for some response from his passengers.

"I like darkness," Dieter said at last, "but so does the enemy. Military training," he added.

Adriane, squashed between the two men lifted her hand.

"You may speak, my dear," said Rolf.

"You have one headlight and little fuel. People doing bad things or desperate things move at night. The Russians will be on edge. At night they'll be less tolerant and more suspicious. Ready to shoot. In the daytime they are able to assess things. I'd rather wait until morning. If we're dropped off in daylight, they might be able to see us but we'll have a better chance of seeing the land and our objective and avoiding patrols."

Dieter patted Adriane's hand. "You're right. Less suspicious in daylight. Let's find some trees."

Large areas of woodland suddenly deserted them. They finally found a field with a double row of trees for a windbreak. It also had a stone wall. They located a gate and drove into the field. By parking where the trees were thickest, Dieter was able to confirm from the road side that the truck was not visible.

Rolf managed to produce some blankets and a small army field stove from behind the truck seat. Crouched by the wall he boiled some of their potatoes. When cooked he broke them up and added some lard, then salt and pepper.

"It's not the meal of a king. But it will fill our stomachs for the night."

Dieter looked at the old man. "What else do you have behind that seat, my friend?"

"No contraband, just essentials I want to keep out the way. It's the feature of my truck I like the most. Only those who know the secret of the lock can gain access."

"The never tell me," said Dieter

They spent a cool, uncomfortable night under the truck. It rained briefly just before dawn. The day was grey and still. An owl watched them from one of the trees before flying off.

As they were packing and about to leave, six Russian trucks rumbled past heading north.

"That's six less to face on the way in." Rolf looked at his passengers. "Maybe today will be less stressful."

Rolf's prediction seemed to be holding. All cramped into the truck cab for warmth, they encountered only a few Russian soldiers on the last kilometres to Eisenach. They were not stopped, just watched with suspicion. Fields continued right up to the first houses. As they rounded a building they came up behind another truck. It was stopped and the driver was talking to some Russians at a road block.

"That truck is American. The stars have been painted over but it's American."

Rolf looked at Dieter. "Don't build your hopes up. That's Rolf. Yes, another Rolf. He 'found' the truck when the Americans pulled back. It was bogged so they left it.

He does deliveries like me. I'd say his truck is full of
cabbages."
The Russians handed the other Rolf his papers and
waved him through. The officer motioned them forward.
He spoke German.
"What, do you have?" he said.
'Potatoes." Rolf handed over his papers.
The officer glanced at them and then called to one of his
men. After inspecting the load the soldier called back
just a few words in a rather bored fashion.
The officer handed back the papers and waved his arm.
He was about to speak when Rolf said, "Thank you sir,
I'm a regular, I know the way to your kitchens."
The man nodded and they were on their way.
"None of this was here before. I just drove straight in."

The kitchen was quite extensive but reasonably organised. They waited and chatted to the other Rolf. He
smiled when Adriane and Dieter were introduced as
Rolf's son and daughter.
"Of course," he said, "how nice to see you again."
A Russian man appeared. He was large and round. He
had fat smiling lips and gold teeth. He handed out glasses of Vodka and through an interpreter advised that
there would be a delay while they brought up sufficient
baskets in which to unload the produce.
The man sniffed and spat. He wiped his nose then wiped
his hand on his apron. "Okay," he said, before smiling
effusively and wandering off back into his domain.
"Why doesn't he hate us?" asked Adriane.
"Oh I'd say he does," said the other Rolf. "He just likes
his kitchen to be supplied and working so that his life is

untroubled.”

The man then added.

“Come over here, away from all the noise.”

He led the group way from the kitchen to a high wall of a house on the other side of the street. He handed out cigarettes.

“Looks less like a conspiracy if we’re just smoking.”

They all lit up.

“This Rolf has more connections and knows more gossip then me,” their Rolf explained.

The man said, “Well, I hear things. Y’know like not to go near the Russian camp near Sondershausen. They’re all vile bastards to a man. In fact, I may stop this if I can, it’s becoming too dangerous.”

He looked at their faces. “You went there didn’t you. Oh hell, I wish I could have warned you. Was it bad?”

“They took everything,” Dieter sighed. “They beat Rolf, knocked him into the mud. We had to buy some more to complete the run.”

The man reached out and patted the older Rolf on the shoulder, briefly closing his eyes. He then turned to Adriane and Dieter.

“Listen, son and daughter-in-law of my neighbour and friend Rolf. I’m not sure how you talked him into dropping you off but I have some information that might help you. I’ve done several dropoffs. Weeks back when it was fairly easy. It no longer is easy or safe. For the person doing the run and for his passengers. The Russians now will simply shoot you. They got sick of rounding people up. It’s offends their pride to have all these people trying to get away from them and into the arms of the Americans. South of this town is forested and steep.

The trees afford shelter but it is quite an arduous journey through to the other side and when you're through you're still in Thuringia. The quickest route into Hesse and the American Zone is to the west. I mean it's just down the road. So that's the way most people go. And they're caught.

Can I suggest you go into the forest and once you're well inside it, then head west. If you do it right, that will take you into Hesse. That's all I can offer. I'd shake your hands and wish you luck but that would look very odd seeing you are the close relatives of my friend."

He raised his eyebrows and added.

"It's a pity you can't stay. My friend could make use of some help." He paused then said quite sadly, "We all could."

Chapter 30

'The Run'

They were given extra fuel. Rolf had explained that he
may not be able to come back without a top up of his
tank. They exited through the same checkpoint and
once out of the town, on the same road north, searched
for a way to get back to the south and their forest. There
were tracks that obviously led to farms even a road
winding off that looked very promising until they noticed the remains of the broken road sign. It announced
the name of the road and then in smaller letters advised
that it was a 'no through road.'
Rolf was concerned that they would be seen rolling
slowly along and that would arouse suspicion.
"We seem to be getting further away and there's nothing," he commented. "If we'd known we could have
looked for something on the way in. We're five kilometres out now."
As they rounded a bend with a clear empty road to the
north, Dieter pointed to several large old oak trees at
the side.
"Is that a road? Behind those trees?"

Rolf nosed the truck in and indeed, partly hidden by the trees and bordered by stone walls was a neat unsealed road. There were no houses, only open empty fields.

Rolf stopped the truck to survey the possibilities.
"I don't know. It's rough further on. Look it just wanders off across the fields. It may not go anywhere. Farms have these roads. Often they just lead to a few farmhouses and end."
Dieter shuffled round in the cab and squinted at the sun. He muttered to himself briefly.
"East ..... west. Look, I think it's worth trying. It does wander but if you look in the distance, it wanders in the right direction. If it goes all the way round it could bring us out at the eastern road and the forest. If not, perhaps close enough for us to leave you and head across country."
"Or we could drive for some time to a farmer's front door."
"Either way," said Adriane, "I doubt the Russians would be much interested in such a goat track."
Rolf revved the motor.
"Well I have a full fuel tank and a whole day to spare. Let's see if this soldier has an eye for a country road."

They motored along with no hint of an outcome.
The road ran through several fields. In one, a man was ploughing with a horse drawn steel plough. He waved as they passed.
"Does he think we're one of his neighbours or is he just friendly?" asked Adriane.
Out of sight of the main road their track became rutted

as it suddenly descended to a small stream. Facing them on the other side a little way up the rise was a farmhouse and yards. A man and a woman were in the open side area with some milking cows. The road curved away and climbed back from the stream.

"I suppose they built their house there for the water supply. A stream is very handy."

Dieter looked at his benefactor.

"As long as your neighbours upstream don't let their cows piss in your water."

Rolf glanced at the young man.

"You're too cynical. Farmers don't do that to each other. We have to exist together."

"It's a pity us Germans are not very good at that," said Dieter, "when it comes to Europe and the world."

They drove on in silence. Rolf's initial fears seemed realised when twice more they came upon a farmhouse or a farm entry but each time the road appeared to end and then curved away and continued. It finally slipped around and headed along the side of a ridge, back in the direction of the main road they had left. They could see some of the open farmland they had crossed.

This section also seemed less travelled. It was overgrown in parts.

"I wonder," Rolf opined, "if we have somehow entered somebody's property? This seems to me more like a large unused field with simply an access road."

"It doesn't appear to be going anywhere," Adriane admitted.

Just as they began to despair that this path would end

or take them back to the start, it did an abrupt left hand turn through an earth cutting in the top of the hill. They stopped and found themselves perched on a high, steep hill that ran straight down through the fields where, marked once again by a clump of oak trees, it casually joined a main road into Eisenach. On the other side of that road was a deep forest.

"Good God," Rolf exclaimed. "You people are blessed. I gave this road no chance."

With the object of their interest in sight, caution set in. Rolf moved the truck a little way back into the cutting. It was decided they would wait, to see what traffic and other movements took place on the road. Once they committed down the hill to meet the road, they would be exposed. It was best to know what chance they had of doing the whole operation unseen.

Early in the day only one vehicle passed along the road in the next ten minutes.

"Could our luck hold?" Dieter whispered as they all sat gazing ahead.

"From what I've seen of others, you two have been more fortunate than most of the people on the roads," offered Rolf.

In the brief silence that followed, Adriane said, "If we were truly lucky, there would be three of us."

Dieter lowered his head in guilt.

"Dare I ask?" said Rolf. There were three of you at the start? Don't answer if it is painful."

It was but they told him the story of Hauke Kluge leaving out details of the apartment and the food. Just a simple version while they waited and counted cars. When they finished Rolf rubbed his eyes.

"So sad, so sad. We started a war and now we suffer the consequences."

As he spoke, two large trucks came into view from the direction of Eisenach. In the back were Russian soldiers. They rolled past slowly and then just below the vantage point they stopped. Out of the forest came two soldiers waving to their comrades on the truck. When the soldiers reached the truck they were involved in a discussion. They were then pointing down the road.

"I know what's going on here." Dieter was quite animated. "They're leaving troops along parts of the road each night. Hidden in the edge of the trees. Waiting for people trying to go through the forest. I'd say they tried this section last night with no luck. I doubt they're even aware of this road we're sitting on. Judging from all that pointing I'd say they're going to set up further down. There's a road meets this one. You can just see it."

After more talk and a number of the Russians seeming to look at a map, the two soldiers from the forest climbed aboard the front truck and the small convoy rolled off down the road. They watched and Dieter's prediction came true. Far off at the intersection, four soldiers were despatched into the trees and the trucks continued till they were out of sight.

Now the whole area before them was devoid of any movement. No cars, no trucks, no people, soldiers or farmers.

"Well," said Rolf, with a suddenness that broke the silence, "It's now or it's never for you two people. Get your cases from behind the seat. Change back into your

suit Dieter. I'll hug you both before we proceed and wish
you every luck. Once I'm down that hill and on the road,
I'll stop briefly if it's clear for you to jump out. Don't
look back, don't wave, just get into those trees. Perhaps
someday you can send me a letter and tell me of your
adventures and your continued good fortune. If I don't
hear I will still think of you and assume the best."

Dieter finally stopped. He was panting. With the two
suitcases he had struggled without hesitation through
the trees and up to the top of a long ridge. Behind he
had heard Rolf's truck roaring away as the man turned
to head back to the sanctuary of the old farm road.
Now he flopped down at the base of some thinner pines
on the narrow edge of the ridge. Adriane struggled up
behind, carrying the Beck briefcase. The man realised
he had not looked back, even to check on his companion. His soldier's instincts had just driven him on to a
point where he felt secure.
As Adriane lay beside him he patted her hand.
"Well, we're in, at least."
"Why did we struggle up a hill?"
"If I was a Russian soldier I'd be up here. Ridges are easier to navigate, you can see where you're going and you
can see anything going on below. So we'll stay on ridges
wherever we can."
"That's good. I'm tired and hungry and thirsty. Less hills
is better."

For the rest of the morning they moved cautiously deeper into the forest. The terrain was quite steep in places,

explaining why it had remained a forest. They found a
very small stream with apparently clean water but had
to climb down to it, drink all they could and then climb
back up to the ridge they were on.

By late morning Dieter decided they were far enough
into the area to make their turn to the right and hopefully cross into Hesse. The sun was hard to see at times
and their direction had been a series of guesses. He had
counted their steps and hoped he had not been fooled
and they were in fact going in a circle as so often happened in battles.

The theory about the presence of Russian soldiers had
remained intact, though occasionally they could hear
very faint voices drift on the breeze. They spoke in whispers.

"I confess, I'm not certain of my bearings. Trees, terrain, ridges, they don't help setting a course. With the
sun overhead ..... well it doesn't help either. A compass
would be a great asset right now."

They rested and ate some of the dry tasteless food they
had left. Then they moved away on Dieter's new course.
It was harder to progress because most of the ridges
now ran across their path.

After two hours of struggling through the untidy landscape it suddenly levelled out and the trees became
larger and more sparse.

Dieter looked around. "We're either through or we've
walked back into Eisenach. I really don't know. If I knew
the time it would give me some idea."

Ahead lay some open areas with grass and forest flowers.

"Wherever we are, I don't think many people come by here. Let's sit and wait a little while. I want to be sure there's nothing happening in this area. If we're close to a town or not."

After fifteen minutes of silence interspersed with minor forest noises and birds they stood once more.
They moved forward, out of the trees, feeling vulnerable. Once across they came upon another much larger opening. Sunlight filtered by the trees made the scene quite pretty but difficult to see the other side.
"Wood smoke," Dieter commented. "I can smell it. Not sure if that is a good or bad sign."

Moving out into this cleared piece of land filled the two travellers with some foreboding but as they traversed the flowers and felt the sun they relaxed. It seemed quiet and unthreatening.
Suddenly Dieter grabbed Adriane's arm and froze.
Ahead and quite close, coated in a halo of late afternoon light they could make out the silhouette of a man with a rifle. He stood still in the far edge of the trees. It was impossible to discern any details of the figure or tell if he had seen them. They waited, realising that they too were spotlighted by a shaft of light. Then the man spoke.
"Y'all walk forward real slowly. Don't make any sudden moves and we'll git along jus' fine."
Dieter and Adriane tried to understand what the man was saying.
Two other figures joined the man. This time he motioned them forward.
"C'mon you two. Ain't gonna bite."

At that moment a loud call came from behind. A Russian voice. A shot was fired. Both Adriane and Dieter dropped to the ground. Immediately in front of them a burst of fire rang out and angry American voices called out.

His face buried in the dirt Dieter said, "I think they're firing into the air. I hope they are."

A verbal exchange was taking place above them in Russian and English. The English speakers sounded much more aggressive and angry. They understood virtually none of it but the Russian voices then faded.

Next, some boots were standing by their faces.

"C'mon you two, let's go."

Dieter and Adriane walked ahead of the three soldiers. Bayoneted rifles pointed at their backs. They trudged across more open grass area with sparse tree cover. Then they stopped while their captors held a brief conversation. They were patted down and their luggage searched. Dieter's knife was removed from the base of the briefcase.

"Nasty," said the soldier, as he threw it away into the bushes.

After this the original soldier moved back into the trees and the other two motioned for them to continue walking.

"I really can't go much further," Adriane sighed. At that same moment one of the soldiers took her suitcase.

At first she thought he was going to throw it away but he pointed ahead and continued to carry it while his companion did the rather casual gun pointing.

After a short distance the trees thinned out and they

saw the outskirts of town.

Adriane dared to whisper. "Are they American?"

"Yes," said Dieter, "and we're in a village. I think we're through."

Chapter 31

'Rolf'

As he headed back up over the strange little road Rolf
felt good. He smiled and wondered about his recent
passengers. Despite their days together he realised he
knew little about them. It did not bother him. In this war
and its consequences everybody had secrets or pre-
ferred not to expose themselves too much. Trust of your
fellows had died early in Hitler's reign. Everybody devel-
oped a degree of paranoia. It mixed badly with national
pride and xenophobia.
He had decided to return on the back road rather than
risk being asked any questions by going through Eisenach. The farmer ploughing his field was now sitting,
looking at his finished effort.
He gave him another wave. It seemed more obvious that
only those who lived along the road, actually used the
road so it was automatic to wave assuming the person
going past must be a neighbour.

Rolf paused at the main road. He waited and watched.
Traffic was light. For many minutes there would be
nothing at all. In a lull he headed forward and hoped his

timing was right. He entered onto the road that would take him home and rolled quietly along. Nobody visible in front or behind. He thought again of the girl Adriane and the quiet soldier Dieter. He missed their company and hoped they were somewhere safe.

His mind wandered to his own family, to his wife waiting for him and to the two sons he would never see again. Both killed in the early days of the war when Germany was winning everything. Their memories were already fading and the initial anguish had subsided.

There seemed to be more traffic on the road now though it was still sparse. Russian trucks. The occasional staff car. And very occasional German cars.

At one point Rolf turned into a short road to a house he knew from before the war. It was more a nostalgic visit than one of anticipation, so he was surprised to see the house he remembered still there and smoke coming from the chimney of some sheds at the back of the house.

The woman and her daughter and her elderly father were all still occupying the house and 'yes' they remembered him and 'yes' they were again making some sausage and cheese again. Rolf paid them in Reichsmarks which they both knew were of little value. He promised to bring them some produce from his farm. They were happy with the transaction. They would rather 'give food to fellow Germans than have the Russians take it.' Hence their production was low key so as not to alert the occupiers.

Rolf drove only a little way from their door before stop-

ping and trying some of the cheese and the sausage.
He thought how pleased his wife would be when he
returned with such things for their larder. Then out of
habit he unlocked the seat mechanism and stowed the
bounty out of sight.

Once more on the road he realised that the military
traffic had increased and noted with some concern that
he was approaching Sondershausen. At least this time
he would be passing and not be entering their stinking
camp.
A kilometre further on he could see some soldiers
on the side of the road. As he neared them an officer
stepped out and waved him to stop. Only one soldier
stood up to follow the officer round the truck. He had
his rifle slung and seemed disinterested. The officer
enquired in rough German the purpose of his trip. Rolf
explained about delivering food to the Russian kitchens
and said he had the paperwork.
The officer stepped back from the truck as Rolf picked
up the papers.
"No need, old man. Go, just go." He waved him on with
an air of tedium, as if the whole business was a waste of
his time.

Rolf was pleased. They were relaxing. Perhaps the initial
hatred had at least subsided and life could become
bearable once more. He revved the old truck's engine,
the thought of home had become more tantalysing.
Now he was passing the Russian camp. On both sides
the fields were covered in tents and the paraphernalia of
war and army equipment. He kept moving wishing to see

the last of the ugly place. It at last began to thin out and he felt relief as the road cleared.

Round a slight bend and Rolf had to brake. A car blocked his way. It was a little German car, stopped in a short row of traffic. About six cars ahead, the blockage was caused by a truck that had been stopped by the Russians.

Rolf peered at the scene. Everybody sat in their vehicles not moving. This was not a situation where anybody would alight, enquire or complain. You just waited.

A number of Russian soldiers surrounded the truck ahead. They were involved in a strong argument with whoever was inside. They seemed drunk and belligerent.

'That truck is American. I hope this doesn't become some sort of incident between the different forces.' Rolf thought. Then he spoke out loud.

"Good God, that's Rolf's truck."

He stumbled past the stopped vehicles toward the scene. Perhaps he could intervene and calm the situation. His friend had a fiery temper. And driving an American truck made him really stand out in any situation. Always being stopped. He would have taken issue with some minor matter and it had no doubt escalated.

Now the soldiers had the door open and were reaching inside. Their language was slurred. They were full of vodka and bravado.

"They must bring that damned drink in by the tanker load," Rolf mumbled as he headed toward the group. Two of the soldiers had their arms in the cab. They dragged a ranting, screaming little man from behind the wheel.

"You disgusting pigs. You are a disgrace to your country. If we Germans have to be defeated it should not be by drunken, mindless swine."

It is doubtful the Russians understood a word of what the man said but they could pick up the vehemence with which he spoke. Then he spat in their face.

The Russian soldier with his gun pointed at their captive pulled the trigger. He shot Rolf, the friend of Rolf in the stomach. He then shot him again in the heart. The man died immediately.

Only a few metres from the scene Rolf screamed in a mix of horror, sadness and anger. Standing, his hands outstretched, he called out. "What have you done? You bastards, you can't do this, stop this killing ...."

These were the last words of Rolf whose friend Rolf had just died. The same Russian soldier turned, his head to one side in a show arrogance and indifference and fired twice into the old man's chest

Rolf shuddered as the bullets hit him. He was not aware of falling but he was briefly aware of being on his back and looking up into the clear blue sky. He was confused and very cold. His mouth moved but he could not speak. Then it ended.

The Russians kept the American truck and used it. They simply pushed Rolf's old truck off the road. It sat there and rusted away for many years. They would have stolen his sausage and cheese and the other items behind his seat but nobody was able to unlock the device and so it was forgotten.

His wife waited at their home. After a week she knew he
would never be coming back to their farm where they
had lived all their married lives. She wept quietly at
night and held his pillow to her face.

Chapter 32

'Moving On'

Adriane Gerst and Antek Beck. Their names were taken and some initial information. They had barely time to walk into the town from the forest when they were loaded into a jeep and taken, with their luggage, on a ride to another town full of American soldiers. They passed a small contingent of German soldiers being marched along the side of the road.
"They're Luftwaffe," Dieter said. "Must be an airfield nearby. They didn't look particularly unwell or mistreated."

Once they'd stopped in a central square, Dieter shook his head.
"I'm not sure where we are. I'd ask but maybe it's better to be silent for now."
Many of the houses, they noticed, had white sheets or cloth displayed from windows and on doors. In a square, there were a lot of khaki coloured trucks with a white star on their doors. Most were transporting US soldiers but one, half empty had civilians, men, women and children seated or sleeping in the back.
They were stopped beside that truck. Their captors

motioned them to wait. They walked across the square
and spoke to another older man. The three soldiers and
the other man all looked back at the captives. He nodded and salutes were exchanged.

The older man walked across to them and spoke in
German.

"I'm Corporal Yates. US Army. We're temporarily set up
in this area. I assume you're trying to get down south or
west. Where are you trying to go?"

The answer of course was 'anywhere away from Berlin
and the Russians' but Dieter had to choose. How far
was far enough? How far was not too far?

"Kassell," he said, "we have family there."

The man looked at them for a moment.

"Well it's your lucky day, my friend. Once I've interrogated you we might get you there. You could be leaving
within an hour. You can wait in this truck here with
these other people or go to that big tent there and get
some soup and bread. It's not bad."

Adriane looked at Dieter. His face was alight. He was a
different man. It seemed they had made it through. So
quickly. So easily. Had they missed something?

Corporal Yates put his hand up.

"Okay, but first, your names once more, for my list."

He held up a wooden clipboard and raised his eyebrows.

Dieter stared at the man. He had seconds to decide
again. Should he become a captured German soldier or
stay in character?

"Beck. Dr Antek Beck. This is my wife Adriane."

The Corporal did not react in any way. He ran his finger
down some sheets of paper. He finally looked up, gave a

little half smile. "A doctor eh."
"Of philosophy," added Dieter.
The man wrote on his clipboard, nodded to himself.
"And where have you travelled from?"
Again Dieter felt a stab of uncertainty. Before he could
stop himself, he said, "Berlin."
The man made another notation. "We are definitely
going to have a talk, later."
Then stepped aside. He held his hand out and pointed.
"Soup?" he said. "When you've finished, hop in this
truck and wait."

In the tent they were handed two slices of white bread
and a bowl of hot chicken broth. It had lentils and spring
onions and small pieces of real chicken. It was thick and
rich.
They sat on a wooden bench seat at a trestle table and
slowly spooned the liquid into their mouths. American
soldiers were sitting about eating, smoking, talking.
They all seemed so relaxed.
"Oh God, this is good," Adriane said, "not since the farm
........" She trailed off.
"I seem to have a lot of chicken soup ...."
When they had finished, Dieter looked across the table.
Their eyes met. They looked down at their bowls. "I can
only ask," said Dieter.

In the corner he approached the cook sitting behind his
table with the pots steaming on a small flamed burner.
He held out his two bowls
"More?"
The cook stood slowly and easily.

"Sure."

He ladled out two more helpings, filling the bowls to the brim. He reached behind one of the pots and slid six slices of bread across next to the bowls, then almost as an afterthought he reached back again and put down a knife and an open tin half full of yellow butter.

"Knock yourself out fella," he said. "It gets tipped out in about half an hour. It's getting a bit old you see."

Dieter did not understand.

"I guess you don't see. Well off you go. Come back any time."

Dieter made two more trips for the food. Adriane sat and stared at the butter. They melted some in the soup to add another layer of enjoyment.

Dieter looked around. He looked back at the cook, deeply engrossed in a magazine.

These were the people who only months before had done their best to kill him.

Chapter 33

'Bad Hersfeld'

The people in the truck had terrible stories to tell.
Of suffering, misery, death, starvation and rape. All the
women and girls told of repeated rape at the hands
of the Russians. Of them returning night after night to
repeat the process. How some had suicided rather than
take any more.
Adriane and Dieter listened and provided sympathy
while both aware of their incredible good fortune thus
far. Nobody asked of their circumstances. They were too
traumatised to be overly curious.
When one of the women began to sob, an American
soldier sitting near the tailboard turned and angrily
snapped. "For Christ's sake will you all just shut up.
I don't want to hear anymore whining. Verstehen Sie!"
Nobody did understand, until a girl said, "The guard
says he doesn't want us to talk anymore. We must be
quiet."

The truck started its engine. They moved off again
through the countryside.
"Doesn't look like we're to be interviewed after all,"
Dieter commented.

The trip took awhile due to US Army traffic.

"Bad Hersfeld," Adriane read as they entered a new town and moved through the streets.

There seemed to be local people about. Some were taking the white sheets from their windows. The square was cobbled in grey stone. It was large and American trucks were parked round all sides. American troops were moving about, all intent on some task.

The truck guards jumped down and indicated that those on board should stay where they were.

The truck's engine stopped again.

Two other trucks rolled up beside there own. These were both full of refugees. Even some men in the remains of German uniforms.

"What are they?" asked Adriane quietly.

"More Luftwaffe. Fairly high ranks I think. I wonder where they came from?" Dieter patted Adriane's hand. "We wait. I can't see there's much to worry about here."

"Fritzlar," said a woman next to Adriane.

"Pardon?"

"Your companion asked about the Luftwaffe men." They're from the Fritzlar base. I worked there as a clerk. The Americans are using it now."

"Oh," said Dieter. "Thank you."

Fifteen minutes later they saw the figure of Corporal Yates approaching.

"So we didn't leave him behind," muttered Dieter.

He was accompanied by six soldiers with rifles and bayonets. They went to the truck furthest away. They could not see but Corporal Yates could be heard addressing

somebody in the truck. He appeared to be holding an enlarged photo on his clipboard. Whoever had been spoken to was arguing fiercely. The exact words were indistinct. The Corporal would not be swayed by the man's denials and kept refuting his claims. Finally he ordered the men onto the truck. A struggle ensued.
It became quite severe until one of the soldiers used his rifle butt several times to the captive's body and he slumped in their arms. Dragged from the truck the man was hefted away between two soldiers. Another climbed down with the man's suitcase and followed. They all disappeared into a large building on the left. It seemed to be the main focus of the US Army personnel.
"I don't want to finish up in there," Dieter confided.
It was Adriane's turn to pat the hand of her companion.

A soldier walked up to the trucks a few minutes later. He seemed neat, with a pressed, tidy uniform. He announced in German.
"You will all be billeted in the building over there."
He indicated with a wave of his arm to a three storey house at the end of the area. It looked like small hotel.
"We will walk you across, one truckload at a time. Tonight and tomorrow you will be processed and you will be given a status. If any of you are attempting to deceive us or if any of you know of anybody here who might be of interest to us I suggest you tell us all that we need to know. Failure to do so could result in consequences."

"It seems we're not going anywhere. Corporal Yates lied."

Dieter looked at Adriane as they walked across the square.

"Perhaps it's his way of keeping things calm."

Inside, on the first floor of the building, Dieter and Adriane sat on a single bed they had been ordered to share for lack of room. The building's original purpose was not so clear after all. Perhaps some civic purposes. It had been cleared out to make room just for beds.

In large groups they were marched downstairs to a room with trestle tables and fed bowls of a stew with bread. Nobody seemed interested in talk. Perhaps afraid that conversation could be seen as some sort of collusion. They all ate in silence.

After the meal they were allowed a short time in another large room to wash and clean themselves from a series of round tin basins. Hot water, soap and towels were supplied. Dieter marvelled at the efficiency of an army that could spare such items for refugees and the former enemy.

Waiting on a bench for Adriane to wash herself, he removed the dreadful shoes of the real Dr Beck and massaged his feet. He flinched not realising just how much they had crippled his toes and ankles. A GI standing nearby, his rifle slung behind, watched him with a degree of mild amusement. Dieter gave him a half-smile and shrugged indicating to the shoes in an air of resignation. The soldier gave a snort and beckoned to him with his index finger. At first Dieter did not understand. The soldier repeated the process.

"Leave the shoes, buddy. Come with me. Hergekommen."

They walked together down a corridor and entered a

room piled from floor to ceiling with army supplies. Boxes, crates everywhere.

"Hey Stevie," the soldier called. "Where's all the reject boots?"

The man Stevie pointed with the pencil he was holding to a row of crates. Once again Dieter was beckoned forward. Behind the crates, piled up the wall was a giant pile of used army boots.

"See if there's anything that suits." The soldier left Dieter and stood talking to Stevie who had that exasperated universal look of an army clerk.

Some of the boots looked as if they had come all the way from Normandy on the feet of a US soldier but others were relatively new. Dieter tried about four pairs before he found some that were a good fit.

"Hey!" Stevie called out and threw something to Dieter. A new pair of thick black woollen army socks.

Walking back Dieter summoned up a little English. He shook the soldier's hand. "Danke, Sank you, very much." The soldier gave another of his half smiles and wandered back to stand at the washroom door.

Adriane looked at the new boots. "Must have good soles. They make you look taller."

That night as they tried to sleep, curled together on the single bed, Dieter leaned over Adriane and said, "If we survive our processing tomorrow, there's something I want to ask you." He then drifted into sleep while Adriane lay awake wondering what it could be that he needed to ask.

Corporal Yates was in their room. A soldier beside him banging an empty jam tin with the back of a bayonet to wake everybody.

"We have a lot to do today, people. Please get ready and go downstairs for some breakfast. There are medics set up in the washroom. If you have any medical problems, any wounds, cuts, bruises, coughs, rashes that need attention, please have them attended to while you have the chance.

You will be called throughout the day for a processing interview. Can I suggest you be honest with us and then we will all get along just fine."

Slowly, the bleary, half-awake people filed downstairs.

"I wonder what today will bring?" said one stout haus-frau. "They're too nice. I don't trust them."

"I have a toothache," said a man. "Do you think they do teeth?"

Sitting about in the square, in the sunshine, Dieter and Adriane, their backs against a wall, watched quietly as more people appeared. Some had fresh dressings.

A woman, in a family, held a young boy with a large bandage on his leg.

"They cleaned and stitched him," she told another woman. "Gave him a needle, but still he screamed. I think he was just frightened."

Adriane looked Dieter up and down. "You may be comfortable in your new boots but they don't look that good with your suit, Dr Beck."

The first of the refugees were being walked over to the

main building. Names were called and they were escort-
ed away. There seemed no particular order to who was
called. Random or just as they appeared on some list.
Adriane looked at Dieter. "Are you worried?"
The man stared at her for some seconds. His face was
twisted in a way she had not seen before.
"I've seen things. Things no man should witness. Or
could forget. I wonder how long the Americans will stay
nice? My unit passed Buchenwald and some of its other
'subsidiaries'."
"What's Buchenwald?"
"It's why I don't want to be a German anymore. Why I
fear for the future. Why I feel so empty. When I joined
the army I was full of the nobility of the cause. We were
liberating large parts of Europe. A liberation that would
bring the benefits of being part of the larger German
state. I realised fairly quickly that not all the liberated
people were going to find our rule to their benefit. Many
were rounded up and taken away. We were told they
were criminals and riff raff."
Dieter paused and took a breath.
"Buchenwald is an extermination camp. It's a giant
complex whose sole purpose is to kill and destroy thousands and thousands of people. They were gassed, shot,
starved to death ...."
"That can't be right. Surely we'd have heard?"
"A lot have heard. They chose not to listen. And there
were many more extermination facilities just like the
ones we saw. If you'd witnessed these poor wretches.
Standing about. waiting to die. In a very mechanised
German way."
"Oh God." Adriane looked at Dieter. "This is not right."

"You know the worst of it," Dieter added. "The ones doing the killing were convinced it was all fine and for a greater good. They were proud of their 'work'.
We bunked with some of them one night. They laughed and told us how on their days off they would select a few dozen men, women and children and take them into the woods for some fun. They would say if these people could run off before 30 seconds they could go free. He said the adults knew they were doomed and did not even try to avoid being shot but the children would dodge around and made a real game of it.
They liked winging them to slow them down and then they would ...."
Adriane was crying.
"Please don't tell me any more. This is too horrible.
I can't take any more sadness. I'll try to help you forget."
Dieter hugged the girl to him.
"You're all I've got," he said, "But I'm not sure I can forget. Then he added, "The Americans must know of these things. What is their plan?"

As the morning progressed Adriane fell asleep on Dieter's shoulder. He was pleased to see that most of the people who were called were not gone for long and came out with some papers. They were taken into the house to collect their possessions and then to a different part of the square to wait once more.
In the warmth and with nothing to occupy his mind, Dieter too closed his eyes.
"Adriane Beck. Wo ist Adriane Beck?"
Dieter woke. Adriane too was blinking. "Here," she said, raising her arm, "I'm here." She climbed to her feet and

joined the group moving away. She looked back at Dieter
gesturing. Why were they being interviewed separately?
He watched her heading across the square as another large group emerged with their papers. There was
a brief holdup at the door and then she disappeared
inside with the rest of the group.
His assumption, now foolish in retrospect, was that
they would be interviewed together and that he could
control the answers they gave. He hoped Adriane would
reinforce their story.

The last group that had emerged as Adriane entered the
army building, now filed into the sleeping quarters to
fetch their belongings. As they passed, Dieter noticed
one elderly man smiling at him. The man nodded in
quite a friendly manner and continued to look. He was
unknown to Dieter.
When they emerged a few minutes later the man again
looked at Dieter. He was about to speak when the guards
ushered them on across the space to sit near one of the
trucks.

A soft peace settled over the area. The sun rose higher
and became warmer. The people who had been first
through their interviews were loaded into a truck. After
sitting awhile with its motor running the truck suddenly
moved off and was gone.
It was now that Dieter noticed the smiling man talking
to a guard. There seemed to be a lot of explaining and
lack of understanding. Then another person joined the
conversation and after a short time the guard seemed to
give up his resistance. He waved his hand sideways and

the smiling man began making his way across the space toward Dieter.

When he reached Dieter he hitched his trousers and sat down against the wall. Leaning forward he held out his hand. "Hullo, my name Eric Graf."
Dieter shook the man's hand. "I'm sorry sir, I don't know you."
"No, no," said the man, "Of course you don't. But we both know Adriane, it would seem. I just noticed her as we passed. You are with Adriane Gerst aren't you?"
Dieter hesitated. He considered this could be a trap and the man was working for the Americans. He decided to take the risk. "Yes, I'm with Adriane. She is my wife."
"Ahh. Wonderful." The man sighed. "I'm not sure how long I have. Somebody who could speak English helped me out just then with that American soldier. They tell us over there that we will be going shortly. I'm trying to get to my brother. It's my only chance. There may not be time."
"I'm sorry. Time for what?"
"To say hullo to sweet little Adriane of course. We were neighbours. I read her stories. She sat with me at our kitchen table many times. She loved our pumpkin soup. I watched her grow." The man paused. He squinted. "May I boldly ask how well you know Adriane? I assume your marriage is recent?"
"We've been together for some time. In Berlin. We got out. We hope to find somewhere to go."
"Then you know her well? You know what happened to her?"
"Yes, everything. All her story."

"Ahh," said the man again. He seemed relieved. "That's good. I feel quite proud you know. Our little secret. Our little Jew. The whole village protected her you know. All of us. Not one said a word. As far as those that needed to know, did know, she was a daughter of the Gerst family. She helped her cause be being so sweet, so pretty. An angel in fact. Tough, clever, a good worker. She would visit us for cake and coffee. I let her pick books to read. Helped her with the big words." The man stopped. "Where is the rest of her family? I left before them."

Dieter sat next to Eric Graf. He felt numb. This news sitting in his mind. He became aware of the question. And he did know the answer.

"Oh, I'm terribly sorry. They are all dead. Murdered by the Russians. Adriane watched it all from a field. That is why she came to Berlin."

Eric Graf let out a cry of anguish. He clutched his forehead and gave little sobs. "Oh my God," he said at last. "We were just farmers. That's all. No harm to the Third Reich, no harm to Stalin, just farmers. God, God, God, why? I went to school with the Gersts. We were at each other's weddings. What a stupid waste this has all been." He lapsed into silence.

Across at the trucks the group from which Eric Graf had emerged were beginning to climb into a truck. The man looked to be in a panic.

"Oh," he said in some distress. "She's not out. I'm not going to see my Adriane." He wrung his hands. "I can't tell my wife about the Gersts. Now I'll have to tell her we have missed Adriane."

The truck sounded its horn. Across with the group the soldier waved his arm to Eric Graf. As he stood, Dieter looked up at him and decided to ask a question.

"What happened to Adriane's family?"

The man looked down. "Oh, so she didn't tell that bit. She didn't tell you that? Well, she was only two or younger. Perhaps it's a part she wants to keep. They drowned. Simple as that. One of those silly accidents that should not happen. In a car at night. The bridge on our small river has an odd sharp bend before you turn onto it. The parents and Adriane were driving through at night. He was a draftsman apparently. On their way to a job I think. The car went in the river. By the time some people reached the car the parents were dead. Frau Gerst said she would care for Adriane. They had been trying for a baby for some time. She took on the notion that she could keep Adriane. Checks were made. No relatives came forward. The town council voted. Papers were prepared and the secret began. Jews were just people then. Only later did it become necessary to be careful. Strangely, Frau Gerst then had her babies. Two sons. She named one of them Eric for me." The man stopped at the memory, then he added, "But they all still loved Adriane."

The truck blasted its horn again and the soldier waved angrily. All the people were on the truck.

"Life is just endlessly sad," said Eric. "Please tell Adriane that the Graf's send their fondest love and will continue to think of her." He turned to go then looked back at Dieter. "Please give your word young man. You will love and protect our girl and give her a decent life."

He waited.

Dieter nodded. "I will, Eric Graf. You have my solemn word. I will do that."

The man marched away. At the truck he gave a brief wave as he climbed aboard. The tailgate slammed and he was gone.

"Ulla Zirkel, Oskar Glanzer, Antek Beck, Kristin Sohner, Reinhold Glanzer. Kommen Sie bitte mit mir."

Five people stood and followed the young German-speaking private to the door on the other side of the square. The door from which Adriane had not yet emerged.

Inside they were walked upstairs to small room with chairs around the wall. Dieter had hardly been seated when he heard the name again.

"Dr Antek Beck."

He followed the private along the corridor. The man opened a door and held out his hand to indicate entry. Inside, behind a small desk sat Corporal Yates. At his back Antek had noticed an American MP guarding the closed door.

"Please, Dr Beck, sit down."

Once seated Corporal Yates looked into Dieter's eyes until he became uncomfortable.

"Our little chat, Dr Beck, will be brief. We're just here to establish identity and then send people on their way. Nothing nasty." He paused and tapped his pencil on the desk. On a large manilla folder. "Unless of course, you're somebody we're looking for. Then things are quite different. There are people from your armed forces and people from your government and people from your industry and others, who we very much want to talk to. People who have done evil things, horrible things, people who have ordered such things. There are a lot of very bad people in Germany at the moment Dr Beck. We want to bring them to justice. We're also looking for the men and women who have been the 'inventors' of your Nazi war machine. The clever people who made many of the weapons that have been used to kill so many people round the world." He paused again. "People like you, Dr Beck."

Dieter could feel the skin on his face becoming hot.

"So, Dr Beck. What a coup it is for me, to catch one of the men from Peenemunde. One of the perpetrators of the rocket attacks on Europe. I'm surprised you continued using your name. You're not a doctor of philosophy. You, are a very clever, possibly evil scientist. An engineer in fact, specialising in aerodynamics. And some justice certainly awaits you."

Dieter could take no more. He felt sick. Tough soldier he was but he could feel a terrible mistake was about to be made. He held up his hands, staring at the Corporal.

"I'm not Dr Antek Beck," he blurted out. "I'm Dieter Falke. Oberleutnant in the 9th Fallschirmjaeger Regiment."

Corporal Yates sat staring back at Dieter Falke. Then he gave a little chuckle. "Pleased to meet you Lieutenant Falke. I admire men who jump out of aeroplanes. Very dangerous. Of course you're not Antek Beck, you look nothing like him."

The corporal took a large photo from the manilla envelope and held it up. It showed a tall thin man with a tiny black moustache. He was in a striped suit, glancing sideways at the camera, holding a cigarette. He had thin framed, rimless glasses. He looked every inch a scientist.

"Now," said Corporal Yates, "I'd like to know why a German soldier has turned up at this base not only using Dr Beck's name but carrying what seem to be some of his belongings and I suspect, wearing some of his clothes. You must admit that's pretty curious. We didn't find anything hidden in his shoes. Would you like to tell me a whole lot more Lieutenant?"

Chapter 34

'The Corporal'

After two hours Corporal Yates called for a break.
He had listened to Dieter's story. He had questioned and
checked every part of it. His life in Dresden. Univeristy.
His leap from a plane in the Battle of the Bulge. His rear-
guard fight all the way to Berlin. The death of his entire
family in Dresden. His friendship with Hauke Kluge.
His final battle in a hopeless last stand in the streets
of Berlin. His discovery of the bombed building and
his meeting up with Hauke and Adriane in the top floor
apartment. Their life together in Antek Beck's apartment.
Their plans to leave as a family. The SS snipers arriving
and the storming of the building by Russians. The death
of Hauke. Their fleeing from the Russian territory.
He did not mention killing Russian soldiers in the street
or the apartment.
Corporal Yates was suspicious. "You seem to have an
inordinate fear of the Russians, my friend. They're allies
of America. Why did you need to get away from them so
badly? Why not just stay who you are? I believe they're

letting regular soldiers go home. Why become Dr Beck? Logic would suggest you have much more chance of moving from place to place as a defeated, demoralised soldier than as a man who could be of considerable interest to the Allied Armies.

What do you say about this? Your story is all quite believable except for your decision to be Beck. What do you say?"

Dieter decided to stay with his account. "I've found many decisions in life are rendered insensible in retrospect, sir. At the time, talking with Adriane and the boy, we thought we would appear of less interest if we were just some nondescript family of refugees. What could be less interesting than a doctor of philosophy?"

This response brought a slight smile to the Corporal's face. It was here that he called a break.

Dieter was left in the room with just the MP. He was given a mug of coffee and some biscuits. After fifteen minutes, Corporal Yates returned carrying his own coffee. Behind him, ushered in by a guard came Adriane. She looked at Dieter, her eyes neutral.

"You may sit side by side but do not speak and don't look at each other."

The American sat looking through his notes. Finally he looked up again.

"Now here's the interesting thing. I've spent a fair amount of time with both of you. And despite my best efforts your stories match up quite well. So, I must assume that you've either rehearsed everything to perfection or you're telling me the truth. I tend to think the latter. I also feel you're leaving something or things out of your story."

"I assure you ...." Dieter was silenced by the Corporal's upturned hand.

"While I was having my coffee it occurred to me that your story really doesn't matter. If you are who you say you are then I have no real interest in you. But I do have a lot of interest in Dr Antek Beck and hell people, you spent weeks living in his apartment. A place that is not available for me to visit. Protocol you see."

He paused.

"So here's my offer. You tell me every and I mean 'every' detail of that apartment, it's contents, the papers you saw, the books you read, what was in the cupboards, the furnishing, the pictures on the wall, no matter how insignificant you think it might be, I want to know. I want you to walk me through that apartment. I want to think I'm there."

He paused and leaned his face on his hands.

"Now here's the deal. If and only if, I think you've been suitably helpful, I'll organise transport for you to somewhere safe and I'll see if I can find somewhere for you to live."

He paused again, then decided to add to his pitch.

"Need I remind you that there are millions of displaced, lost, homeless and often starving people out there on the roads. From what you've told me, you seem to have avoided most of these problems and here I am making you an offer that will deliver you even more grace."

"Or you could take us to the nearest woods and shoot us."

It was Adriane who had spoken. "After we've given you the information."

Dieter looked at Adriane in surprise, then to the Corporal.

"It's not the way we work, ma'am. At this point in time I have no great love of the German people but you have my word as an officer in the United States Army. I will follow through on my offer."

"But you will shoot Dr Beck if you find him." said Dieter.

"Boy oh boy," said Corporal Yates. "None of your business really but no, my friends, nobody is going to be shot. We will give him a chance to impart his knowledge to our people. He's a very clever man. Simple. We'd like him to work for us. Bring himself and his family over to meet our scientists and they can all work together. That will be his only choice mind you. So don't hold back because he's one of your countrymen. It won't be good for any of us."

Adriane spoke again. "Then there's something I'd like to give you."

Both the Corporal and Dieter looked at the girl.

"What?"

"Can I go to my suitcase?"

Corporal Yates looked at his subordinate. He spoke in English.

"They have suitcases? I thought it was just the briefcase?"

"We checked them, Sir. Clothes and some food."

In German he said to Adriane.

"What is it you're going to get?"

"A quite fat notebook." She paused. "Hauke liked it. I brought it along as a little surprise for him when we ended our journey. It still has a lot of blank pages. It just occured to me that the notes in it may be of interest."

"Oh you think so!"
Corporal Yates motioned Adriane and his junior officer
out the door.
"Go. Look very carefully this time. Bring anything of
interest."

Eating their evening meal, back in their quarters, Adriane asked, "Is their anything we forgot to tell him?"
"I don't think so."
"I'm sorry I cried."
"Don't be concerned. The man understood."
"I kept seeing Hauke as we talked."
"He was everywhere in my thoughts too. I remember he did like writing and doing little sketches."
"The Corporal seemed to like the notebook. I wonder if they'll find him? Did we give them any clues?"
"It's hard to say."

Later as they sat watching the sky in the twilight, two old men joined them. They brought out four chairs.
"Don't sit on the cold ground," they said, "you may as well be comfortable."
The conversation was stilted. The old men were executives from Krupps armaments. A particular interest for the Americans it seemed.
"I don't trust them," said one. "They are hunting people. All sorts of people. Don't fool yourself that they are going about the country giving refugees free rides. It's a filtering process. They have lists."
The other man added, "Why does it matter? The war is over. Germany is destroyed. Why don't they let us live in

peace now? We could do quite nicely if they'd go away and leave us alone."

Dieter looked from one to the other.

"I don't think that's how it works in wars. The winners don't pack up and go home. There will be retribution. Quite a lot I'd imagine. I'm no longer a proud German."

"Have you forsaken your Fatherland?" said the first man.

"I've seen what we've done. I've spoken to others. Been told of terrible things. If even half is true, the world will not forgive us or leave us in peace. No wonder they have lists. The Russians I suspect have much longer lists."

There was silence. All four people awkwardly looked at the sky.

A first star had appeared.

"Funny," one of the men said, "after all we've been through, the world is still here. It always has been. We just stopped noticing it."

He reached into his coat and took out a leather case. From it he took two small silver cups and a silver flask.

"We'll have to share. I only have two cups. I had my little travelling flask with nothing in it. Now it's full."

He looked around.

"It's whisky. Scottish whisky. I traded it with a British soldier for a medal I had. I thought, who needs a medal for productivity for a factory that no longer exists? Now ......"

The man poured out the liquid into the two cups.

"A toast. Either it's a bullet in the forest or some sort of future. Prost."

Chapter 35

'Transport'

Four days later, the young private who spoke German
came to see them after breakfast.
"Our records show that when you were first in contact
with us you indicated that you wished to go to Kassell,
because you have family there. I assume that was a lie?"
Dieter saw no point in disagreeing. "Yes, that was a lie.
I thought you needed to hear something like that."
The man continued. "It's of no consequence. We have
some intelligence from that region that suggests it
would be a suitable area anyway. There is some avail-
ability." Seeing that his message was not being fully
understood, he added. "To fulfil the obligation Corporal
Yates has with you two, vis a vis, somewhere to live."
He held his hands out, palms upward and raised his
eyebrows. "Well? Does that suit?"
Dieter looked at Adriane. "Yes. Yes, okay that would be
suitable."
"Good," said the soldier with curt nod of his head. I'll
make some arrangements. Be ready to leave this afternoon."

He spun around and walked away. Efficient and officious.
"Things happen quickly with us," said Adriane. "I wonder when our luck will run out?"
Dieter looked at her, then stepped forward and em-
braced the girl, resting his chin on her shoulder. After
a moment he said, "Whatever it is, we'll know soon
enough. Let's pack our few possessions."

At 1.30pm a US soldier appeared at their side as they
sat looking out the window. "Gehen zu Kassell," he said
indifferently. He waited a few seconds. "Let's go. C'mon."
They took their bags and descended to the marketplatz
square. Dieter wore US army pants and along with his
boots and a blue shirt the Americans had obtained from
somewhere. They had also given him a black flight jacket. All of Antek Beck's possessions including his clothes
were retained by Corporal Yates.
The soldier led them across to an old Dodge half-size
truck. It had a tarpaulin covered back with a faded red
cross on a white square. He threw their cases in and
then ushered his two passengers into the back. He was
chewing gum. He seemed disinterested in them, as if
they were an interruption to his life.
The truck had a padded bench seat along one side and a
larger bench opposite presumably to take patients.
They heard the soldier climb into the truck's cab. He
started the motor, then gave a long blast on the horn.
Shortly after. the crunching of boots brought two more
soldiers to the back of the truck. Climbing in they took
up positions each side of the rear. Another soldier
closed to tailgate. They heard him getting into the front
cab.

With a couple of misses of the gears and some jerking
movements, accompanied by curses, they moved off.
The two soldiers with Adriane and Dieter were both
smoking. One wore sunglasses.
Apart from a brief look they ignored the two passengers.

After winding through the streets of Bad Hersfeld
the truck eventually gathered a little speed. Some
fields could be seen outside. They slowed a little then
stopped. From the cabin voices were raised.
"We're here. You go right. I thought you'd done this
before?"
"Okay, it all looks the damn same, sometimes."
The truck shuddered off, turning right. A few more fields
passed and then they entered a forested area. The trees
were quite dense on both sides. Sunlight flickered on the
sides of the tarpaulin.
A short way into the forest the truck began revving its
engine. The driver changed up and down through the
gears, slowing and then shaking along a bit further.
Finally, with more revving which seemed to produce
very little forward movement, the truck swung to the
side and stopped.
The two soldiers in the back leaned out of the opening.
They were joined by the two from the truck's cab.
All four soldiers then stood a short way away from the
truck and spoke together. They seemed to be trying to
come to a decision. They pointed into the forest. One
shrugged his shoulders.
The two guards from the rear then returned.
"Out of the truck, you two. Last stop. You're not going
any further."

Neither Dieter nor Adriane fully understood but it was obvious they were meant to alight. Once out the soldier in sunglasses said, "Go for a walk. Stretch your legs." He pointed into a clear area next to the truck. "Go on, get over there were we can see you."
Dieter took Adriane's hand and they walked into the clearing. There were some fallen trees on the far side on which they could sit. It was a bright, pleasant day. War had not touched this place. Already, small yellow and white flowers were sprouting on the forest floor. Dieter looked over his shoulder, back to the truck. The two soldiers had their rifles out and were doing something with them. He gripped Adriane's hand tighter and leaned toward her.
"There's something I need to ask you. I keep putting it off but it's urgent and I want to know."
"What?" asked Adriane, feeling the tightness of Dieter's grip.
"Simple question but hard to say. Can't wait, now. Adriane, will you marry me?"
After a slight pause, Adriane looked up at Dieter with a beaming smile and said, "Yes, of course I will." Then she looked puzzled. "Why is it urgent?"
"I wanted to know before .... I think they're about to shoot us."
Adriane gave a gasp and looked back to the road. The two soldiers had their rifles across their chests in the ready position. The passenger from the front was watching them. The driver was using a big walkie talkie.
She could see it all. Once the final go-ahead was received, the rifles would be raised and their lives ended. They would be left right here amongst the flowers in the

forest.

Frantically she grabbed Dieter and said, "Hold me. Please hold me. Don't let me go."

They stood in the centre of the clearing with the light on their heads, the warmth on their shoulders, the smell of pine and early spring about them and waited for the end to their brief lives together. Both had their eyes closed and their heads bowed and pressed together.

Dieter thought, "We make an easy target this way. Hopefully it will be quick."

He considered running but the clearing was large, they would not make it into the trees.

Despite facing death so many times he felt sad that now he was going to be shot this way. Not heroically with some greater purpose but just wasted. A job to be done. A matter to be cleared up and finalised. He felt anger that after all of the life he had lived, he now held somebody that he realised he really loved without conditions and he could do nothing to help her. He felt anger too that the Americans had lied to them, had built their hopes up with a deal and now they were going to prove themselves to be a miserable and unworthy lot.

Minutes passed without a sound. A bird called and fluttered through the clearing. It gave a squeak above their heads and then joined a companion and they flew off. Dieter lifted his head. He could feel Adriane shaking in his arms. He stole a glance. He felt sick with anticipation. He realised they were both perspiring. He blinked to clear his eyes. The two soldiers were sitting on the truck's tailboard. They were smoking. Their rifles lay on the ground.

The truck passenger sat on the running board writing on some paper attached to a clipboard. The driver had the truck's bonnet up and was peering into the engine. Sitting on the fallen trees at the far side of the clearing, the two passengers now heard the sound of a truck engine through the trees. Eventually another Dodge ambulance pulled in behind their vehicle. A man alighted. He walked round to the open engine compartment of their truck and looked inside for a minute, then looked underneath. Even at a distance he was obviously a mechanic. There was a discussion and some pointing. A bit of backslapping from their driver, as if he had just pulled off a good deal.

"Hey, you two. Move it. C'mon!" Suddenly things were happening again.

Their driver was calling across to thcm waving his arms. Their luggage was being thrown into the back of the second truck.

As soon as they were seated the soldiers jumped in and the tailgate was slammed shut. This second vehicle pulled away without effort and powered along.

"Trust Brewster," said one soldier.

"Yeah," said the other. "Six of these to choose from and he picks the dud. Told ya it was the clutch."

"Bet Sammy got that baby going as soon as we left. Nuthin' he can't fix."

Adriane understood none of the conversation, so she tried a smile. The soldiers looked at her briefly then ignored her. She looked instead at Dieter. His face was still pale.

She leaned closer. "Is the offer you made still standing?"

"Of course it is. You'll have to forgive me, I'm not too

brilliant at relationships."

"It's odd," said Adriane, "Corporal Yates didn't query our situation."

"Well, he either didn't care or he was quite insightful. In the end he probably didn't care. We were just two people with some information."

As the truck moved closer to Kassel they passed US Army traffic. There were quite a number of refugees along the roadside. They were not necessarily moving, just camped by the road. There seemed to be collections of furniture and oddments of household equipment. The faces of these people seemed resigned to their tenuous existence.

The soldiers were commenting.

"Hell, what an existence."

"Guess it doesn't pay to go starting wars."

"Have you seen Kassel?"

"Naw, haven't been there."

"Bombed the crap out of it, I tell ya. Real mess."

Now they turned off their road onto a smaller road on the left and began making their way through the countryside. The terrain became hilly. They wound past farms and fields. Some clean and untouched, others damaged or burnt. Dieter could no longer contain his curiosity.

"Entschuldigen Sie mich. Wohin gehen wir?"

The soldier with the sunglasses looked across. "What's that fella? Where are we going?"

"Ja, Ja."

"Willingen. We're going to Willingen." The soldier added

an aside to the others. "Providin' o course da driver has some freakin' idea how to get there." The soldiers all smirked.

Dieter turned to Adriane. "Willingen?"

"I don't know it," she said.

At 4.30pm the truck, having made its way round several detours and backtracked past the town, ground to a halt on a high part of the road. There were discussions from the cab. The map was produced once more.

"Is this it?"

"I dunno. Seems about right but how do you tell?"

"Is there anybody round we can ask?"

"Hey, hang on, look, there's some guy waving. Way over, next to the house. This must be it. Open the gate."

Doors slammed and the truck drove in an opening, under a covered entrance between two stone walls and proceeded along a neat gravel road for a short distance then swung round and stopped.

A man was speaking in German. Another voice said, "Oh this is where it gets difficult. Hang on buddy just hang on."

The passenger from the cab appeared at the back. He beckoned to Dieter and Adriane. Once they had climbed out he said, "None of us speak German. It's over to you two now. Here read this."

Of course he spoke in English.

He handed Dieter a thick white envelope and motioned for it to be opened.

Dieter pulled out about five sheets of paper all in German. The top sheet was titled United Sates Army of Occupation, followed by a typed message.

A man appeared round the side of the truck. He held out
his hand. "I'm Egon Kingele. I represent the local com-
mittee. I'm also your neighbour. I have to make sure you
are here and that you understand that this is where you
now live. Is this all clear to you?"

He was a squat man with big shoulders and huge fore-
arms. He had a bald pate, ringed by black hair and a
large drooping compensatory moustache. He wore dark
blue trousers tucked into gumboots and a shirt that
may have fitted once but now had a stomach to contend
with.

Eliciting no response he continued.

"I don't know why the Americans put you here but if you
sign my paper they will pay me. Who knows, we may
talk about all this one day. My house is just there. Not
too far. We could wave if we get along or ignore each
other if we don't." He gave a little gurgling laugh to indi-

cate his attempt at humour.

For the first time Dieter Falke and Adriane Gerst looked around trying to adjust to the information and their situation. They were in a paved courtyard. To their left stood a tidy two storey farmhouse. Old and tired looking but rather nice. Its lower level was made of stone while the upper floor was timber. Next to the house was what appeared to be a good-sized vegetable garden, though it was obvious at a glance that all the produce therein had been taken. There was also an orchard. Past the garden and set back was a giant barn. One side was in fine condition with large wooden doors. The right hand side of the building was charred and damaged with the blackened frame timbers showing the previous extent of the building. The buildings were on the top of a small hill. To each side the land sloped gently away providing a view across other farms and fields. Opposite the gate where they had entered, stood a substantial pine forest.

"I'm sorry," Adriane said, "we didn't know about this until we arrived just now. It's hard to grasp it all."

The truck driver could take no more.

"Oh for Christ's sake. I don't know what you krauts are blathering about and guess what, I don't care."

He grabbed the piece of paper from Egon Kingele's hand and led Dieter by the arm to the bonnet of the truck. He produced an indelible pencil from his top pocket and jammed his finger on a line at the bottom of the form.

"Sign the damn thing already." He made writing motions with his hand and then gave the pencil to Dieter while nodding and smiling as you would with a slow child.

Dieter signed.

"Right," said the man, handing the paper back to Egon.

"That's it ladies. We done our bit. We delivered the goods and the guy got his paper signed. We're done. We're gone. You're on your own. Don't know. Don't care. Thanks for yer sparklin' company."

The Americans all climbed hurriedly back in the truck. The motor revved and they moved off, only to stop after a short distance.

One of the soldiers climbed down from the back and dragged a cardboard box from under the seat.

He walked over and dumped it on the ground.

"From Corporal Yates. To keep you alive for a few days. Yeh, I know, don't understand a word I'm saying. All I can say is you two musta done the man a huge favour."

He pointed at his mouth and then at the box.

They watched the truck roar off with unnecessary haste.

In the silence Dieter turned to Egon Kingele, his new neighbour.

"Thank you for your help. Do you mind if we leave our details for another day? As we said, we knew nothing of this until now. We seem to own a house. It is .... a lot to absorb. What do we have here?"

The man smiled. "No, of course not." He looked about. "This place has eighteen acres. Both sides of this are yours. At the end of your field is a nice creek. Your neighbours beyond have thirty acres. They grow hops for the local brewery. Beyond them is a pig farm. I have forty acres and I grow everything I can. I have some prize winning pigs as well."

"Were they bombed?" Dieter indicated to the barn.

Egon shook his head. "No, they stored fresh hay. It combusted and set the building alight."

"What happened to the people here?"

"A little too much enthusiasm for war I would say. Their two sons joined up and were both killed. They were very keen members of the party. They died in what was probably the last bombing raid on Kassel. Attending a party meeting. I have to be honest, they were not nice people."

He screwed up his face and inclined his head and asked, "Are you a farmer by any chance?"

"No," said Dieter, then he looked at the girl beside him. "Oh well Adriane is of course. She grew up on a farm but me ....."

Egon drew a breath. "Well, you'll learn. You'll have to. Between this lovely girl and me perhaps you'll become excellent. It's peaceful here. This area has survived. Time to reflect. If you see what I mean. You help me and I can help you. Eh?"

Then he added, spreading his arms.

"And some day if you feel like sharing, I would be most interested to know how this all happened. I am naturally a curious person." He shrugged. "And I talk too much."

He reached into the pocket of his pants and handed Adriane a big iron key. "Perhaps you would like to open the door of your house. I'll leave you in peace now."

As he walked away, cutting down through what was their land, Dieter called after him.

"Are there any priests in the area?"

Egon stopped and turned.

"Yes. Two in fact. Are you troubled?"

"No," Dieter called, "I want to arrange a marriage."

Chapter 36

'Willingen'

The cardboard box contained a dozen, full day, army ra-
tion packs. They carried it to the porch. Adriane turned
the key in the substantial old oak door. The lock clacked
open. They had to push the door. Inside, in the small
entranceway paved in stone, Dieter put the box down
and took Adriane by the shoulders. He looked at her.
She looked back.
"Are you sure? I need reassurance."
"Yes," she said, "I'm sure. When you're not being a soldier, you're the nicest man I've ever met. Marrying you
would be wonderful." She added, "Do you know we've
never really kissed. I mean properly."
Dieter Falke, Wehrmacht soldier and man in control,
looked abashed.
As they kissed and he felt her young body against him
he made a pact within himself to never reveal his knowledge of her past. It helped his feelings. He felt that this
was love. He felt he belonged to something once more.
Holding somebody who wanted to be with him was the
most wonderful sensation.

At almost the same time, in the recesses of her mind, Adriane decided she would never speak of her ordeal at the hands of the monster Brunek. She thanked God he had not made her pregnant.
Now they both held secrets that would see them to their graves.

They walked together into the parlour. The room smelt dank, closed and unused. It needed windows open and air to circulate. It had a huge lounge set around a fire-place. The lounge chairs were covered in rich dark rose coloured tapestry. Beyond, in a large nook with a step up, stood a big dining table and eight chairs. The furniture was all solid and dark. Through the bay windows they could see the fields. Their fields!
"This is a big house," commented Dieter.
"I feel like a trespasser."
"I suppose we will for while. It would be good to replace their items with our own but we have nothing. So we'll have to pretend. When I saw the barn I thought, is it just me or is there some irony in the fact that we have inherited another building with a side missing."
"Another magic room." Adriane looked up at Dieter.
"Our boy would have loved this one even more," he said.

As the evening came they explored the house, ate some US Army rations and wandered through the various rooms. The larder was bare unlike their previous abode. Probably cleaned out by the neighbours. The bedroom, where they would sleep together that night, lay untouched. It had a grand view of their little orchard.

Much of the family's possessions and personal affects
were still there.

"We've only met one but I suspect these locals are an
honest lot," said Dieter, "it's a good sign."

As was their nature, the pair were as pragmatic as ever.
With their previous experience of living in another person's world they accepted their surroundings, put any
issues aside and saw only their future and their possibilities.

August 1946

Egon had brought them a leg of pork and ten minutes of
local gossip. In return he left with tomatoes and eggs.
Dieter was on the roof of the barn tying down the last
of the new shingles. It was whole once more. He was
immensely pleased with the result of nearly a year's
work. The timber alone had taken months to locate and
obtain.

The garden next to the house was full of vegetables.

A limited batch of apples had appeared on the trees of
the small orchard by the barn. Egon advised them that
they needed to be fertilised properly. It would be a few
years before they had a bumper harvest. The previous
owners had not looked after the orchard.

Only one crop grew in their fields but they were happy
to look out across a sea of high green corn in the main
field near the house. Egon's idea.

"Corn grows fast and it's easy. Everybody likes corn.
People, cows, turkeys and geese. It keeps in storage.
Perfect for you."

Their farm owned two cows, ten chickens and one rooster.

Surviving the winter was not easy. Their two neighbours helped with what they could spare and both Dieter and Adriane had repaid them with their labour. Little was said of the previous owners or the circumstances that led to their own occupation of the farm. They would tell their whole story when the time was right. Egon was keen to know so they had given him basic information. With the radio speaking of ongoing trials and retribution it was a time to say little.

Dieter gathered that the last owners of their farm had been avoided because of their Party connections. People who could do you harm if they were upset.

Egon had turned into a make do parent for the newly weds. Beaming in the little local church as he presented Adriane for her marriage to Dieter. His wife Martha had sat in the pews dabbing her eyes and proclaiming how much she loved weddings.

Many displaced and desperate Germans and other races roamed the country for some time. They asked for food that Dieter and Adriane did not have and slept in their barn, too sick or tired to move on. One stole a chicken. Their last visitor was a lost soldier. He had stayed for some weeks, working hard round the fields but always with a desperate, melancholy demeanour. Then he received news that his family were safe and had changed back to a revived, reborn human and departed hurriedly to reunite with them.

Now on this bright summer day in early afternoon, Dieter realised he had not seen any refugees or beggars for a month.

Perhaps as the weather warmed and the nation adjusted to peace they were all at last finding a place to settle and make a future. He looked down to the house and the yard. Adriane was hanging out some washing. The sun shone on her slim pretty figure. In the town she was given some nice, cotton frocks from a charity group. She became feminine again.

Egon took them into town in his truck whenever they wanted a lift with him.

Adriane's figure was changing in shape. From his vantage point Dieter could detect a slight bulge on her abdomen. It filled him with a joy he had never known before. The weary horrors of his past would be with him till his last breath but for now they were pushed to the back as the sun shone, birds sang and there was no smoke on the horizon.

He sat on the barn roof admiring the extensive views he was afforded by its height. The roads and fields were all empty. Those who might be seen about were probably having some lunch. The day was warm and still with no breeze. The earth sparkled beneath his gaze.

As a person born and raised in a city he found secret enjoyment in the idea of space and a certain amount of room. Of walking more than twenty metres and still being on his land. Sound, or the lack of it was another phenomenon. The world did not rush into his ears in a mix of life and machinery. Humanity kept its distance and so did its need to make noise. Cities hummed and vibrated. They did not rest at night as did the countryside. Here sounds were afar and indistinct. Not a cacophony. Each was recognisable. Somebody calling out, a cow, a goat, horses being prepared for the day, the clang of metal, somebody hammering. At night the earth was still and silent. It was possible to see stars.

For a moment Dieter considered all of the events in his life. Particularly since 1940 when his existence came under threat by the decisions of a man who led his country into a form of hell.

He and his wife were orphans of that hell. It had taken everything they knew and loved and left them alone with only each other. He could not therefore say that they were 'lucky', just more fortunate than most.

Something caught Dieter's eye. He turned his head. At a distance, way off on the road, a sole figure was making it's way up the hill. Perhaps he had decided too soon that all the refugees were gone. It could of course be a local. Though most people did their walking early in the morning or in late afternoon to avoid the summer heat.

He lost interest and went back to his musing. Adriane looked up and they waved.

"You should get down now. You'll fall asleep and slip off." She laughed. It was a good laugh.

Having a person who cared about you and loved you so unconditionally was an experience that Dieter still found beautiful. A few times he tried to put into words his own joyful feelings of affection for his wife. They were stumbling, badly formed expressions but as part of her love Adriane understood and their bond only increased.

He smiled as he looked down at her hanging more of their washing on their line. The peace he felt would have to go unexpressed.

He lay back, hands behind his head. High up in the blue sky, the faint sound of some large aircraft droned overhead. Probably American, probably cargo planes.
His country was divided into zones. He thanked good fortune for the decision to leave Berlin and get away from the Russians. They were not to be trusted.
He squinted at the sky to make out the four black specks moving above. His eyes closed.
At once he was transported to a cold forest. Wet, filthy and afraid. The jagged blasts of light from the American shell fire had stopped. Their planes roared overhead. They owned the skies and could seek and destroy anything in their path. Now the Americans were in the woods, looking for the last of the German paratroopers. He could fight. Kill some Americans. What was the point? It would save nothing and prove nothing. Whether he was dead or alive, Germany would fall and the humiliation would begin.
August Haas lay beside him. The small indentation in the ground afforded little protection. Together they had flopped into it as the shelling began. The other men had scattered.
August rolled over and looked at his friend.
"Dieter, you know, I don't give a shit about the Americans. They can have this damned forest and all the others between here and wherever they're going. All our officers are dead and we're next. What do you say my friend. Lets, ... let's 'disappear.'"
Dieter's eyes had grown accustomed to the darkness. They were on top of a slight slope. To their left appeared

to be a long deep channel. The sort of terrain that would allow advancing troops to move forward unseen. He motioned to August to be quiet and pointed to the area behind. He thought he saw a shape in the channel. As August turned and lifted his head to peer back into the darkness, there was a flash and a crack. Just a single shot. August gave a grunt and fell directly on top of Dieter. Blood rushed from his face and over the pair of them. No chance to run. Await capture or death. Voices came closer.

"Did you get him?"

"Yup, pretty sure."

"Better check."

The sound of slithering across dirt and leaves. Voices right above.

"Oooh yeh. Clean shot. Let's go, stay low."

The boots stomped away and Dieter lay for some time under his dead friend. When he pushed him off and sat up, he thought he would be seen and shot. Nothing happened. Figures passed by, nobody noticed him.

He sat with his friend, numb and alone through the night. As morning approached, he straightened August's body. Sat him quietly in a dignified slump, as if asleep. He rose. Dusted off the leaves, wiped his face. He tapped the helmet of August Haas.

"Keep sleeping my friend, I'll look out for us."

Dieter Falke managed to rejoin the remnants of his unit later that day.

Now he opened his eyes again, on the roof of the barn. The planes were gone and the ghost of August Haas with them.

His attention switched back to the road. The figure was now near the top of the hill. The walk would be easier down the other side.

As the person approached the big stone pillars of their covered gate it stopped and stood there looking about. It took something from a pocket and appeared to compare some written information with their gate. For a while it just stood. A wavering image. Uncertain in vision and in itself apparently. Then walking forward this traveller opened their gate and closing it neatly behind began walking along the roadway to their house. The person was not particularly big. Weary perhaps from a long journey.

As Dieter watched he had an odd sensation. Some trick of memory. He squinted and looked closer at the person's walk. It made him curious.

He leaned over and called to Adriane.

"There's somebody coming. Another lost soul I suppose. Nobody local. Can we spare some food?"

He noticed Adriane was stopped in the yard below. She was staring fixedly ahead, watching the visitor.

They both continued to peer at the approaching figure in the bright light and waited.

Chapter 37

'Correspondence'

August 7, 1945
United States Army of Occupation
From: Major - James A. Madden - 15th Intelligence Unit -
Maulhausen
To: Brigadier General - Thomas Fitzhenry

Brigadier General Fitzhenry
It is with considerable pleasure and pride that I can con-
firm that our unit has in custody one Antek Beck, chief
dynamics engineer from the Nazi Rocket Program.
As you will be aware Sir, a considerable effort has been
expended in locating the persons who worked on this
Program and I consider the apprehension of this individ-
ual to be a major achievement for the United States of
America.

I believe it is our intention to remove the captured senior Peenemunde and Mittelwerk personnel to the US mainland with all haste. I await your advice on when and where this transfer will take place.

Sir, I would also like to bring to your attention the splendid work carried out by our Unit's Corporal Rainer Yates.

His detection of a refugee carrying some belongings associated with Dr Beck, his excellent handling of the situation and his subsequent analysis of a letter, photos and other information obtained from this person gave him enough information to work out a location where we might have found Dr Beck.

His assumption proved correct and we were able to make the arrest.

I recommend that he be given an award for his outstanding work and the consideration be undertaken as to whether he can receive a solid promotion as well.

In addition -

A notebook handed in by the refugee couple contained quite detailed random notes and sketches by Antek Beck on such matters as the initial work and eventual success of the V1. How they overcame the guidance issues for the V2. The bombing of Peenemunde in 1943. (In which Beck was nearly killed.) Establishment of production at Nordhausen. (He was heavily involved with further refinements with Mittelverk Gmbh which are detailed.)

Judging from this Beck seems to have great knowledge of the flight capabilities of the rockets. He travelled to France to set up launch sites, made modifications to ensure successful launches. With the parts, equipment and rockets we are shipping back to the US, his cooperation will be very valuable.

The notebook along with all other information collected has been forwarded by courier under strictest security.

It should be also recorded here that Dr Beck has indicated his willingness to be relocated with his family to the United States and to cooperate fully with our personnel.

July 25, 1945

Field Notes Diary - Captain Boris Chaban

Berlin - Sector E

A distressing incident occurred today when four Soviet regular soldiers were cut down by sniper fire while attending our canteen around mid day. The fire was coming from a partially damaged building in a side street at a considerable distance from the canteen.

The perpetrators were obviously well trained marksmen. The first group of our men to reach the building had some difficulty in gaining access due to a missing lower stairwell. Once inside they were subjected to heavy re-sistance from what turned out to be some four remnant officers from The 1st SS-Panzer Division Leibstandarte SS Adolf Hitler (1st SS-Pz.Div. LSSAH) the unit directly associated with the protection of the German Fuhrer.

Of the five Soviet soldiers who entered the building one was killed and one wounded on the stairs. One of the SS soldiers was killed at this stage. Our three remaining soldiers pursued the Germans and killed one more on the final flight of stairs.

The last two Germans had now entered an apartment at

the end of the corridor on the uppermost level. When our soldiers reached the apartment they found these last two German soldiers dead on the floor. They immediately came under heavy fire from the occupants of the apartment. Two of our soldiers were wounded when it appears the person's gun jammed.

Our remaining soldier was advancing on the man when a boy lunged at him with a knife. Our soldier brought the boy down with his bayonet but was subsequently taken down and rendered unconscious by the man in the apartment.

The apartment occupants then lifted the boy onto their lounge and appeared in great distress over the boy's condition.

They sat with the boy for a while but then decided to leave. Before they departed they checked the condition of our unconscious soldier and attended to our wounded soldiers and made them comfortable.

It is through the account of one that I know what transpired in the building. It is his opinion that the family were about to leave the apartment when they were caught up in the melee that took place. He doubts they knew who was entering their apartment or for what reason.

It is also his opinion that they left because they believed the boy to be dead.

When we evacuated our wounded soldiers from the room our Medics attended to the boy and while his situation was

*grave and his pulse very weak they were able to success-
fully transport him to our sector hospital with the soldiers.
Surgeons worked on all of them. The boy too at my request.*

*All are making good progress. I plan to speak to the boy in
the next day or so to try to shed further light on the circumstances of the whole affair.*

*The apartment where these events took place is of great
interest. Examination of the contents including documents
and files revealed that the apartment is owned by Dr
Antek Beck, who it transpires is a major figure in German
rocket research. He is sought by Moscow for his
knowledge. All Russian checkpoints have been issued with
details of the man in the hope of apprehending him.*

*It should be noted that a man and woman going under the
name of Dr Beck did pass through our checkpoints a few
days past.*

Immediately after the incident at Beck's apartment.

*It is certain that these people were the occupants of his
apartment whom our wounded man saw leave, however
it is clear that they were just using the apartment (it was
remarkably well stocked with food) as a staging post and
to escape the fighting in the streets.*

*No doubt they did not realise the importance of the man
whose name they 'borrowed' considering it a good
disguise to assist their journey.*

Dearest Rolf

*We hope this letter reaches you and finds you in good
health. We promised to write to you if we were
successful in our quest. There are many things to tell you.
We have a small farm near Willengen. Considering the
state of the world over the last five years we must consider
ourselves very fortunate. I'm sure our good fortune has
rubbed off on you and things are much improved.
We'll say no more for now. There is a story for you but
we thought we would just see if we could make contact at
first.
Please write and tell us your news.*

Much love and affection
Adriane and Dieter Falke

Returned to Sender.

The apartment on level 8.

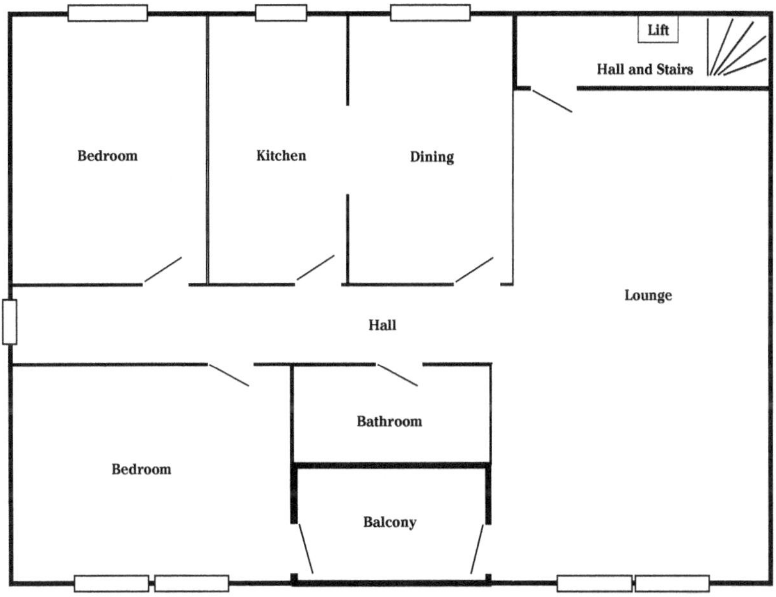

www.ingramcontent.com/pod-product-compliance
Lightning Source LLC
Chambersburg PA
CBHW051007180726
48291CB00006B/2007